Afraid of Everything

Also by Karen Jones Gowen

Farm Girl

Uncut Diamonds

House of Diamonds

Lighting Candles in the Snow

Farm Girl Country Cooking:
Hearty Meals for the Active Family

Afraid of Everything

Karen Jones Gowen

WiDō Publishing
Salt Lake City • Houston

WiDō Publishing
Salt Lake City, Utah
www.widopublishing.com

Cover Design by Steven Novak
Book Design by Marny K. Parkin

Print ISBN: 978-1-937178-59-8
Library of Congress Control Number: 2014953328
Printed in the United States of America

To Mother and to Becki
Two of our busiest, happiest angels on the Other Side

One

I HAD EXAMINED THE BUSINESS CARD UNTIL IT was faded and bent. It had been in my wallet, gone through the wash in the pockets of my jeans, and most recently I'd kept it next to the landline on the front hall table. I'd tossed it in the trash once or twice, only to pull it out later.

Gloria Chavez.

A name branded on my psyche. I picked the card up from the kitchen counter, framing it delicately between my thumb and forefinger after quickly washing the smattering of breakfast dishes. Half a cup of non-fat Greek yogurt with a fourth a banana and sprinkle of granola. Two cups of coffee, black. The dishwasher, stainless steel to match the stove and refrigerator, looked pretty but sat idle. If it had hands, it would've been languidly filing its nails.

The kitchen was now as spotless as an appliance showroom. I leaned against the granite counter top, staring at the card.

Gloria Chavez.

I had to beat back the chills coming over me when I saw the name, fingered the card, re-read it for the millionth time. I had memorized each number and word, making the thing itself superfluous.

It was a test, a dangerous ride. It was me at age ten, climbing onto the roller coaster at the Wisconsin State Fair, experiencing intense stomach pains as I anticipated the imminent death of myself and everyone else strapped into the precarious cars. While the others smiled and hooted in expectation of thrills and entertainment, I saw a monster designed for terror. The roller coaster would shortly hurl us toward the open sky, where we would moments later come crashing to earth in a bloody heap of combined flesh.

And there was Mom and Dad, cheering me on from the sidelines. "Good girl, Helena! It will be fun, we promise. Go on now. Don't look so worried! We'll be waiting right here for you when it stops."

It was only the kiddie roller coaster, safe as anything. My parents had brought me to the "nice man," who would help me climb into my place and strap me in. The man with his crooked, yellow teeth, his greasy, scarred face and hairless wiry arms, and the way he touched me on the bottom when he boosted me up and into the swinging seat. I shrank away from him, desperate to avoid his touch as he fumbled around my midriff for the safety belt crumpled next to me.

"What're you afraid of, darlin'? This ain't nothin' yet. Wait till it starts." He made wild circular gestures with both arms, imitating the roller coaster veering out of control. He looked me over, tightened and fastened the strap firmly across my waist, patting me down discreetly enough so that my doting parents, watching and waving below, wouldn't notice anything amiss.

"You sure are a pretty little thing, ain't ya?" he whispered close to my ear.

He gave a final smirking grin before turning away to help the next one in line. Where he'd touched me burned like acid, and I trembled in revulsion. At least when the roller coaster crashed I wouldn't see the man again, have him grabbing my arm and elsewhere to help me out.

I no longer ride the roller coaster, of course. I didn't need a State Fair with its leering carnival men and terrifying rides when the normal events of each day were nerve-wracking enough.

Such as the prospect of calling this woman. This Gloria Chavez.

My home in a Pasadena subdivision was a safe haven. It was a place where I could manage, with extreme caution accompanied by a predictable routine, to achieve a particular degree of calm. However, if selling the house would somehow fix my current dilemma, maybe cure me completely in the process, I was willing to consider it.

"My appointment is in two hours," I said to Annie, always more edgy than her brother. I ran my hand up and down her soft fur until it lifted with static electricity. She jumped off the loveseat.

"I'll need an hour to get there, don't you think? I know exactly where it is, over near the shopping center at Old Pasadena. A thirty-minute drive from our house, but you never know with delays. I'll head west on the 210 and take the San Fernando exit, driving the rest of the way via surface streets. Or I could get on Colorado and take it straight there. No, on second thought, I don't want to accidentally end up at the mall, so forget Colorado Boulevard."

I slipped the card into my wallet. "If there's extra time, I might call this Gloria person. If I feel right about it. Meanwhile, I'll tidy up. It'll help to calm me down."

Annie kept leaping off and onto the loveseat while I stood there chatting with the two of them, no doubt anxious about my leaving.

"Don't worry, Annie, you'll be fine. You need to relax and keep Amos company."

I lifted Amos from the floor, my signal for cuddle time. His tummy fur was soft on my bare arms, his legs limp in anticipation of curling in my lap. His heaviness balanced me. It would be nice to cuddle a moment with my babies in the family room, our favorite spot.

"You came right when I needed you, didn't you, darlings? Lucky for me Angela's little girl was allergic. And that Angela could talk a worm onto the hook."

Nurses are natural caregivers and everyone else she'd asked already had more animals than they could handle. I had repeatedly declined to take the year-old cats—what did I need with something more to worry about—but Angela kept after me.

"Helena, *please,* you're the only one left," she had insisted. "I guarantee you won't regret it. Amos and Annie are easy to take care of, very clean and well-behaved. You know how cats are, and these two are the best. Spayed, up-to-date on their shots, plus they each have their own personal travel case when you need to take them somewhere. They're no trouble, Helena, I promise."

Angela had been right, of course, and thankfully I had finally agreed to take her cats, both of them. I'd figured I was doing a big favor to a friend, being a considerate, helpful person, and instead I was the one who had most benefitted.

Today I was too nervous to sit for long. Amos and Annie must have sensed it. They kept pacing across my lap, not settling down, batting paws at each other's faces and doing their growling-talking thing, engaged in their own peculiar sibling, best friend communication.

Finally, I gave it up and stood, quickly swiping the cat hair off my tan linen pants. It was warm for March, and I'd decided to wear a long-sleeved, tailored white shirt with casual pants and slip-on brown flats. Of course, I'd take a jacket, always prepared for getting icy chills regardless of the weather. My hair was in a ponytail, keeping it out of my face. I couldn't stand to have loose hair tickling my skin, especially when I was tense about something in particular.

"Enough for now, kitties. You two play. I've still got a few minutes to do a quick tidy up and vacuum."

I went after the cleaning while obsessively checking the clock, and I finished exactly as anticipated. Despite dreading this appointment and highly anxious about leaving the house, still I felt compelled not to be late.

Checking the bathroom mirror, I unclipped the barrette holding back my shoulder-length brown hair. Such boring, nondescript hair, and were those a few additional gray hairs? I brushed through it once or twice and redid the ponytail, tightening it up. There. Smooth sides, no mess. I fluffed out my bangs. I would worry about the gray later.

I ran back to the family room and gave my babies another cuddle. "I promise to come back soon. Be good, don't argue, and wait for me right there. I'm going to need you when I return."

They stretched out, sunning themselves while fanned out on the loveseat, right where the morning rays coming through the patio door would shine on them until noon. My cats awed me with their intelligence. They knew how to enjoy life way more than I did. No wonder ancient Egyptians had worshipped cats as gods. Humans could never hope to have such insight into what constituted a blissful existence, not to mention the grace and poise while achieving it.

I paused at the hall closet on my way to the garage, pulled out the sticky roller and ran it over my pants to remove any remaining cat hair. Finally I was ready, with forty-five minutes to spare, as long as nothing bad happened.

I backed out of the garage onto my drive, glancing over at Trudy and Tom's to see if Trudy was outside yet this morning weeding her flower beds. I noticed a few long strands of grass poking through the purple ice plant next to the front walk, but no Trudy. Mom would want me to go over after my appointment and help my neighbor with her weeding.

"Trudy likes doing it herself, Mom," I said. "If I weeded her ice plant it would seem pushy, as though her yard wasn't tidy enough to suit me."

"Never pass up an opportunity to do good, Helena," Mom said. Not really, but I heard her voice in my head as clearly as if she were saying it.

I paused in my driveway, in my car, gazing at my house—my *home,* as they said here. It always sounded strange to my ears. In Wisconsin a house was a house, no matter how long you'd lived there. In California, people said *home* even before moving in, as in "I'm looking at buying a home." As though a home was something you could buy. You bought a *house.* You created a home. It took years, and in many cases the home never materialized. Or perhaps it did, briefly, before evaporating like the morning fog.

I wasn't sure my house was a home yet. Probably not, but I loved it anyway.

Eight years I'd lived there, buying it after Simon left, to free myself of painful memories and get a fresh start. It was a typical California tract house that I'd upgraded and taken excellent care of it inside and out. The landscaping had filled out and set off the place to perfection.

I visualized a for sale sign in the front yard. It did not make me happy. No way could I do this.

I checked the dashboard clock and decided on the route I'd take, planning which side streets to go in order to avoid the hospital. It would add an extra ten minutes but no matter. There were too many other things stressing me out right now. I absolutely was not going to drive past my work on top of everything else.

Two

AS I ZOOMED TOWARD MY DESTINY ON A relatively clear freeway, I mentally prepared for the first session. Normal family, check. Decent, good parents who loved me, check. Conventional religious background, check. No funny uncles, check.

I hadn't liked thunder and lightning, but what kid does. To me, crashing thunder had been the sound of the world ending. Lightning would strike our TV antenna—out of all the houses with TV antennas in town, it would most certainly hit us—causing the house to burst into flames. I'd run to my room, slam shut the door, and crawl into bed with the covers over my head, expecting to smell fire and planning out my escape route for the moment I did. This was after I got too old to run to my mom and dad's bedroom and hide in their closet.

I had disliked surprises or sudden loud noises. The phone or doorbell ringing in a quiet house had unnerved me. I'd want to disappear, fearing some unpleasant visitor, despite it routinely being a neighbor stopping by or the Avon lady or a friend coming over to see if I could play.

I'd never had more than one or two friends at once, to avoid confusion and potential conflict. Having a lot of friends was too complicated. If they all wanted to play at once, I'd have to choose and possibly hurt someone's feelings. Or what if they wanted to play with each other and leave me out? One friend, maybe two if we got along well, was plenty.

I had lived in constant fear of being made fun of at school, since kids tended to pick on the oddballs. I tried to fit in and avoid being targeted by acting as normal as possible. I made sure to bathe every night and wash up in the mornings, to always wear clean clothes so I wouldn't smell. I was a quiet child, passive, didn't rock the boat.

"You smell!" was the most common taunt I remembered. Certain kids had weird odors, and they'd get victimized for it.

"How can someone smell like fish every single day?" I asked my mom one day after school as she ironed my dad's shirts. "There's this girl at school who everyone picks on for stinking like dead fish."

I watched as Mom sprayed the clothes with water, then touched the flat, hot face of the iron with a wet finger and heard it sizzle. I couldn't fathom how she kept from getting burned. She would explain how you have to pull your finger away quickly. That it's not really the skin in contact with the hot surface but the moisture. She would show me how to spit on my index finger, encourage me to try, but I couldn't bring myself to complete the task. Moistening my finger with saliva and tentatively approaching the iron was as far as I'd get.

I can still remember the feeling of distress coming over me at the thought of it. The dread reaching up like a snake uncoiling in my gut, trying to strangle the breath out of me, to snap at me with vicious jaws the second I dared touch the searing, sizzling flat of the iron.

"Maybe her family eats a lot of fish for dinner." Mom moved the iron over the back of a shirt. When she was ironing, with the steam rising up and the fresh laundry scent filling the room, it would slow her down. She'd actually listen instead of saying "hmm mmm and okay" as she zoomed around the house and garden getting things done.

"I suppose her dad might like to fish on the lake, and so they eat a lot of bass and blue gill," she said. "The aroma does have a tendency to cling to the curtains and furniture. It's why I don't cook fish very often. If her family does, and their whole house smells like it, the girl will, too."

"Everyone in class says she stinks."

"I'm sure she can't help it."

"She doesn't have any friends," I added.

"Oh, that's too bad," my mom said with a sudden frown. After all these years, I could still see the distraught expression on my mother's face as she visualized the friendless child. "I'm sorry to hear it. Maybe you could be her friend, Helena. You could invite her over to play after school, and we can have her stay for dinner. Would you like that?"

"I don't think so. I doubt if she would come anyway. She doesn't talk to anyone. If I asked her, I'm pretty sure she'd say no."

"If one day you'd like to bring her home, it would be fine with me. You don't even need to ask first," Mom said, stretching one of the sleeves of Dad's shirts flat on the board then spraying it lightly with water. When she lowered the iron, it hissed and crackled on the damp fabric. I watched the steam rise up as Mom expertly slid the iron up the sleeve, straightening out the material to avoid pressing in wrinkles.

"I probably won't though," I said. "She keeps to herself and hardly talks. I wouldn't know what to say to her. Besides, I don't want to get picked on either."

"Helena, you wouldn't. You come from a nice home, you have nice clothes and you're always clean and polite. You could set the example of friendship." Mom gave me the expression I knew too well, the one that meant she was not pleased.

I so often held back when Mom wanted me to go forward, whether in friendships or tasting an unfamiliar food or experiencing a new challenge. She'd say to me, "Go ahead, Helena, it will be fine!" I'd balk and frown and fuss in resistance, until finally Mom either forced the issue or gave it up. If she compelled me, I was upset. If she ended up yielding on a point she believed in, then she was upset.

"I'll get teased if I'm friends with someone who smells bad," I insisted, arguing my case. Mom gave the one-shoulder shrug, her typical gesture for when she disagreed with me but had decided to let it go.

I never did talk to the girl, or befriend her. At some point during the school year she simply disappeared from class. One day she was gone, no longer attending our school. The teacher didn't mention the girl, which was strange since teachers normally would comment briefly on where a student went when they left during the school year. No one asked about her, either.

Birthday parties had panicked me, too, with so many people together in one space. Not real friends either, but kids invited by your mom. The party where my mom made me invite my whole third grade class was the one I had agonized about the most. A few kids had started asking the entire class to their birthday parties. For some reason, Mom decided I should do the same.

Thinking back on the day, it wasn't as bad as I'd expected. Most of my classmates came, although not the girl who smelled like fish. She was still in my class then and had received an invitation same as everyone else. I got lots of nice presents, but nothing as good as what I already had in my bedroom and play room: Barbie dolls, a talking Crissy, an Easy Bake Oven, Etch-a-Sketch, the Mousetrap game.

My mom had organized games and favors for guests, followed by a giant cake decorated with balloons and flowers made of frosting. Nobody made fun of anything. In fact, they had seemed to enjoy my party and my house and my mom. Several of the popular girls began treating me like I was one of them, an unexpected and uncomfortable development since I didn't know how to act like a popular girl. I was relieved when, after another week of school passed, these girls went back to playing with each other and left me alone with Cora and Mandy, my two friends at the time.

As I reflected back on these incidents, I wondered when it began. When I first became aware of the distress that was ever present, either inside of me or outside, waiting to attack. What others saw as ordinary events—being invited to a party, going to sleep at night, attending school, responding to a grown-up—I saw as potentially terrifying incidents to avoid with whatever power I could muster. Or if unable to avoid them, at least shrink into myself so completely as to be essentially invisible.

Reflecting on my growing up years and remembering the frequent panic that had accompanied the most common activities, I was at a loss. Maybe the therapist would find something.

The drive was uneventful and I arrived at ten-thirty on the dot, thirty minutes in advance. After turning off the ignition I sat in my vehicle in the parking lot, hesitant to get out and go inside the building.

I pulled the realtor's card out of my purse. Gloria Chavez. She was supposed to be one of the best. Someone at work had given me her information. I didn't remember who, as those last few days had been such a blur. I vaguely recalled a conversation where I'd made a comment about putting my house up for sale and creating a big change and someone, probably Angela who knew a million people, had handed me the card and said, "Call Gloria. She'll take care of it."

Sitting in my Toyota Corolla where I felt warmed clear through and protected from the outside clamor, I didn't want to leave. Forget the therapist, forget the realtor, ignore everything in the world but the isolation, the quiet, and the healing sunshine.

However, I managed as usual. After enjoying an additional ten minutes of my solitary sauna, I reluctantly went into the building.

Three

"HELENA CARR," I SAID CURTLY, INTRODUC-ing myself the second I walked into the room. I waited awkwardly, confused about what to say or do next.

After greeting me with a handshake, embarrassing since my hands were cold and clammy, the therapist gestured toward a luxurious arm chair and I quickly made my way to it.

"Welcome, Helena. I'm Dr. Ruby Brown. Please have a seat and get comfortable. Or would you rather I call you Ms. Carr?" She lowered herself gracefully into the matching chair across from me.

"Helena is fine, but thank you for asking," I responded, feeling incredibly nervous and out of place. I looked around to avoid eye contact while attempting to compose myself. I crossed my legs to help control the shaking.

Dr. Brown's office was decorated in restful taupe shades. There were golden oak accents and live flower arrangements scattered about, including one on the table next to my chair. Its fragrance, reminiscent of springtime back home, relaxed me a little.

"Sorry to make you wait so long. The forms my secretary gave you, the tests and so forth, were to help in analyzing and diagnosing your particular form of anxiety." Dr. Brown ruffled the pages of the papers I'd filled out. "I've gone through your results, and we can talk further. To get to the bottom of this and come up with a treatment plan."

She gave me a moment, and I paused while considering what to say without sounding foolish. Nothing. I had nothing. I felt incredibly self-conscious, unable to speak.

She cleared her throat. "I much prefer live flowers, don't you?"

"Oh, yes, always. These are lovely. Are they from your garden?" I asked, at last finding my tongue and gushing forth about the flowers.

She chuckled. "If you can call Costco my garden. It might as well be, the way I wander through their produce department. I can never resist getting one or two arrangements from the flower stand."

"That's a nice routine," I said without conviction, while mentally adding up how much the four bouquets in her office would cost if she replaced them once a week for freshness.

"Well, Helena, it appears you've come to me because of an incident at work?"

I turned away from the bouquet of daisies and finally looked at her directly. Dr. Ruby Brown was an attractive, slightly heavy black woman. Approaching fifty, I suspected.

She wore large bifocal glasses with red frames, conservative clothing—a mid-calf, orange and yellow print flowing skirt that looked comfortable yet captivating, and a light brown turtle-neck sweater. Her over-sized gold hoop earrings and chunky matching necklace perfectly set off her outfit. Dr. Brown's hair was extremely short, cropped close to her head. Although at first glance the gray and black appeared to be blended evenly, the gray was definitely gaining ground. She had a charismatic smile that exuded warmth and friendliness. I began to feel slightly more at ease.

She continued, allowing me a few more moments to collect myself. "You know, at its basic level, anxiety is not a bad thing. It's a hormonal response to dangerous situations, evolution's way of benefitting humans in the face of danger. Perhaps to make you feel better, it's been proven that people with low anxiety levels have a greater risk of death than those with average or higher levels. If it is any comfort."

She picked up a yellow legal pad from the table in front of her and put the papers I'd filled out on top of it. I nodded, understanding what she was saying, without knowing how to respond.

Dr. Brown glanced down at the papers again. I had a feeling she knew exactly what was there, but was buying time and trying to relax me by waiting. Or maybe she wanted to give me a chance to speak up, something I was hesitant to do.

"You test for a high level of General Anxiety Disorder," she said finally. "It can make certain situations extremely difficult for you, as I'm sure you're aware. For instance, are social situations a problem?"

"Yes, definitely. I avoid them like the plague. I always worry I'll say or do something stupid or embarrass myself in some way."

"Do you have particular fears or phobias? Things or events you have an excessive response to?"

"Flying. I'm terrified of flying. If I have to get on an airplane, I've got to take something first to calm me down. And to help with the nausea and headache."

"What do you take?" she asked, probably wondering if I was a druggie. I admit, at times I'd wondered if something heavier duty might help me. Being a nurse and administering pain medications as part of the job, one couldn't help but consider it.

"Over the counter, nothing prescription. Extra-strength for the headaches. Benadryl to help me sleep. It knocks me out, which helps if I have to fly."

"Other fears in particular?"

"Besides the parties—ugh, I hate a party almost more than anything—I'm afraid of road trips. I can manage driving locally, no problem. I even enjoy it. I'm okay with the freeways, any kind of driving when I know where I'm going and it's familiar. But to take a road trip of several days? It's torture. I can't do it. I guess when given a choice, I'll take flying, because then I can medicate myself and sleep through it."

"I see. Makes sense. Casually, we tend to use anxiety and fear in similar ways, when clinically they have different meanings. Anxiety we define as an unpleasant emotional state, uncontrollable and not easily defined. You might feel general anxiety without knowing why, without realizing what it is you are anxious about. You may have physical symptoms, such as headaches and stomachaches, without actually being sick."

"Yes, sounds familiar. I wake up anxious. Sometimes in the middle of the night. People at work were telling me to cut back on the coffee, when seriously, it's coffee that calms me down."

"You drink a lot of coffee?" she asked, making a notation.

"I don't think so. I mean, the typical two cups first thing in the morning. I'm never very hungry for breakfast, but I want my coffee. Black, first thing. Then mid-morning, when I visit my neighbor or if I'm on break at work, I take it toned down with milk or cream. Do you think that's excessive?"

"It might be, given your state of anxiety. Cutting down on the caffeine could help lessen your anxious feelings. It's one of the first things to try."

"I don't know. Coffee relaxes me. In fact, I'm feeling nervous thinking about having to give it up."

"You're not ready to take that step yet, I understand. This initial visit is for us to go over possible diagnoses, causes, treatments. We don't need to jump right in with any drastic measures."

"Good." I smiled, realizing as I did it was the first smile that had broken through what had undoubtedly been a very tense expression since I walked into Dr. Brown's office.

She smiled back at me. "You have a lovely smile, Helena. I hope before we're done today, I see it a few more times." She set the forms down on the table, still keeping the yellow pad on her lap. "Now, let's talk a moment about fear. Unlike anxiety, fear is an emotional and physiological response to a recognized external threat. For instance, when you came in today, you were clearly exhibiting signs of fear. Avoiding eye contact. Clammy skin. Hesitant to respond to direct questions. Since we've chatted awhile, do you still see me as a threat?"

I paused, not knowing how to answer the question. Truthfully, I saw everything and everyone as a threat.

"I hope you'll relax and be honest, Helena. This isn't a test, I promise. You already filled out your tests and now we are getting to know one another."

I took a deep breath. "I don't see you as a threat. I mean, not really. No more than usual." Dr. Brown laughed, as though she knew what I meant. It encouraged me to continue. "There's something about your voice, the calm environment of your office. It doesn't feel like an office, more like a comfortable sitting room. The apprehension has lessened."

"I'm glad to hear it," she said.

"I know what it means to be afraid, trust me, Dr. Brown. What happened at work—it was like a trigger, and my job was the war zone. I couldn't go back."

"Rather like post-traumatic stress, I take it. Are you ready to talk about it?" she asked in a soft voice.

"I think so. That's why I'm here, isn't it? I guess I'm finally ready to discuss it with a professional." I stopped, not sure if I was ready. Blurting things out was not my typical pattern of conversation.

She waited a moment longer, calm and patient, before prompting me with a hand gesture. "Go ahead, Helena. Whenever you're ready."

"It was at work, although this is an ongoing problem. A serious thing I've dealt with for as long as I can remember. No matter how much I try to talk myself out of it, it's always there, my own personal shadow of gloom."

Dr. Brown nodded. "It's called General Anxiety Disorder. It affects three percent of the population, more common in women than men. A few of the symptoms are exaggerated worry and tension, often expecting the worst, even with no apparent reason for concern. Would you say you are overly concerned about money, health, and family, as well as work?"

"Definitely. I wake up in the morning afraid of the day. Afraid to take a shower. Afraid to leave my house, to open the mail. What if there's bad news in one of those envelopes? The things I'm afraid of, you'd laugh if I told you."

"Try me." She gave me a direct stare, as though in challenge. Only in a nice way. Dr. Brown really did make it easy.

"Okay, just off the top of my head . . . I'm afraid of answering the phone, afraid of making a call, afraid of going to the doctor, afraid of getting up in the morning and going to bed at night, afraid of stepping outside, feeling like everyone is watching me. Afraid of getting in my car, and once there, afraid of getting out. I'm afraid of weighing myself, of going to the gym."

"Those last two I can identify with," she said with a laugh. "Go on."

"Afraid of taking a pill, of eating or of not eating, especially in public. Afraid of going to church because of all the people. Shall I go on? It's ridiculous, but I can't seem to stop the cycle."

"Yet you were married, raised a family, right?" She picked up my information form again, where it would say I was divorced, one daughter. "You've been gainfully employed as a labor and delivery nurse for . . . what's it been?"

"Twenty-five years, give or take. I guess I've learned to live with it. Until now. Oh, and after the divorce I had a pretty hard time as well," I admitted.

"When the anxiety level is mild, people with General Anxiety Disorder can function socially and at work without terribly serious problems. Although avoiding certain situations, such as flying or road trips or parties, as you mentioned. Despite the discomfort, you're still managing. You've been one of the lucky ones."

"What do you mean, lucky?" I did not feel lucky. Cursed was more accurate.

"Able to live a normal life despite your illness," she said.

"Illness? I'm sick?"

"GAD is considered a serious mental illness. For people with it and other anxiety disorders, worry and fear are constant and overwhelming and can be crippling, as you've experienced. The good news is, Helena, there's treatment. Counseling, therapy, and medication, if necessary. The exact cause is unknown, but family background, hereditary factors and life experiences can definitely contribute."

I crossed and uncrossed my legs, rubbed my arms to take away the chill. "This is very interesting, Dr. Brown. It's not the first time I've heard of GAD of course, having a medical background. For some reason I never applied it to myself. Stupid, I know."

"Not stupid at all, considering the stigma mental illness has in our society. It's a shameful and unfortunate fact of our culture. Now, first off, Helena, I want you to call me Ruby. I have a Doctorate in Clinical Psychology, and I worked hard to get the title, make no mistake about it. I want to assure you, I am thoroughly qualified to help you, but I don't need the distance of a high-falutin' doctor label with my clients. We're going to deal with a lot of personal things as we meet together, and we may as well begin on a first-name, friendly basis. Are you okay with that?"

"Certainly," I said, and when she didn't immediately respond, I filled the awkward silence with a question. "Do you think you can help me? Overcome my fears, at least the ones concerning the hospital, so I can return to work and get my life back?"

"I certainly hope so. Of course, there are different kinds of anxiety disorders and phobias. First, we'll want to identify what kinds of fear you experience, or if it's a phobia of something particular."

"I am generally afraid of everything, I guess you could say. When I had the incident at work, it gave me a phobia of the hospital. Things escalated. I used to handle and control the anxiety fairly well, I think, until then."

"That's a true insight. A trauma or significant event can be a trigger and create an anxiety disorder in people who have an inherited susceptibility to it. Or exacerbate the disorder already there, to make it impossible to continue as before. Are you afraid of anything specifically, perhaps one thing more than another?"

"No, just generally. Simon, my ex-husband used to tease me about it. 'Helena is afraid of everything,' he'd tell people, laughing at the idea of it, like I was some kind of circus freak."

Dr. Brown—Ruby—tapped her pen against her forehead like she was freeing up brilliance. I waited for her to tap out an idea or two that might help me out.

"What scares you the most, Helena?" she finally asked.

"The idea of Simon leaving me used to haunt me," I said. "Before that, it was the possibility of my daughter getting abducted, until she grew up and became an expert at Tai Kwan Do."

She waited. I hated when people did that. Wait and wait until you answer your own questions. My dad had been a salesman and he used to say, "Whoever talks first, loses. One of the first rules of sales."

Ruby broke the silence. Score one for me. "What would you say scares you the absolute most, right now? Aside from being here, of course." Another low chuckle. "Before you answer, Helena, I want you to relax into the deep armchair, close your eyes, breathe deeply. It smells good in here, doesn't it? It's scented lilac, and then of course the flowers are very fragrant. Focus on your breathing, feel yourself sinking into the chair, let it support you. No worries, you are safe and protected. Visualize a place where you feel relaxed. Where you feel safe."

I closed my eyes and immediately thought of my hometown, and there on the outskirts of town was the meadow next to the lake where my dad liked to go fishing. A rickety dock was at the end of the sloping meadow with a wooded area to the left of the dock. Mom, Dad and I would take picnics on summer evenings, and I'd run along the bank trying to catch frogs.

Finally I began, knowing there was no other way. "I suppose it would be having my stability and secure footing pulled out from under me. It's why this experience at work has me so shaken up. If I can't do my job, then what?" There, I'd asked *her* a question.

"Is there a transition you could make within the framework of your career, one that might feel like a safer environment for you? Go into teaching perhaps?" Ruby asked.

I nodded. "I considered it. I'd need to go back to school and get a few additional classes to qualify. Except teaching nursing is so much different than being a nurse." I stopped to gather my thoughts. "I'm a reserved person. Not a talker. Getting in front of people with everyone staring at me, having to be the supposed expert in my field, would terrify me. It doesn't feel like the right move right now."

"Of course." Ruby paused, and I willed her to go on. With her finely-modulated, slightly husky voice, she should have been a public speaker or radio announcer, instead of sitting here hiding her talent under a bushel while serenely waiting for clients to open up.

"First, we need to address the immediate situation at hand," she said. "We'll work on finding an effective treatment so you can go back to work and not have a panic attack whenever you walk into the labor and delivery room."

"Yes, please, I need a treatment. Please. I can't live without my job. Without work, what else is there? Not to mention the loss of income."

A vista of emptiness and boredom expanded before my

vision like the arid stretch of a desert and there I was, a tiny little canteen at my side, taking one step after another, traipsing alone across the endless landscape. If I ever managed to leave my house, that is.

She licked her pencil tip, preparing to write something down in the yellow pages of her legal pad. I liked how she used pen and pencil instead of tapping her notes into a tablet. It was homey and comforting. She had a yellow pencil to match her yellow legal pad. I imagined her typing the notes out after each visit on an old-fashioned typewriter. Although, I had noticed her receptionist had a very nice Macintosh.

"It appears you've made work your security blanket, Helena. Does this sound about right?"

"I suppose so, especially since my divorce. It's been work. And my two cats."

"What made you decide to be a nurse?"

I paused, thinking, and she prompted with, "Was it a desire to help people?"

"Help people? I suppose so. I really liked science, especially chemistry. But you can't very well have a career in chemistry, can you, so I chose nursing."

She nodded, willing me to continue. I relaxed into my chair, remembering how it used to be.

"When I was a kid, women's lib was brand new and most little girls still thought their career choices were limited to teacher or nurse. I chose nurse because science was my favorite subject. Secretly, I wanted to be a doctor, but I had this idea only boys could do that. By the time I realized otherwise, I was committed to nursing."

Ruby made a few notes on her pad of paper, and then smiled up at me. "Helena, I feel certain I can help you. It may take some time. If you're okay with me, I'd be happy to see you on a regular basis."

"Sure, I'm fine with you. You're easy to talk to, and I definitely need to get this worked out in my head."

"This has been a brief, introductory visit, as I said, to make sure we're both comfortable with each other. Why don't you come back next week, and we'll get into things more deeply. I'd like to learn more about your experience at work. How does that sound?"

"Good. I'll be here."

"I'd like to assign you homework your first week." Her endearing chuckle again. "Bring me a list of ways you could face your fears. For instance, crazy things you might consider doing, totally out of your comfort zone."

"I've already been thinking of a few things along that line." This was my chance to go wild about my future, at least on paper. I could call Gloria Chavez. Definitely something for the list.

It was settled. I'd come once a week to see Dr. Ruby Brown, who would help me get over my apparently serious anxiety disorder. I'd get back to normal, or at least *my* normal, and return to work. Although as I left her office, the familiar creeping dread closed in on me like a cloud, smothering the brief light of hope I'd experienced in making this first appointment.

I couldn't help thinking: If this doesn't work, then what?

Four

I N RESIDENTIAL PASADENA, FRIENDLY NEIGH-
bors were something from the past, like black and
white television and clunky black phones setting on side
tables. We came home at night, pulling into the garage
and shutting it tight behind us. Get out of vehicle, enter
house, avoid neighbors.

There were people right across the street from me who
I'd never laid eyes on after eight years of living in this
house. Trudy and Tom, my next-door neighbors, were
different—an older couple, originally from a small farm-
ing town in Idaho. They enjoyed the outdoors, did their
own yard work, took walks together in the early evening
and sought out friendships in the neighborhood.

When they first moved in, I'd find myself wandering
outside to see them, like they were some kind of other
worldly visitors I was drawn to. I had three days off each
week, and by the third day the hours stretched endlessly
and made me uncomfortably sensitive to my solitary state.
The cats had each other; I had no one. Maybe I should
have gotten just one cat instead of two, one who had only

me for companionship. Jealous of my cats, that's how bad it was some days.

I sauntered out front to see if the mail had come yet. Trudy was often outside weeding her flower beds this time of day. I glanced over. Yes, there she was. Human-kind at its best, gesturing and smiling at me.

"Good morning, Helena," she called out, waving her spade in the air. "Beautiful day, isn't it?"

"Lovely," I called back. "How are you?"

"Wonderful!" She stood and stretched. "I'm ready for a break. Do you have a minute to come in for a cup of coffee?"

"Sure, I'd be delighted." Ignoring the mailbox, I trotted over. It was early March. The warm air scented with juniper and honeysuckle wrapped around me, carrying an irresistible invitation to take a long walk. I'd go on to the park after visiting with Trudy.

Trudy dropped her spade and gardening gloves where she'd been digging and ushered me inside, through the open garage and into the kitchen. She and Tom were in their mid-sixties, as friendly as they were old-fashioned. Tom had a booming voice and liked to tell awful jokes involving puns. Not nasty-awful but unfunny-awful, where you found yourself laughing mostly at his enjoyment of telling the story.

Trudy offered me freshly baked blueberry muffins and real cream in a little pitcher with painted-on blue pansies circled around the top edge. The sugar bowl matched it.

"Passed down from my Swedish grandmother," she explained, handling the set with loving care. "I like to use them, not keep them in a box stored in back of the closet. What's the point of having family heirlooms if you don't allow them to enrich your life?"

I wouldn't know. I didn't have family heirlooms. My mom had been obsessed with reducing clutter. She tossed out things faster than she could replace them. Her rule was "For everything that comes into the house, two must go out." After she was diagnosed with cancer, her greatest concern was that Dad would never again throw anything away and he'd grow ancient and helpless in the big house, letting stuff accumulate until all he had left of their spacious home was a tiny space to hobble around in.

"The least I can do for him is make sure the place is cleared out before I go," Mom had told me on the phone. I imagined her as she must have been those final weeks, walking with crippling pain, taking another small grocery sack of "junk" to the garbage bin out back. She said she wouldn't let Dad take it in case he peeked inside and pulled something out he couldn't bear to part with. She'd de-clutter when he wasn't looking. Normal trash she would toss in the kitchen garbage can and let Dad do his manly duty emptying it, while the clutter got her special treatment. She alone was allowed to touch it, for fear it would spin its magical tendrils around the unsuspecting and end up back in the house, entrenched forever and taking up precious space.

"I'm having a barbecue this Saturday, Helena," Trudy said, interrupting my thoughts. I nodded and smiled, pretending interest while still engrossed in my memories. "I do hope you'll come," she continued. "Just a few neighbors over, some people from Tom's work, and my nephew who recently moved to California from West Virginia. I'd like you to meet him."

That caught my attention. It sounded like a set-up. Trudy, who'd been happily married for over four decades, had a stubborn fantasy about fixing me up. She saw my expression and followed with, "Don't worry. He's only twenty-five. Besides, I learned my lesson after the last time."

"Thank you," I said. "I guess it's safe enough since he's practically the same age as my daughter."

"Perfectly safe. Poor Daniel . . . he's got issues, as they say. I feel bad for him. He's my sister Bernie's son, the sister who died of breast cancer, so terribly sad, and left him just a boy. Maybe that had something to do with it, I don't know. They say it's one of those things nobody can control or fix, but being left motherless at such a young age can't help anything."

"I'll be glad to meet him," I said automatically, thinking of how horrible cancer is the way it steals away mothers.

"Although I do know a couple not quite as young men who'd be perfect for you. . . ." She looked at me sideways.

"Trudy!" I hadn't gone on a date for years. There had been one or two awkward blind dates set up by well-meaning friends, including Trudy, until I put a halt to the tediously unpleasant routine. Forced excursions with incompatible partners was not my definition of a good time.

"Why not, sweetie? There might be someone waiting just for you, the perfect man, if only you'll put yourself out there to find him. You must get lonely sometimes."

"Yes, sometimes. But I can't go through the whole middle-aged dating scene. And I have my cats."

Trudy shook her head at me. "Yes, you have the cats. Oh, dear. You say the word, Helena, and I can fix you up. No pressure."

I hemmed and hawed, and finished my blueberry muffin.

"Then you will come on Saturday?" Trudy persisted, as she refilled my cup with coffee.

"What time and what can I bring?" My way of saying possibly, without actually saying it.

"Six-thirty. We'll have hamburgers, hot dogs, potato salad, sliced tomatoes. No need to bring a thing, I'm sure there will be more food than people the way it is."

"How about if I bring lemon bars? I've been craving them lately and don't want to make a pan just for me." Maybe I'd go. Maybe I'd bring lemon bars.

"Sure, if you want to. You know how I love your lemon bars." Trudy moved the plate of muffins closer to me and I took another. "But really, Helena, I know how busy you are. If you don't get a chance to bake, it's no problem. I'll have so much food the way it is. I don't want to put any more pressure on you. I want you to come either way, with or without a dessert."

"I have plenty of opportunity to bake since I quit my job," I said, then wished I hadn't.

Trudy got the familiar, concerned look on her face, the one where she feels sorry for me and tries even harder to include me in her regularly scheduled social events.

"I'm enjoying the freedom," I quickly added. "It's much easier now to get my walks in. To clean house. Play with my cats. Did I tell you I'm thinking of putting the house up for sale?"

"You did mention you had the name of a realtor, but I had no idea you'd decided for sure or not. Oh, honey, if this happens, I'm going to miss you terribly. You've been such a good friend to Tom and me."

Was she kidding? "Trudy, I come over on my days off and drink your coffee and eat your goodies. I'm not sure that counts as being a good friend."

"Yes, you are. If you move, I'm going to miss you. So there." She got up from her chair across from me at the kitchen table and gave me a hug. "That settles it for Saturday. I won't take no for an answer. This could be the last party I get to invite you to as a neighbor. Although I hope we'll always be friends, no matter what." She sat back down awkwardly and wiped at her eyes with a napkin.

I was deeply touched by her words. "I'll be there, I promise." I meant it this time, one social event I wouldn't back out of. "Besides, I can't become a hermit. I used to get that way on my days off. Some days all I did was venture outside to come over here."

"I'm sure you'll soon find you're busier than ever. That's how it was with me when I retired. I wonder constantly how I managed to work forty hours a week with everything there is to do."

"I know what you mean. After Simon left, I couldn't imagine what in the world I'd do with myself because it seemed he took up so much of my waking moments. Same with Cassie going off to college."

I could see the California sunshine peeking in through Trudy's kitchen window, around the gently waving, white lace curtain covering the open window.

"What a gorgeous day," I said, feeling almost hypnotized by the curtains weaving in and out, in and out. The fresh spring green of the aspen tree outside the window made playful shadows on Trudy's kitchen counter as the leaves turned in the breeze. I stood and carried my dishes to the sink. "Thank you, Trudy, for the coffee and muffins. I should go. If I call the realtor, she'll want to come through and examine things. Time to de-clutter!"

I sounded exactly like my mom right then, with the excited note she'd get in her voice when she was ready to clear out a room. I could see her bustling around the house with her secret cargo headed to the outside garbage bin where Dad wouldn't find it. I missed her. I would always miss her.

I'd take a walk first, then come home and call my dad, see how he was doing. I doubted he'd ever get over the loss of her. Even worse than my grief at losing my mom so young—she was only seventy-two—was seeing Dad lost and empty. I should call him, I thought, feeling the familiar stab of guilt. Usually, he called me.

Trudy and I said good-bye, with one last assurance of yes, I'd make it to the barbecue, with or without lemon bars. I took off down the street toward the park, to walk and think about Mom, who for some reason had come strong to my mind as I'd watched Trudy's curtains being so gently caressed by the morning breeze.

Five

WHEN MOM DIED, MY GRIEF CAME LIKE A silent howling creature, one whose throat was cut before it could scream. Sorrow was too mild a word for what coursed through me like a living being of destruction. Although it was just a feeling—how could a *feeling* possibly be so powerful and encompassing—it stunned me into immediate stillness.

I was at work when I got the call. I didn't say a word when the grief hit me, but I knew it was palpable to the others in the room because of how the noise level reduced. There had been chattering, snickering exchanges of gossip and teasing among my co-workers at the nurse's station. The second I got the news, the silence became a wave spreading out from where I was on the phone to those in the immediate area, and then on down the hall.

They could sense some part of what I was experiencing, this raging, growing creature passing through them, over and around them, putting a pall on the atmosphere. They knew it, whatever it was, and they were aware for just a moment. It gave me a small satisfaction, in a perverse and mean way, knowing my despair went outward to share itself to my unsuspecting coworkers, giving them a sudden sense of lowness. For them, it was a bad mood coming on inexplicably, when a second before you're joking around and feeling perfectly fine.

Remembering made it come back to me, the horrible day I got the news of her death. It was a shock that brought me to my knees, the other nurses rushing over to see what happened.

One day she was herself, complaining about fatigue and weakness but otherwise the same woman she'd always been. Busy, active, talking a mile a minute to her friends on the phone, and then she got the report from her recent doctor visit. The death sentence. Cancer of the uterus spread throughout her body, infecting my mother with its deadly horror while she, unknowing, had gone about her daily routine, wondering why she hadn't been feeling up to par.

As I pushed through to the park near my neighborhood, I managed to level out emotionally. Mom was somewhere else—happy, I was sure of it—in a better place. Clichéd though it sounded, it made me feel better to imagine her there, wherever it was.

I arrived home feeling renewed and ready to get started on the de-cluttering Mom had taught me how to do so well.

When Mom had first gotten sick, Dad mentioned a few times how nice it would be if I could come back home and help her. She was not herself, he would say. She was tired a lot, weak, and unable to keep up with the house and the usual activities she had always enjoyed; the gardening and decorating and making quilts or afghans for the various charities she was involved in.

Back then, I didn't know how I could have left my job, the house, my two cats and everything and return to Wisconsin for any length of time. I had offered to pay for a cleaning service, to help Mom out, but Dad turned it down. He said it wasn't the cleaning, it was having me there.

I really couldn't see how my presence would help, or what I'd do about my job.

Going back and forth for the short term would be way too much traveling. I'd have to fly, and flying required me to face death. When I walked on to a plane—shaking, freezing cold despite wearing a sweater and coat no matter the weather—I believed it was the last act I'd ever make. Everything in my world had to be put in order beforehand, because in all likelihood I would not get off alive. I'd only been on a plane once, when Mom and Dad had their fortieth wedding anniversary party at the house and I'd flown back with Cassie.

Dad had suggested how good it would be for Mom if I came back to help out for awhile. I'd hem and haw and say, "We'll see. Maybe when I can get more than four days off a week. I'll see if I can come at least for a long weekend. Or maybe when this contract ends, before the next one starts."

I was a traveling nurse and went from contract to contract, sometimes getting several weeks in between jobs. "When my schedule allowed," I told him, but in reality I hadn't planned on going. I figured he was exaggerating

Mom's condition. She had rarely been sick a day in her life. Dad was overreacting, and it was nothing but age catching up to her at last.

Then she got the diagnosis and within two weeks, she was gone. Cassie and I flew out again, for the funeral.

At the funeral I couldn't believe it was real. How was this even happening? When she was buried, my guilt felt like it would bury me. I cried in Dad's arms, apologizing for not coming sooner, filled with regret for not being there for her. Or for him. He hugged me and patted my back like always and said don't worry, he understood. People always feel a sense of guilt with the loss of a loved one. It was normal what I was feeling, he said.

As I stepped inside my house, the home phone rang and I brazenly picked it up. Usually I let the machine get it, disliking the interruption of answering calls in the middle of something. I said hello, not quite able to mask the irritation that comes with having a ringing phone disrupt one's thoughts.

It was Dad. "Oh, you *are* there," he greeted me.

Strange, I thought, when I had been thinking of them. "Hi, Dad. I just barely walked in."

"Glad I caught you. It's been a while since we talked."

"Didn't we talk last week? Remember, you called on Saturday?"

"Yep, like I said, it's been a while. Guess who I just heard on the radio?"

"Uh. I have no idea."

"Rita Greenwood! She was doing a plumbing ad for Hipple Plumbing and Heating."

"Who's Rita Greenwood?"

"You know, that lady at church who's so friendly. Talks to everyone? She brought meals over after your mom passed. Her husband's a dentist, doctor or something . . . maybe it's an eye doctor, I can't remember. Something medical. They've got three little kids. Two boys and a girl. The girl's just a baby. Toddles around up and down the aisle at church. Friendliest little thing you ever saw."

"Oh, right." I had no idea who Rita Greenwood was. I hadn't been back to the hometown since Mom's funeral, and before that for the anniversary party. My parents had always come out to California for three weeks every winter, to get away from the cold. Three weeks was all Dad could stand of the traffic and the crowds before he got homesick for small town life and rushed back to Waunegee.

"She was talking about her plumbing and how they had a problem with their toilets flushing right. Until she called Hipple Plumbing and had them install their toilets that can now flush anything, and now Rita Greenwood is one satisfied customer. . . ." Dad was droning on in the way I knew so well.

I glanced at the clock. This could go on forever, and I certainly wasn't in the mood to hear a pointless story of someone I didn't know and her toilet problem of all things.

"Dad," I interrupted. "I really can't do this right now. I've been thinking of Mom, missing her, and I can't listen to a story about plumbing and toilets flushing or not flushing. Please!"

My dad never talked about he felt, only about superficial subjects he couldn't possibly care about. It bothered me how he had never really acknowledged his grief about Mom. She had been the love of his life, married forty-eight years, and yet when she died he devoted the two weeks after the funeral to organizing his workshop in the garage. I'd seen him sorting screws and nails and bolts into random piles. All the years Mom had asked him to please clean up his exceedingly messy work area, and finally he decides to make a show of it after she's gone.

"Never mind, then. I thought it was interesting, that's all." His voice reflected his disappointment. I tried to redeem the conversation, to ask how he was doing, but it was no good. We both were deflated and off track and finally Dad said, "Well, I'll call you again."

"Yes, we'll talk soon. You know you can call my cell, Dad. You've got the number. You don't have to always call the house phone and try to catch me here. In fact, I rarely pick it up. Not sure why I did today."

"I've got your cell phone number in the book in case of emergency, but I don't want to bother you when you're out driving or shopping or at work or something. I figure if you're home and you're not busy then that's where to reach you."

"Dad, you know I'm not working right now. Remember, I told you."

"That's right. Something about a baby dying, wasn't it? That's too bad, Helena. You take some time off and then I'm sure you'll be ready to go back, as good as new."

Lately Dad couldn't seem to remember things very well. He'd always been a better talker than listener the way it was. The typical salesman. I gave up, not wanting to correct him about my experience at the hospital. He wouldn't remember anyway. "Okay, whatever you want to do, Dad. Bye, I love you."

"Well, then, Helena, I'll let you go. It's snowing here. They say it may snow through the night, but we'll see. Looks like it might turn into freezing rain by morning. We could sure use some spring. Everyone's tired of winter by end of March. I've got my lettuce seeds planted though, did it on Saturday."

"Where did you plant them?" I asked to be polite, while gritting my teeth at the prospect of another long, pointless story. Dad lived for his garden and could talk forever about what he planted and how it was doing.

"In the front yard, directly under the living room window. I dropped them right on top of the snow and then pushed them down a bit with the shovel. They'll work their way into the soil as the snow melts and the ground thaws, and I'll have leaf lettuce before Mother's Day!"

"Okay, right, Dad. I really do need to go."

He said good-bye then, still sounding like a hurt puppy. I shouldn't have been so short with him—my poor, lonely dad. Only he never acted like he was lonely. He never discussed Mom or anything about his feelings, always masking everything beneath those long, rambling, pointless stories about people I didn't know or care about. And I had tons to do to get this house ready for Gloria Chavez, if I ever got up the nerve to call her.

I'd call Dad next week, when there was more time to talk.

Six

*I*ATTENDED TRUDY AND TOM'S BARBECUE ON
Saturday as promised. Trudy introduced me to as
many people as she could before rushing off to see to the
salads and her apple crisp, fresh out of the oven with a
topping that wasn't crunchy enough for her liking. Since
others had brought in desserts as well, I didn't feel bad
about not getting around to making the lemon bars. As
Trudy had said, there was plenty of food. Maybe not more
food than people as she had predicted, but definitely
more than enough to go around.

Tom stayed busy at the grill, hailing guests as they
came into the backyard. It was an all-American feast,
with hamburgers and hot dogs, potato salad, tossed green
salad with ranch dressing on the side, and frosty pitch-
ers of lemonade. Neither Trudy nor Tom drank or served
alcohol at their home. A few of the new attendees seemed
rather confused, digging through the cooler of ice for
beer and instead finding a vast array of canned sodas.

It was one of the many qualities I enjoyed about
this couple from Idaho. They had moved to California

without becoming Californians, without putting on any airs of cuisine or sophistication, preferring instead to maintain their down-home roots. The only reason they'd come in the first place was for Tom's employment. Once he retired, they planned to return to Idaho and live near their families—brothers, sisters, nieces and nephews, kids and grandkids. It was a huge extended family, and Trudy missed them.

Trudy approached with a young man in tow, a ruddy-faced, blonde fellow smiling in a welcoming way. "Helena, I want you to meet my nephew, Daniel, fresh out of West Virginia. He's my sister Bernie's son, the one I told you about. Recently moved to the area and barely knows a soul. Keep my neighbor company for a bit, will you, Danny? Helena's a shy sort and may run away on home if she gets nervous."

Daniel invited me to sit with him at a small white table under a magnolia tree. "This is such a nice spot," he said with enthusiasm. "Let's take it before someone else claims it. I love this tree. Reminds me of home. Sorry about Aunt Trudy. You know, saying that about you. There's nothing wrong with shy people. Some of my best friends are shy people. I quite like quiet folk. They give us motor mouths more of a chance to do what we do best—talk your ears off."

I sat down, glad to have a talkative companion to take over the burden of conversation. After a moment's silence, as we both added condiments to our burgers and settled in with our brand new companionship, I said, "Trudy is right, though. I suppose I am shy, especially compared to an outgoing person like your aunt. I don't care much for social gatherings. She knows it but is always good to invite me over for her parties . . . although I usually don't come."

"But you came to this one." Daniel took a big bite of his hamburger, wiping away dripping ketchup with at least three napkins wadded in his hand.

"Yes, I've had a lot more free time on my hands lately. Guess I was getting a little bored."

"I know what you mean! I love it out here in California, but sometimes there are too many people. I often find myself retreating to quieter places. Until I get bored with my own company and need to get out among the living."

"Did you move here permanently from West Virginia?"

He nodded in response, managing to say around his mouthful of hamburger, "If anything is permanent. Sometimes I wonder. I've been here five months, longer than Aunt Trudy seems to remember. And I do know quite a few people already. You know how aunts can be. They think you're still a little kid at twenty-five."

I continued with the questions, to keep him talking. "What's it like there, in West Virginia? I'm from Wisconsin myself, a town called Waunakee. I imagine it must be similar?" I picked at the salad and took a tentative bite of my hamburger.

He took a long gulp of lemonade. "I wonder if this is fresh-squeezed, do you know? I can't tell. As a Southern boy, I should be able to recognize fresh-squeezed lemonade when I taste it, as a matter of principle."

I shrugged. "Probably frozen. How would Trudy have had time to make homemade lemonade with everything else?" I waved toward the crowd of people, the seating arrangements tastefully assembled, the long banquet table filled with food.

"It tastes fresh, so I wondered," he said. "Anyway, let me ask you this. Do people die young in Wisconsin?"

"Not particularly. I think we're from pretty hardy stock in Wisconsin, what with the Scandinavian and Polish influence, and those long hard winters to toughen us up."

He bit into his hamburger again, and I took the opportunity to do so as well. It was embarrassing to eat in front of people I didn't know well. I usually avoided it, but I was hungry and the food was delicious.

"Either die or get out, those are your options where I come from. I chose to get out," Daniel said around a mouthful.

"Die young? What do you mean?"

"The coal mines. It's pretty much the only work there is, and you don't work underground breathing in coal dust the livelong day and enjoy a long and happy life."

Daniel's accent was gentle and slow, with dips and rises, like the green valleys and hills he came from. "I love your accent. Is that how everyone talks in West Virginia?"

"I guess," he said. "I don't notice since I've lived there my whole life. Until I came to California, that is. But thank you for the compliment." Daniel laughed—a warm, sweet sound. I imagined if I'd had a son, he would be like this boy. I thought about him losing his mother when he was young. Awful, horrible cancer.

"How can it be that different from Wisconsin?" I asked. "Small town America must be pretty similar, regardless of the area."

"I don't think so. In high school we used to have sausage links coated in pancake batter, then deep-fried and served with syrup. I'd mix my syrup with a little bit of brown sugar. And speaking of syrup, there's the cough syrup. Now that was a big part of my childhood."

"I'm sorry to hear it. Were you sick a lot?" He must've been frail and ill as a child, maybe due to breathing secondhand coal dust.

"No, but I do like cough syrup. It comes in handy for so many things, like when you need to sleep. And as an anti-depressant. And when you have a cough, of course. When I first got out here, I missed my cough syrup. I managed to finagle a prescription for a huge bottle with codeine and, funny thing, I didn't know I had to measure the amount. I was swilling it for everything until I realized my head wasn't right. I called the pharmacist and he set me straight."

He laughed and then hurried on. "Don't worry, I'm not a drug addict, it's just that I'm from West Virginia. My grandmother would save up as many of the teeny tiny alcohol bottles from airlines she could get a hold of, and we'd play bartender when we visited her house."

I had to smile at the way he stated it so matter-of-factly.

"It's surprising we kids weren't alcoholics. She'd give us red wine with cranberry juice at seven p.m. and we'd go straight to sleep. Wake up around ten the next day. My grandmother loved her remedies. I guess I got it from her."

I could have listened to him the rest of the evening, but other conversations kept chiming in, jarring me, making me feel unbalanced. Until Daniel would start in again with his sweet voice, accented frequently by a gentle, humorous laugh, and the chattering around us would recede into the background.

"Yes, my grandmother was quite odd. I imagine I could tell stories about her forever. But I don't want to keep you. In case you wanted to run on home, or run away, to hear Aunt Trudy tell it," he said with a teasing grin.

"Your aunt Trudy knows me pretty well. I live alone with my two cats, and things can get pretty quiet there. I like coming over to visit her."

"What do you do for work, if you don't me asking?"

"I'm a labor and delivery nurse. Or I used to be, that is," I said.

"You changed careers?"

"I quit."

"Really? You're too young to retire. Was it for health reasons, if you don't mind me asking? I've heard nursing as a profession can be terribly hard on a person," he said.

"I guess you could say that. Emotional reasons, anyway. There was a near-death experience, I almost lost a patient, and it practically did me in. I mean, you'd think I could handle it. I've been in nursing now for twenty-five years, I should be a pro, right?"

Daniel shook his head. "I can imagine it would be tough, the things you see. I know I couldn't do it. I happen to have this extreme sensitivity to the suffering of others. It can get quite inconvenient like with certain kinds of employment. I recently quit a job helping senior citizens navigate the new Medicare regulations. I couldn't handle the sorrow I felt at their confusion over the loss of benefits and the higher costs. I wanted to change every-thing back for them and make it all better. But, well, that wasn't my job description."

"I thought I'd get over it. I went to counseling. I don't know what's wrong with me. Why I can't go back." My voice wavered as I tried to get control of my emotions.

Daniel reached out a hand and touched my arm. "It must be very difficult. After all those years in one job, to think it's over."

I nodded, a lump in my throat. I didn't want him, or anyone, feeling sorry for me. I should stop talking. And then I blurted, "It is hard. It's the most difficult thing I've experienced in my entire life. Worse than my divorce. I had no idea this would happen to me, how I'd be too afraid to do my job. I guess that's why it's so tough. The one thing I felt I had control over, the one thing that didn't scare me or overtake my mind with fear." Daniel's blue-gray eyes stayed on me as I ended with, "If I don't have my job, what else is there?"

"Are you okay for money though? You've got a savings to tide you over, I hope."

"Yes, I do. Money isn't the problem, although I always worry about money regardless," I replied, before realizing I probably shouldn't discuss my finances with someone I barely met. "Let's face it. I worry about everything and without a job to distract me I'm like a feather floating around in the breeze. I could land anywhere, and I don't mean that in a good way."

The other guests seemed aware of the intimacy of our discussion and stayed away. The loud, intruding dialogue had drifted off into the breeze. It was like a special gift. A bubble of isolation enveloped the two of us and I was alone with Daniel, the one person I had sincerely confided in. I had not shared this much with Trudy. Or Cassie. Definitely not Dad. I doubted if Ruby with her training and skills would be able to consistently open the wellspring of emotional turmoil like this young man had done.

Surely Daniel must feel uncomfortable with my raw openness. We didn't know each other, and I was twenty-plus years older than him. Yet he didn't break eye contact, didn't appear restless or annoyed or bored. He sat quietly across from me at the little white cast-iron table, his half-eaten hamburger forgotten on the paper plate, the sliced dill pickles falling out the sides of the bun, and my plastic glass of lemonade sitting across from his plate, like a mismatched couple.

"The job market isn't exactly booming where I come from either," Daniel said, "unless you want to be a coal miner. And I did not want that for my future. Coal miners spend their lives underground and die young. So I came out here, got a job right away. Nothing really great. I worked at Lowes, and it paid the bills."

"Do you still work there?"

"No. I am currently unemployed, unfortunately. Like you, I guess." He smiled and burst into his sweet laugh as though it were a song. The idea of being out of work didn't seem to bother him in the least. "I have several promising interviews next week, and I'm sure I'll have something before too long. Hopefully real soon, because I need my paychecks. I miss going to the opera."

"The opera?"

"Yes, I love the opera more than anything. It's always refreshing to encounter something more tragic than myself."

"I wish you luck on your interviews next week, Daniel," I told him. "You're a delightful person, and I'm sure you'll get a job soon."

"Thank you. I'm sure I will. Actually, I normally get anything I interview for. I think it's part of the problem. It's like being offered too many choices at the feast, and so my tendency is to take everything and get stuffed. Maybe if my choices were limited, I'd have an easier time deciding on the right side dish, you know what I mean?"

I nodded, with a sudden understanding. "Maybe it's what fear has done for me. Limited my choices to make it easier. Maybe this is why I hold on to it the way I do."

"You have a lot of fear?"

"Oh my, yes. I'm afraid of everything," I said.

Daniel laughed his warm laugh that seemed to say "I know, I understand, and you are very clever for having said so."

I smiled back at him. "I can't tell you how much I've enjoyed our chat, Daniel. It was exactly what I needed."

"I quite enjoyed it as well. It was good to meet you, Helena. I wish you the best in working out your issues. I have issues of my own, so I can identify. That fear thing? I know what it's like."

"You do?" I felt a sudden kinship with him and wanted to know more. "Are you afraid of everything too?"

"Not everything, but right now there's one specific fear I have, and it is holding me back from acting when I should. I need to talk to someone, and I'm afraid."

I waited, wanting him to feel comfortable enough to share with me if he felt so inclined.

He leaned in and said in a conspiratorial whisper, "Let me ask you something."

"Go ahead."

"Do you believe it's possible for a person to change things about themselves? You know, something so deeply ingrained in them, emotionally, mentally and physically, it seems to be part of their internal make-up, their being. Who they are and have always been?"

I stared at him, unbelieving. It was like he had been inside my head the past few weeks. I managed to stutter, "I . . . I . . . don't know . . . not sure, really. I hope, I hope it is possible."

"I do, too! I've got this thing, this problem I want to change. I've been to counseling. I even joined a church. So far, nothing. I have this idea it still might be possible to root it out of me. If I do, will I still be me?"

"Same here, Daniel. I'm in therapy right now for General Anxiety Disorder. I have no idea if it will work, if such an extreme personality change is possible. I'd like to think it is."

He brushed crumbs off his side of the table. "I know this woman back home, an older woman, a friend of my grandmother's. This woman was the orneriest person you ever laid eyes on. She could cuss like a coal miner and take on anyone in an argument till they backed down, she didn't care who you were. You could be the mayor of the town, the governor of the state, and if she had a bone to pick with you, you better watch out. Her husband was afraid of her, her four sons had married and moved far away. Neither they nor their wives wanted anything more to do with her, never mind she was their mama. She was a force of destruction, pure poison, until the day she came down with a bad case of the flu."

"The flu? Did she die?"

"No, and I wouldn't be surprised if the whole town didn't wish she would. With each passing year, she had got meaner and ornerier and mouthier."

"What happened?"

"She got a terrible high fever. They said it was up to 106 or something to kill a normal person. She was burning up, buried under a stack of heavy quilts. Her husband was watching at her bedside to hear her last words and bid her farewell. The sons had gathered as well, and maybe a daughter-in-law or two, I'm not sure."

"Did she last the night?"

Daniel grinned. "Listen to this. She not only lasted the night, she woke up in the morning with a smile on her face. No one had seen her smile for as long as they could remember. She said she saw Jesus and he had told her to straighten up or the burning of her fever would be nothing compared to the fires of hell."

"Oh, my goodness. Do you believe it?"

"I don't know. It might have been a dream, a delusion from the high fever. It doesn't matter because whatever it was turned her overnight from the worst person in town to the best. From then on, she was completely different: kind, charitable, soft-spoken, pleasant. She stayed that way until the day she died for real, ten years after."

"Amazing. Wouldn't it be wonderful to have a magical experience like that? It gives me hope just knowing it happened."

"I know!" Daniel exclaimed. "Something so sudden, complete and dramatic, you are never the same afterward."

I was getting ready to ask him more about it when Trudy approached and pulled him away. "Daniel, can I steal you away from Helena for a second? I'd like you to meet the Sandersons from Tom's work."

After wishing each other luck and promising to keep in touch through Trudy, Daniel and I parted ways. I was done with the party after that and walked across the front lawn to my own place. I had enjoyed myself more than I'd expected. This often happened. What I dreaded would turn out to be surprisingly enjoyable while what I expected to be wonderful would bring disappointment.

As a result, I often reminded myself to simply live in the moment: happiness is a choice, lose the expectations, enjoy each day for what it brings, good or bad. I had sayings like these posted on plaques around my kitchen and in the bathrooms.

One year I'd bought a calendar with an encouragingly positive saying for every day of the year. I couldn't bear to throw them away with each new dawn, thinking, I need to remember this. I wished there was a way to stamp the helpful quotes on my mind and not forget them. I imagined myself with positive affirmations tattooed all over my arms and legs, and figured it wouldn't help any more than the plaques hanging in the rooms of my house. I would see the words but nothing would change.

I thought about Daniel's story of the meanest woman in town who overnight had undergone a complete reversal of personality. I wanted to believe such extreme change would be possible for me, and clearly Daniel wished the same for himself. I suspected it would take more than affirmations and positive sayings to do the trick.

At home, I turned on my computer and once again Googled "trading houses." I might do a short trade with someone far away. Yet another plan to mull over.

I clicked from one lovely photo to the next, imagining where I'd go if I had the nerve. A non-English speaking destination would mean language lessons, a purpose and focus, a productive way to spend the long days in a foreign environment. I'd found charming places in the Irish countryside, in small English villages, in New England seaside resorts—"guaranteed secure, our applicants thoroughly screened, credit check and references required." Funny how anything promising safety and security made me doubtful of that very thing.

The realtor card was lying next to my computer, the name Gloria Chavez seeming to shout at me. Perhaps selling my home would be the thing to trigger a reversal of my condition. What if, like the woman who got the flu, I could change as quickly? It would definitely require a drastic measure.

Selling my house, for instance.

I would do it. I would call Gloria Chavez.

As I dialed the number on her business card, my hands shook so bad it took three tries to get it right. It reminded me of those nightmares where someone is trying to get into your house, and after running around locking the doors and windows, always one step ahead of the bad guys, you run to the phone and dial the police. Only you can't dial for the shaking and the fear; and time and time again you try, while the bad guys are breaking through the glass of the window right next to you.

As I listened to the phone ringing through, I felt weak and faint, like I was about to take a sip of a magic drought that would turn me from a toad into a princess. Or a princess into a toad. I wasn't sure which.

Seven

PUTTING THE HOUSE UP FOR SALE WAS A giant step. More than a giant step. It was rebuilding a city. I was rather proud of myself for going ahead with it. And hopeful. Yet there was the familiar pull of guilt.

Why couldn't I have done anything like this when Mom was sick? Before she died?

I could have, I really could have, in hindsight. Instead, I hadn't gone out once, in spite of Dad's hinting around. Couldn't do anything for Mom but for myself, why yes, of course, I'd actually sell my house if it meant a cure. But there had been no cure for her.

I'd go out and see Dad—I would do it. Since I was facing my fears, I might as well include air travel. Visit Dad, go see Cassie while I was at it. Or I could take a long trip someplace exotic. I'd add these ideas to Ruby's list.

The doorbell rang. It was the realtor, Gloria Chavez. After quick introductions, she suggested a walk-through of the house. "So we can see where we're at with appraised values?"

"Of course," I said, moving out of her way.

Gloria swooped through my home like a bird of prey eyeing each delicious morsel. "The crown molding is top of the line. It's not often you see crown molding like this in a den. Love the granite countertops! The herb garden in back!"

On and on and on. She seemed to think she could sell it yesterday.

"It's very clean! Usually I suggest a re-paint before we list, but this is pristine. Did you recently have it done?"

"Three years ago, I think." I didn't want to admit I scoured the walls once a month.

"I am stunned," she gushed. "This place is great, Ms. Carr. May I call you Helena? Modern, clean feel to it, good neutral colors throughout." She punched something into her smart phone, intently punching and frowning and winking, like she and her phone shared secrets known only to the two of them.

I took the opportunity to regard the place, visualizing how a prospective buyer might see it. Neutral earth colors, shades of beige and dusty green—it was spare, clean, soothing and peaceful—my retreat from the outside world. Well-chosen paintings of modern art on the walls, accent pieces with bright colors to contrast with the softly shaded walls and white-beige carpet, deep dark leather seating to welcome me home and give me curling up spaces with my two cats.

Amos and Annie had disappeared quickly as soon as they caught the energetic vibes of this intruder. Of course they'd run and hide. I didn't have people over, not even Trudy. The cats were used to a quiet life.

Gloria was in her mid-forties, I'd say. She had bleached blonde hair, a ton of make-up skillfully applied, wore skinny jeans and high heel boots, with a fitted red leather jacket over a white silk blouse. It felt like she might crash over me, run me into the ground then step on me with those boots. She was the picture of the strong, rich, independent business woman. I felt myself shrinking smaller and smaller the longer she was in my house, despite her wide smiles and compliments, and despite the promising aura of dollar signs following her as she strode through the rooms.

I should have felt reassured, knowing my house would sell quickly in the hands of such competency, but I kept fighting the urge to run off and hide with my cats. I knew they'd be under the bed in the guest room, waiting in their dark cave for the electric woman to leave.

When I suggested we sign the papers without further delay, Gloria snapped her fingers. "Great! Looks like your home will definitely appraise above the market value, what with the upgrades. And since there were recent sales in your neighborhood in the one-mil range. Shall we sign the agreement, or do you want to wait until I crunch the numbers and can give you an exact appraised value?"

"I'm ready to sign," I said. "And then you can go ahead and get it listed for whatever you think makes sense."

"Fabulous!" Gloria responded in a flurry of energy involving an iPad, a briefcase, a contract and a lot of clicking and snapping sounds as her heels hit my ceramic tile. She moved to the dining room table where she opened and shut her case like some people bite their nails. She ran her hands over the table. "Love this polished mahogany!"

I fearlessly signed everything she laid out for me. I noted it with satisfaction and decided to mention it to Ruby at our next session. Gloria would take care of the house, I would take care of the sorting and packing up, and the future would take care of itself.

Gloria departed in a flurry of assurances of success, of a quick sale. She'd deal with everything, and I was not to worry about a thing. I let out a huge sigh as I closed the door behind her. Where were my kitties? I shook the box of cat food to bring Amos and Annie running.

I curled up with them in the living room, in my leather sofa that was dark green like the deep woods of Wisconsin, pulled Mom's hand-knit, rose cabled afghan over us and stroked their fur as they each found their usual spot: Annie curled into a ball in my lap, and Amos sprawled against my legs.

"It's done, kitties. Gloria will take care of it. She said I don't need to worry about a thing, and funny thing is I believe her. She kind of reminded me of Mom, you know? She had that super take-charge personality where with her on the job no one has to worry about a thing. Did you feel it, too? Only way skinnier than Mom, more hip, and with a whole lot more make up. I take that as a good omen, don't you?"

Eight

AT MY NEXT APPOINTMENT WITH RUBY, SHE started right off by checking to see if I'd done my assignment. "What did you come up with?" she asked all excited, like we were planning a party.

"I put my house on the market," I blurted.

"That's huge! I had no idea you were thinking of doing something so drastic. Good for you! What are your plans?"

"It's not like it will sell fast in this economy, although to hear the realtor talk it will go next week. That's how they are though, all rah rah, gung ho, I can sell your house no problem. I figure while getting used to the idea, I'll have time to think about my next move. You know, the *lack* of a plan is one way of facing my fears, I think. I've always been so security-oriented it feels very positive to make a jump into the darkness like this."

I had a few other vague notions playing around, such as not only visiting Cassie in Houston but actually moving there. Perhaps settling into a completely new environment would make me feel okay about nursing again.

When I mentioned it to Ruby, she responded doubtfully. "I'm not sure a move is enough in your case."

"I'm a pretty tough nut to crack, huh?"

"I wouldn't put it that way exactly. However, it's apparent you've carried fears from childhood to the present, multiplying them along the way. They are such a solid part of you, one single event could trigger paralyzing and crippling psychosis. Similar to what your experience at work did, which by the way, I still need to hear about. You've been able to function fairly well up to now, and you might continue to do so. Then again, perhaps not. This is my concern."

I raised my eyebrows at this grim prognosis. "You are scaring me a little."

She chuckled and shook her head. "Sorry, didn't mean it to sound so grim. But I want you to understand the importance of managing your anxiety disorder."

"I think I do understand it. That's why I've come to you."

"It could be selling your home might provide the catalyst to get you beyond fear-based paralysis. So might a major move out of the area. But you do realize it might not be enough?"

I shrugged. "We'll have to see, I guess. I'm not sure I'm ready to do anything more drastic. I mean, this idea feels pretty intense the way it is. And to tell you the truth, I've tried pushing myself my whole life, in an effort to 'get past the fear.'"

"How do you feel about selling your home? Are you experiencing any anxiety? Finding it difficult to concentrate, to leave the house, having any nightmares?"

"A little, except I'm not excessively afraid, believe it or not. Maybe because Gloria seems confident it will go well and I'll get a good price. I wasn't sure at first I'd do it. I called to have her give me a quote or an appraisal. Once she was there, she kind of took control and I was rather like putty in her hands."

Ruby frowned. "Do you feel you lost control of the situation? Any regrets about signing the papers?"

"No, nothing like that." I reflected on how Gloria had made me feel like my mom was there bustling around and taking charge. I didn't want to share the image with Ruby for fear it would make me seem childish and inept. Instead, I came up with some random mumbo jumbo to sound good.

"It was more how the confidence she had in herself and in my property carried over to me, and I felt less worried about the decision. I still feel good about it. I think she's very capable and will do everything right, get me a good price, run the paperwork through quickly and smoothly," I rambled.

"When it sells? What then?" Ruby asked.

"I'm thinking of a few options."

"I hope your options involve a new situation, even if it's not moving to—what was the city you mentioned— Houston, I believe? Unfamiliarity with your surroundings could be helpful if you can handle it."

"I should at least go to Texas and visit my daughter. She's been wanting me to come down and see their place. My dad lives in Wisconsin. I could go stay with him."

"These visits would not be unfamiliar, would they?"

"I've never been to see Cassie. She's been asking me to come for ages."

Ruby cocked her head. "How long has she lived there?"

"Since she was married, three years ago. They got married here in Pasadena then moved shortly after. Keith, her husband, had a job offer. Course it didn't last and he's doing something else now. Typical. Anyway, that's how it happened."

Ruby looked at me in surprise, before quickly moderating her expression to one of mild interest. "You've never been to her home?"

"No, I have not. And please don't judge me for it. I can't stand road trips and I'm afraid to fly, remember?"

"Sorry, Helena. I wasn't judging, only trying to get a feel for the situation. How is your relationship with your daughter?"

"It's great. Our relationship has nothing to do with why I've not been out to see her. Cassie calls me often, we talk on the phone, and she comes out to California to visit me once or twice a year when she can afford the ticket."

"Do you call her?" she asked, persisting in this line of questioning about my relationship to my daughter.

I patiently answered, following the rules of being a good therapy patient, despite knowing she was off track. "Not as often as I should. I'm not much of a phone person. Ringing phones annoy me, and people always seem to call at the most inconvenient times. It's like they know you're busy and that's when they call."

"How about your dad? Do you talk with him?"

More with the family issues, of which there were none. "He calls me at least once a week. My mom died two months ago, and of course he's still grieving for her. He'll call for no reason, just to ask what I'm doing and tell me what he's been up to. He's lonely."

"It's nice he feels he can talk to you," Ruby said. "I'm sure it's a comfort to him during such a difficult period."

"My dad's a retired salesman. He can talk to anyone. He could talk to a tree if he wasn't wearing his glasses and mistook it for a person, and the tree would probably talk back." This line of conversation was going in the wrong direction. My problems had nothing to do with my family. "My relationships with my parents are—were—fine. Really."

"It's your dad and your daughter then? No siblings?"

"No. I was an only child, same as Cassie. My parents had lost a baby before I was born, and my mother had several miscarriages before me and then again after. They always said I was their angel child and how lucky they were to have me. I suppose I was spoiled, although I didn't feel it or I didn't feel weird either. My parents seemed to dote on me despite my anxieties. They never suggested anything was wrong with me."

"Did you feel close to your parents?" she asked.

"Yes, I suppose so. We were your typical all-American family. No fighting. Happy home. Dinner every night at six p.m."

Ruby was writing something in her notebook. "Any anxiety disorders in your family history? Your mom, perhaps? Or aunts, grandmothers?"

"You don't believe me, do you? I guess it's typical for people in counseling to complain about their parents and their dysfunctional childhoods."

"Why shouldn't I believe you?" She smiled up at me with an innocent expression.

"Because therapists always think everything begins in childhood, with family struggles, and you are probably no different."

"It is the first place to look, yes. If you say your home was a happy one, I accept that. I see no reason for you to hide anything. I mean, it's okay if you aren't ready to tell me something, Helena. This isn't a Federal investigation. I want you to feel safe and talk only about what you're ready to discuss." Ruby spoke so sweetly and softly, it was difficult to stay upset with her, even when it seemed she was needlessly prying and going off on tangents with her questioning.

"I have absolutely nothing to hide," I insisted, "and I say this in complete honesty. My parents and I had a loving relationship. They spoiled me, I suppose. You know, tried to make my life perfect in every way. They didn't want me to suffer any discomfort or to want for anything."

"Can you give me an example?"

"I'd make a comment to them about casseroles, for instance. How I did not like casseroles, because then you can't separate your food and eat it one item at a time, my preferred way. In a casserole, the meat, vegetable, grain and sauce are mixed up together and you are expected to eat them together as some kind of indistinguishable mush. You know how it is. It was disgusting, and I could never force myself to eat any of the casserole dishes so popular in the 1970's. They looked like dog food served on a plate, with the ingredients blended together in a pile of goo."

Ruby laughed. "I myself have a particular fondness for casseroles, but go on."

"The day I first remember my mother fixing casserole for dinner, my dad said, 'You know, Martha, I think Helena is right. It's impossible to eat one thing at a time under these conditions. But I'm trying. Here's a green bean!' He held it aloft on his fork. My mom agreed, saying, 'Everyone in the neighborhood is talking about this recipe, how good it is, but I don't think it's that good. It tastes bland, if you ask me.'"

"Sounds like it was one of those cream of mushroom soup casseroles," Ruby mused. "I love those."

"It always made me feel good when both of my parents could see my point and agree with me on a matter of strong opinion, such as my dislike of casseroles. Neither of them insisted I clean my plate, then or ever, and I don't remember Mom making casserole again. They were everywhere in those days, too—at church potlucks, family reunions, or when I ate at a friend's house, there'd always be some kind of blended dish. I'd pretend to have a stomach ache and unable to eat, which wasn't far from the truth, since I had frequent stomach aches and headaches as a child."

I felt I should add more, so Ruby would know where I was coming from. "I can't bear to say anything bad about my mom or dad. My mom recently died, and my dad . . . he is one of the best people I know. To tell you the truth, I don't think I deserved such wonderful parents."

"I understand. We'll move on then." She looked at me with compassion. "I am truly sorry about your mom."

"Thank you." I was nervous. We were getting through the childhood pretty fast. Next would come the marriage, and I wasn't prepared to talk about it.

"How about we move to the present?" Ruby checked the clock on the wall. We still had another twenty minutes. "Remind me again what exactly happened to cause you to quit your job. I understand it was a life-threatening situation with one of your patients? It's important for me to know everything in order to help you."

I'd rehearsed the day over and over again in my head, yet this would be the first instance I'd shared it out loud. I'd wanted to, but no one had yet questioned me about it outright. I was glad Ruby had. Besides, I'd rather talk about work than my parents.

There was nothing wrong with my family and everything wrong with my job. What happened there put me over the edge and it shouldn't have—that was the real problem. I was a professional, graduated from the University of Wisconsin-Madison Nursing School in 1989 and working without a break for twenty-five years. Now here I was, afraid to step foot in a hospital. It made no sense.

I took a deep breath and plunged into my story.

"It was a routine delivery that almost ended in tragedy. It's part of the job. Everything seems so smooth and regulated and antiseptic in hospitals, and most deliveries go just fine. But in reality, people don't understand how close to death a mother can be when she delivers, how treacherous is the journey from womb through birth canal, to finally arrive in the foreign environment of this new world and take those first breaths of oxygen-rich air."

Ruby nodded in understanding, listening carefully.

"The patient was in HELLP Syndrome. Her labs went up but her blood pressure was normal. She was bleeding out of everywhere, every prick in her skin, because her blood had no platelets. She was bleeding faster than they could replace the blood. Before this, the patient had had a vague sensation of pain over her liver. I called the doctor who said, 'Her blood pressure is fine and she's only got one symptom, the slight sensation of pain around her liver. She's fine, no need to order labs.'

"Then the patient starts bleeding out of a previous injection site. I call the doctor back and this time he tells me to go ahead and order the PIH panel and DIC panel. I want him to come in and evaluate the situation but he says no and to call him back when I get the lab results.

"I call him back when I get the results—the liver enzymes are up and the platelets are down—and I tell him the platelets are only forty and the liver enzymes are over 2000. This is serious. It means the liver can rupture, or explode, and you can bleed to death. The doctor says to me, 'We can't deliver her baby until her platelets are back up to 60.' The reason for this is the mom can bleed out on the operating table. 'Don't take her to the OR,' the doctor says.

"At this point, I really want him to come in and evaluate the patient. Platelets take six hours—you get them from the Red Cross—and they have to defrost. You can't just get them quickly from the blood bank. You can transfuse whole blood but you can't get enough platelets this way. I remind the doctor, 'We can't get the platelets for at least six hours.'

"He says, 'She'll be fine until she gets them. We'll wait out the six hours when she gets her one unit of platelets.'

"Except she isn't fine. She has increasing pain over the liver, and I go ahead and redraw the lab without the order. Not unusual for a nurse to draw labs without a doctor's order, it happens all the time, but this is an old school doctor who thinks nurses should just be delivering coffee. He would get very upset for a nurse to take any type of initiative. Yet he won't come in, probably because it was my suggestion."

Ruby is frowning and shaking her head. At once, she and I are women professionals bound together in familiarity with the ridiculous prejudice still existing against us in many quarters, especially among older men who insist on clinging to their antiquated attitudes about women in the workplace. I saw it constantly in doctors of a certain age. I imagine because of both her race and gender, Ruby had faced it way more than I did.

"To be fair," I added, "the doctor didn't know me. I was a registry nurse subbing from another hospital. I'm sure if he had dealt with me before, he wouldn't have been so reluctant to listen." After this nod to tolerance toward the doctor, much more than he had allowed to me, I continue my story.

"The platelets are now 32 and it's only been two hours. I call the doctor again. He yells at me for redrawing the lab without his order. I ignore him and ask as calmly as can be, 'I'm sorry, Doctor, but can I go ahead and prep the patient for surgery?' I know full well, and so does he, the only way to save the mother now is to deliver her baby.

"'No, not until I get there. I'm coming in. Keep the patient comfortable until then. I'll be less than twenty minutes. Don't do a thing further, do you understand?'

"'Yes, Doctor,'" I say as politely as I can manage. It's all I can do to keep from slamming the phone down on him. The charge nurse is at the station, the first time I've had a moment to speak to her. It's a busy hospital and the charge nurse has had her own patients. I catch a breath and quickly tell her what's going on with the patient in Room 3.

"She listens and responds with, 'Dr. Richardson is in the unit, just delivered Room 7. Show him these labs. He'll do something.' And the charge nurse rushes off. I find Dr. Richardson, who says, 'Get her in the OR *now*. Order six units of whole blood. I'll section this patient myself.'

"The patient's idiot doctor finally shows up thirty-five minutes later, but by then the baby is delivered, the mother is fine and the case is over. The patient is in ICU receiving more units of whole blood, and I make myself scarce.

"Somehow I get through the remainder of my shift but when I get home I'm a wreck. Shaking, traumatized, completely devastated by what could have happened. What gets me is these kinds of cases have been happening more frequently lately. My fear was the next patient could die on my watch."

"I understand," said Ruby. "You had an experience which might have been routine except it hit you in such a way, perhaps on such a day, so instead of processing it like you normally would, you turn it into a symbol of everything bad that could happen."

I nodded, thinking she'd pretty well nailed it. "I can't stop going over the what-ifs. What if I hadn't caught the symptoms? What if I'd had more than one patient, like the charge nurse who'd been running around like mad going from one to another? I was registry so they'd only given me the one patient. What if I hadn't talked to the charge nurse at that very moment? What if Dr. Richardson hadn't been there? My patient only had liver pain, usually the last symptom of HELLP, with others happening beforehand like headache, heartburn, high blood pressure, blurry vision, swelling. She had had none of that, only the liver pain. It could have so easily gone the other way."

"Yes, I see," Ruby said. She was the kind of person who made you feel safe to talk your heart out.

"Each day at work from that day on, I was afraid," I said, remembering that awful time. "At first I thought it would fade away, but it didn't. It got worse. Now I can't even drive by the hospital without gripping the steering wheel and feeling like I'm going to die right there or maybe drive the car into a brick wall. It's horrible. Horrible."

"So you quit your job."

"What other choice did I have? And besides, I can't keep on like this. I've got to turn things around, get over the fears that have plagued me my entire life. I used to think when I got older it would fade away, but it's not. Instead it's getting worse. What will I be like five years from now? Ten years? I can't live like this anymore, Dr. . . . Ruby. You've got to help me."

"I'll try, Helena. We will work on it together, and we'll go after some real change, all right?"

"Because of what happened, here I am at forty-six facing a career change, a possibility I had never dreamed would occur since a nurse is always in demand. Except a nurse who wants to run away from blood and hide from potential medical trauma is not in demand," I said. "I'm a wreck, I admit it."

There were other issues besides, and I was ready to address them, all of them, hoping Ruby could draw the poison out of me and provide healing. The guilt I felt over my mom's death. The resentment about my divorce. The fear of getting close to another person again. I wanted Ruby to fix my paralyzing anxieties about work, about relationships, about money, about getting on an airplane, about all kinds of things.

"I don't know where else to turn," I added, feeling pretty low after sharing so much today, at only our second session. Usually I kept everything inside and tried to pretend I was normal.

We ended there and set up an appointment for next week. I was confused about how much longer I should keep coming. It seemed like a lot of talking and discussing and nothing I couldn't think about on my own. As much as I liked her, as easy as she was to open up to, I left that day feeling apprehensive about continuing the sessions. I felt there was something more I needed from her, something she couldn't give me. I wasn't clear on what it was. To be cured, I guess. And she'd made it clear at our first session there were no cures for anxiety. Treatment, yes. Cure, not really.

I wanted to feel normal instead of being a freak who couldn't handle an incident at work. I was a nurse, after all. People die in hospitals. Women die in childbirth. I knew it, had even witnessed it, so what was so different about this time?

My dad would have said it was the straw that broke the camel's back. Maybe it was as simple as that. Just a straw.

Nine

I CAN'T UNDERSTAND WOMEN WHO FALL IN LOVE over and over again. For me it was once, and we were married, and then he fell out of love and found someone else. I didn't. I often think of Simon. I try not to, but I can't help it. It's like he's dead yet his spirit is still with me, you know? I feel more like a widow than a divorcee. They live in Seattle, where she's from. Her parents are there, and I suppose Simon worked things out to get a transfer to make her happy."

It was our third session. Ruby had said she believed my fear of dating may be due to lingering feelings for Simon. Of course, she was right. It had been so comfortable with him. Easy in fact, the way he took charge of decisions, of difficulties large and small, smoothing our pathway through life.

"I try not to think of Simon and her together. Instead I imagine him alone and thinking of me, as pathetic as it sounds. I see him sorting through papers on his desk the way he used to do, and there's a bubble over his head containing my face and images of us together. Our wedding, on our honeymoon, in the hospital when Cassie was born, our new little family in our joyous cocoon.

"I see him going out for a morning run. He's thinking of me. His . . . wife—what's her name?—is a shadowy figure of no definite shape, without a face. Simon's brown eyes are on me, gazing into mine, soft with love, sharp with unwavering interest. I never think of him without seeing those eyes on my face, penetrating my soul, and the loneliness sears through me, always accompanied by his gaze that used to fire my heart."

Ruby nodded sympathetically as I rambled on. Sometimes I wondered if she had secretly hypnotized me, allowing me to so freely and uncharacteristically share my private feelings. Maybe the fruity-scented electric candle she had plugged into the wall was a particular aromatherapy, stimulating clients to loosen their tongues.

"Go on," she said in her soft, low, mesmerizing voice.

"After Simon left to live with his girlfriend—now wife—I was numb. People said I should take some time off—take care of myself, go on a cruise, a single's cruise maybe, party up a storm, get a whole new outfit, meet someone new. Meet a whole string of new someone's, why not. That's what they were telling me at work. I did investigate the cruise possibility before deciding against it. Too many expectant singles, too much pressure. My best therapy was work—twelve-hour shifts, overtime when I could get it, taking other nurse's sick time—until I was certifiably a workaholic."

"I see. This became your pattern for years, a workable routine," Ruby added. "Simon moved out and then remarried, your daughter grew up, and you lost yourself in your work."

"Pretty much," I said. "It's hard to feel lonely when you're working twelve-hour shifts, four days a week, sometimes more when I could get it. I suppose it was inevitable there'd be a crash."

"When your mom died," Ruby suggested softly.

"I wouldn't say it devastated me once the initial shock had passed, or rendered me helpless with grief for weeks afterward. I will always miss her. Yes, she was too young to die and yes, it was sudden, but when one's parents are in their seventies, it can happen."

"Then came the incident at work," Ruby prompted.

We'd gone over it before; maybe she thought I needed to discuss it further. Apparently I would talk about whatever she thought I should, Dr. Ruby Brown with her soothing voice and her fresh flowers and her deep, comfortable armchairs. And her aromatherapy.

"Yes. I nearly lost a mother on the floor and something snapped," I said. "A switch seemed to turn off. I became ineffective as a nurse. My job, what I'd counted on to keep me sane when the rest of my world was crazy, had turned against me. I was afraid to go to work, just as I'd been afraid to go out after Simon left me. I'm still afraid to date. But, Ruby, here's the thing. I can't hang on to the fear of nursing as long as I've held on to the fear of a new relationship. Something has to change."

"It will, Helena. I hope to find a treatment combination to help you face the stressful areas of your life. Work, relationships, getting over your divorce after . . . what's it been?"

"Eight years." I crossed my legs.

"Yes. Eight years. It's time to move on, Helena. You know that, don't you?"

"I'm not sure how." This was where Ruby should take charge and tell me what to change so I could return to work. Next week wouldn't be too soon. I wanted her to talk and talk and let me rest. Like my dad could talk, only he never said anything helpful. His pattern of conversation was to carry on about boring topics involving people of little interest.

Rita Greenwood and her doctor-lawyer husband. The pastor at their church and his two teenage boys who were stars on the high school football team. The woman who worked at the new bakery in town, who'd greet him with, "How can I tempt that sweet tooth today?" She was after him for sure, the vulnerable new widower in town, and my dad didn't even catch on. "She's only being friendly, Helena," he'd told me.

"How did you and Simon meet?" Ruby asked.

"At college, at a party, one of the rare events I got talked into. I didn't party much. I never enjoyed social situations and nursing school is extremely rigorous. You can study constantly and it still won't be enough."

"Go on," she encouraged. "Tell me about your relationship."

"Our first date, Simon took me to see a replay of *Jaws* at the Student Center, first time I'd seen the movie. I was completely freaked out by it and walking home, I practically jumped into his arms at any sound or movement. I clung to him the whole way back to my apartment. I guess he liked it, because he kept asking me out. He wasn't as serious a student as me, so I turned him down a lot due to all the studying. He persisted and we became a couple, stayed together through college. We were married shortly after graduation, and I was officially an adult. Married, my nursing degree, ready for the world."

"And the world let you down, didn't it, Helena?"

"In a way, yes. I'd always done everything right in my life. Worked hard at school, graduated with honors, gainfully employed. I got married instead of living together which was what so many others were doing. My parents would've died. They've always been extremely old school when it comes to morals, hard work, saving money, responsibility, traditional values and such."

"Do you blame your parents for the divorce, Helena? For example, do you suppose if you and Simon had lived together first and gotten to know each other better, things might have gone differently?"

"No, because I'm pretty old school myself. I don't believe living with Simon beforehand would have made him any more faithful to me. Most likely less faithful. I absolutely do not blame my parents and their value system. I blame Simon. Period."

Ruby nodded and encouraged me further. "Go on. I'd like to hear more about your relationship with Simon."

Up until this visit, I had resisted discussing the marriage. Now I'd put it all out there, see if it made any difference.

"Simon didn't want kids. I did. One or two so we could have a normal family life, the typical American family. We argued about it, not so much before our marriage because I was focused on getting through school and starting my career. Afterward, when I figured we were ready to settle down and have a baby, he was adamant. 'Kids are messy. They cost too much. They are annoying. They ruin a relationship. A baby will get in the way of our careers. We'll get a dog instead.' Simon had an answer for any argument. Except I got pregnant by accident, because sometimes that happens when people who don't want a baby are meant to have one."

"Okay, now you're pregnant. How does Simon react to it?"

"After the fact, he was fine with the idea. Suddenly, before Cassie is born, he gets motivated in a way I'd never seen in him before. It was like he had to jumpstart his career and his money-making aspirations while he still had the chance. He seemed to have this idea that he was going to be Mr. Mom and have full responsibility for our child, which was ridiculous. As it turned out, he never changed a single diaper."

Ruby chuckled at that. It occurred to me I didn't know a thing about her. If she were married, divorced, had kids, any of it. She wore numerous rings, along with her other jewelry, but none I had been able to identify as a wedding ring.

"Go on," she said, as though she knew I was speculating about her personal life and she wanted to turn the spotlight back on me, the troubled one.

"After the baby, Simon became your typical 1950s dad, same as his dad had been. Go to work, come home, read the paper and wait for dinner. And here it was the 1980s, not the 1950s. I worked too, so sometimes 'the royal husband' had a fairly long wait for dinner. He took to stopping somewhere on the way home, and we only ate together on my days off. On those days I would cook, and the three of us would sit down together for dinner, how my family used to do. Sometimes he'd be held up at the office, but it didn't matter. On my days off I had dinner ready at six o'clock, and Cassie and I would eat with or without him."

"What brought you to California?"

"There was an opportunity with an old friend of his family's in Southern California, to go into business with a Toyota dealership in Pasadena. Simon's dad provided the investment money—the Carr family is loaded, his dad owns half the town of Whitefish Bay—and we were on our way. Cassie was four when we moved."

"It must have been hard on the grandparents, seeing you move clear across the country."

"My parents were devastated to see their only grand-child leave, and I thought for a while they might retire to California. Instead, they came every February to visit. When Simon and I moved, I'd been working steadily in labor and delivery in Wisconsin, and I qualified to be a traveling nurse in California. Simon was excited by the amount of money I could earn traveling over being a staff nurse. Between the two of us, we were making a high six figures a year when he left me."

"Did you consider moving back to Wisconsin after the divorce?"

"By then, I'd made my life in Pasadena. Cassie had grown up here, and I had no desire to leave. Certainly not to return to the humid summers and freezing winters of Waunekee, Wisconsin. I'm struggling with a lot of guilt right now where my parents are concerned," I admitted, hoping to change the subject from Simon and our past. "Not being there for my mom when she was sick, and I guess you could say not being there for my dad either."

Ruby and I had talked briefly about my relationship with my parents. I think she finally understood it was nothing they'd done or hadn't done as parents to cause my anxiety disorder. I told her about Dad's latest phone call; how he had rambled on for an hour and a half about people in town he'd run into, and what they had said to him and what he said to them. The bakery woman continued her flirting, and he was still clueless. Rita Greenwood and her perfect family remained the most interesting subject in his repertoire.

Ruby listened carefully as always. Finally she said, "You know, Helena, guilt comes for a reason."

"What?" I was surprised. I was used to people reassuring me not to feel guilty about my mom, it wasn't my fault, and how could I have known her apparent bout with the flu was actually her dying of cancer. "What do you mean?"

Ruby took a moment before answering. "Subconsciously you may recognize your faults regarding your relationship to your parents, and it's coming to the surface as guilt. As a way of causing you to change a few things."

I stared at my hands in my lap. "Really? This certainly isn't making me feel any better."

"A therapist's job isn't always to make the patient feel better, Helena. Not like a nurse or medical doctor does.

Sometimes my job is to assist patients in seeing the truth. Which can be hard, extremely difficult to face, and it nearly always brings up uncomfortable feelings."

"Yes, and right now you are making me feel like crap," I said. "Plus I'm not sure I agree with you. Maybe I haven't been right there for my parents every second of the day. Does that make me a bad daughter? No, I don't think so. I think I am a good person despite my faults. I mean, we all have faults, right?"

Ruby nodded. "Yes, we all have our faults."

I rushed ahead in my defense. "I've been trying to live my life in the best possible way, despite my anxiety problems. My parents instilled in me the value of hard work and responsibility and I've been trying to live up to it. You have no idea how hard it is when every moment I've got to fight this . . . this . . . thing inside me, tearing me up, convincing me danger lurks everywhere, and if I'm not careful it will destroy me."

"My intention is to get you to examine the perceived threats from other angles," she said softly. "Because knowledge is power."

"This is what these counseling sessions are for, after all, aren't they? Getting me so I can go back to work, pay my bills, and continue being a responsible citizen?"

"It's something to think about," Ruby said. "That's why I brought it up. Helena, I'd sincerely like you to consider the possible source and purpose of your guilt regarding Mom and Dad."

Our session was coming to a close, and I was relieved. Talking so openly about Simon and telling Ruby about

my parental guilt, which she seemed to think was justi-
fied, had clearly not been good therapy for me today. I
didn't appreciate how she had dumped on me. She was
my counselor and supposed to be finding a way I could
return to work, not finding fault with me.

"I realize feeling guilt isn't pleasant," Ruby went on, "but
like I said, it is there for a reason. It's up to you to decide
what the reason is."

I listened, or appeared to. I was done talking. Ruby
seemed to sense it and wrapped our session up, bringing
it to a close fifteen minutes early.

Before I left, she gave me another assignment. I was to
take a definite step toward the future. Either go on a blind
date or call someone I'd not spoken to for ages or make a
concrete plan for when the house sold.

I said I would, although I was tired of the homework
and of the sessions, too. I had come to get over my fear
of nursing and thus be able to return to work. I didn't
need to start dating or to change my relationships with
my family, all of which Ruby kept harping on. She needed
to stay on task and address the immediate situation rather
than going off on these tangents. I had learned how to
function well enough within the framework of my life.
This recent development, my distress over returning to
work, was really the only thing I'd been unable to manage.

Ten

ON THE WAY HOME I GOT STUCK IN TRAFFIC and ended up at forty miles an hour on the 210. I called Cassie, told her about Ruby's newest assignment and tentatively brought up the possibility of moving to Houston. She was ecstatic.

"Mom, that's amazing! I'd love to have you here! Houston is such a fabulous place to live, so much to see, such a diverse population. I know you're used to diversity in California, but in Texas people are more laid back. If you moved here, it would be so perfect."

Cassie's enthusiasm made me cautious. I couldn't tolerate being pressured to do things I wasn't yet prepared to do. "The house barely went on the market though. There's plenty of time to look around and decide," I responded.

"Look around where? Where else would you go? There's Wisconsin, but I know how you feel about going back there. You always say you'll never again live in a small town where everyone knows your business. How you prefer large cities where you feel invisible. Houston is the ideal solution. You'd be stepping outside your comfort zone by getting far away from Pasadena, and I'm sure you'll have your head back together in no time. We have excellent hospitals when you're ready."

"I'm glad you're excited about it, Cassie, but I'm not sure. I need to feel right about wherever I go." The traffic was picking up, and I felt nervous holding a cell phone while driving. Switching it to speaker, I laid it on the console between the driver and passenger seats.

"What's holding you back?"

"It's such a big decision, isn't it? I don't know . . ."

"Mom, don't be silly. It's not that big a deal. If you don't like it, you can always go back to Pasadena."

So like my Cassie. Not a care in the world. Move here, move there, change again, pack up, switch jobs, lose things in the process, spend too much on moving expenses, end up in a bad neighborhood and have to leave again.

"I'm not as flexible as you, Cassie. Selling my house is more than enough to deal with right now. I'm still looking at a few other ideas and then I'll decide, okay?"

She let out an exasperated sigh, accustomed as she was to my careful, step-by-step methodology. "Fine, but you should at least fly out and visit us. You can look around and see what you think. You have never come to see me, you know, and it's been three years since we left Pasadena."

"What is this? Isn't it the mom who's supposed to be guilt-tripping the daughter, not the other way around?" I let out a fake laugh, feeling overly-sensitive and overly-guilty after my recent therapy session.

"Not a guilt trip. I just wish you had come out to see us in Texas at least once in three years, Mom. Never mind,

I know. You're afraid of flying and you can't stand road trips."

"If I come, I'll fly, and that'll give me another step toward facing a solid fear."

"Great, then I'm going to keep an eye out for ticket prices. Maybe if I get a good deal, you won't be able to resist taking advantage of it. At least come out for a visit, won't you, Mom?"

I noticed a small, plaintive tone creeping into Cassie's usually upbeat voice. "I'm not promising anything, but let's both check out prices and watch for discounts," I conceded.

"Mom, you're too frugal! You've got plenty of money, why not buy the ticket? I'll take time off work and show you around. It'll be fun to go shopping together. We can eat at some of the fabulous restaurants Keith and I have discovered. Texas barbecue is the best in the world."

"Have you forgotten I'm not working now? I don't have the paychecks rolling in anymore, you know," I reminded her. "Cassie, I've got my cell on speaker, and you're cutting out a little. I may need to go. I'm on the 210."

She let out a huge sigh. "Okay, Mom. Fine then, whenever you want. I'll take time off, just let me know. Hey, guess what? I was so close to buying a laptop yesterday."

"What kind?" I felt a lecture coming forth and bit my tongue to stop it. Cassie was a social worker, barely earning enough to make her car payment, who didn't seem to grasp the concept of living beneath one's means. Both she and Keith had entry level jobs with steep student loans to pay off.

"The one that goes from a laptop to a tablet with apps and everything, then you push a button and get Windows and then it's a laptop," she said.

I was relieved it wasn't a high-priced Apple computer. No way should she be buying one of those. "Why didn't you get it?" I asked her, not as interested in why as relieved she had not.

"Not enough money, so I applied for a Best Buy card and they denied me."

"Good. You don't need the debt anyway. Did they tell you why you got denied? You usually get approved for credit, don't you?" She and her husband juggled so many cards and payments I couldn't imagine having to keep track of their numerous monthly payments, having to be sure and pay each one on time to avoid late fees. Not to mention the huge interest build-up on the balances.

"On the application I put my income at $18,000 a year, which probably isn't enough."

"You may have a heavy enough debt ratio to make them turn you down as well," I added. *Thank goodness.* The last thing Cassie needed was another credit card.

"I suppose. I guess I'll just have to keep saving up for it then!"

"I second the motion. Saving up for what you want is always better than going into debt." The traffic was beginning to clear, and I didn't want to be on my cell phone going seventy miles an hour. "I should go, Cassie. I'm on the 210 headed home. Can I call you later?"

"But you won't, Mom. You always say you'll call me back, and then you don't. There's something more I wanted to talk to you about. A question about Keith."

"What about him?" I wasn't crazy about her husband, who was too footloose and fancy free for my liking. His money management skills were nonexistent, worse than Cassie's. He'd lecture her for spending too much on groceries then go buy the latest gaming system without consulting her.

"Hey, watch out!" I touched my brakes. "This stupid car just cut me off," I said, explaining my outburst. "Good grief. The way some people drive. It's an out of state license plate, wouldn't you know it. Figures. They need to learn how to navigate California freeways if they're going to come here."

"Calm down, Mom. Quick question. How can I get Keith to listen to me? I mean, we get in these fights and he shuts down. He won't listen to my side of things in the slightest. I'm aware a couple can't expect to agree on everything, but why can't he at least manage to engage in a reasonable two-sided conversation?"

"I have no idea, Cassie. It sounds like immature behavior, in my opinion. You've been married three years. I doubt he'll change at this point."

"That's a discouraging take on it."

"Maybe. People don't adjust easily, sadly enough. I wish it were different, but it isn't. We are who we are and it's pretty much who we stay throughout our lives. Expecting someone to change, especially a spouse, is unrealistic. We get stuck in our ways, I guess."

I thought back to the conversation with Daniel, about the woman who'd been transformed overnight. I'd momentarily felt hopeful of such a thing occurring in my own life. Now, after three therapy sessions and feeling forever stuck in my own dreary personality, I despaired of the possibility of attaining lasting change in myself or anyone else.

"That philosophy makes my career choice as a social worker fairly bleak, which is probably why I don't see it the same way," Cassie said. "I believe we can change and grow continually. Otherwise, what's the point?"

"You could be right, I don't know. Only it doesn't seem valid from my perspective. I'm trying to improve things about myself and it feels impossible." I pulled around the slow driver from—where was it? Wyoming, it looked like. Or Utah. Yes, Utah, with the orange arches on the license plate. This was making me nervous, trying to talk to Cassie while navigating the freeway.

"Are you at work, Cassie? Maybe I should let you go."

"I'm on break. Don't give up on your therapy, Mom. It's not impossible. You can improve, regardless of where you are now. You believe it too, or you wouldn't be seeing a counselor."

"I may not be seeing her much longer. It doesn't seem helpful. I'm thinking of quitting after the next session."

"I don't think you should," Cassie said. "You told me you liked her. She was easy to talk to. She had good ideas, you said."

"I did at first, only it's the same old thing every week. Talk about my marriage, talk about my parents. Get more social, face my fears, go on a date, blah blah blah. I've been facing my fears for as long as I can remember! Does she actually think this is a new concept to me? Anyway, I need to hang up. The traffic has picked up and this isn't safe. Bye, Cassie, I'll talk to you later."

I clicked off before she could pull me back in. Driving while on a cell phone was asking for trouble.

Anxiety about the idea of traveling to Houston, even for a visit, overwhelmed me. With their excessive financial obligations, Cassie shouldn't take time off work. Not to mention, I certainly did *not* want to be in the middle of things if she and Keith were having problems. Mentally I set aside the idea of going until later. Much later. Perhaps when I got an offer on the house.

My spur of the moment, caught in traffic phone call to Cassie and discussing the option of flying to Houston was definitely outside my comfort zone. I'd add it to the list of completed assignments as soon as I got home.

Eleven

AT MY NEXT COUNSELING SESSION, I OPENED with, "I've been researching things, places I could go. It's been interesting."

"How so?" Ruby asked.

"The visualizing creates anxiety, and then I think it through, which seems to help."

"That's good, Helena. What kind of anxiety are you feeling?"

"You know, the usual. The things we've discussed about my leaving: fear of the unknown, of people, anxiety over the prospect of boredom, how after the initial excitement wears off there won't be enough to interest me. Here's the thing: I think I need a project to give me direction."

"What kind of project?"

"If I knew that, I wouldn't be wondering about it, would I?" Ruby was always asking the same old things. "Sorry, Ruby, I didn't mean to snap at you. I guess I'm feeling frustrated today at my apparent lack of progress."

Why was I still making these appointments? I was tired of answering the same predictable questions, tired of making no improvement. I'd felt better after the brief conversation with Daniel two weeks ago than I had after hours with a professional.

Ruby seemed to sense my mindset and changed directions. No more questions. "A project is an excellent idea," she offered in a kind and gentle tone, as though speaking to a child coming out of a tantrum. "You could have a plan based on your interests or inclinations, like art lessons, write a novel, become fluent in the language if you go foreign, learn the local crafts, make a quilt. . . ."

Therapists were skilled at keeping a balanced relationship and not reacting negatively toward annoying people like me. It didn't matter. I'd already moved on.

When my forty-five minutes ended, Ruby asked as always, "Same time next week?"

I took a deep breath. "You know, Ruby, I think I'd like to try it on my own. I feel like I'm ready. I appreciate your help, and I seriously doubt I'd have come this far without you."

"I agree you've made progress, Helena. You put your house up for sale, you are investigating a dramatic relocation, you've explored your guilt with your parents and your feelings for your ex-husband. It's satisfying when a patient gets to this point, but as a professional, I'd like to feel closure, too. I need to feel I've done my job. That you are ready to move on."

"I *am* ready," I said. "I'm okay, really."

"You understand it's my job to ask the hard questions. I trust you will answer me honestly." Ruby paused. "Are you able to go back to work? It's what I mean when I say moving on, and it was the specific focus of your first visit, as I remember."

"I'm sure I will, once I get back from wherever I'm going. I'm perched at the end of the high dive, ready to jump. I'll be fine." These were the things I kept telling myself. "And there's the insurance. When I quit, I lost the insurance from work, and my supplemental private policy has paid for these sessions up to now. If I keep coming to see you, it will eventually have to come out of my pocket."

"If you're concerned about the money," Ruby let the idea hang in the air for a second before continuing. "If it's your main concern, I'm sure we can work something out."

"Working something out" was professional code for "easy payment plan." I was not interested in going into debt for therapy or using up any of my savings. I shook my head. "After I come back from my trip or short term cure or whatever it turns out to be, if I am still afraid of nursing, I'll come see you."

"If you are absolutely certain, I understand. I can't stop you. If you need to talk again before then, give me a call, all right?"

I agreed, hoping it wouldn't be necessary. "Thank you. I will." I didn't believe in burning my bridges, another lesson my salesman dad had taught me. "Never burn your bridges, Helena," he'd say when I threatened to turn my back on a situation, or a person.

Ruby and I parted on friendly terms, more like a couple of girlfriends saying good-bye until next time than the end of a doctor-patient visit.

I decided not to go home right away. The whole day was ahead of me for celebrating the end of my therapy and the beginning of my new existence, yet to be determined. I stopped at the mall on my way home, thinking I'd look for end of season clothing bargains, maybe browse the bookstore and get a bite to eat. If I ate a late lunch, I wouldn't have to worry about dinner.

The mall was deliciously empty at one p.m. No fashion-conscious, self-conscious teens clumping together as they rush from one trendy store to another like darting goldfish. The briskly walking, early bird senior citizens had long gone home.

It was moms with strollers, in and out of stores, with their fashionable clothes and bags, and their dressed-up infants and toddlers. The mall was the microcosm of middle-class American society, a fascinating diversion to wander languidly around or to sit and observe people. I wasn't a big shopper, never enjoying parting with my hard-earned cash, but I liked to feel part of the scene as long as I was there. I'd pop in and out of stores just to see, when I finished my lunch.

I sat in the food court with my Kung Pao chicken and Orange Julius, watching people come and go, and wondering what my own future plans should be. Immersing oneself in the world of commerce might be restful for the short-term, but not if you're behind the counters eight hours a day or a manager worried about meeting sales quotas.

It was how Simon had been in the Toyota dealership: regardless what sales are at any given moment, it's never enough. There is always the striving to do better, to make more. I'd never have the mindset for such intense determination to be the best, with the best always out of reach and one step ahead of you. I liked nursing, or at least I used to, and I would go back. It was the only job I'd ever had.

I tossed my plate in the bin and joined the throng of shoppers, sipping on my drink and wondering again what I'd do. Funny how something so reliable as employment, that I never gave a moment's consideration to except for calendaring when I was working and when I wasn't, was now constantly at the forefront of everything I did and thought.

I'd find myself thinking as I drove by a garden supply store, "I could work there. It'd be pleasant spending time outdoors, dealing with plants." Or when I ate out, "I like to cook, bake especially. Maybe I could work as a baker. Get a part-time job in a bakery. I should take a class on cake decorating."

I'd imagine myself working here or there and what it might be like to step in for an application and an interview. I'd have to practice first, drive around, visualize parking and then walking in; think carefully about what I'd say. I couldn't go into a place of business like a normal person and fill out an application. It would take days of psyching up for it until, after numerous false starts I might be able to fill out one application. If they did happen to call me, I most likely wouldn't pick up the phone or return the call.

It still felt strange not to have a job, any job. My divorce settlement was untouched, my savings were substantial, the house paid for. I wasn't hurting for money by any means. Not yet anyway. I didn't know who I was anymore or where I belonged. It was unsettling. I had been a wife, a mother, a nurse, a divorced woman—now I was faced with the potential of new possibility, of floating away from the familiar to the unknown.

As I paused to check out the shoes behind the glass window, I saw a pair that called to me. Not the strappy party sandals front and center, because after all, where would I wear them? Not the athletic sports models I always wore at work. Instead I was attracted to the hiking boots in the back row. Leather. Laced up. Thick soles. To be paired with a heavy pair of socks.

I entered the store and found my size, but right before finalizing the purchase, I saw a pair of sturdy leather walking shoes, also lace-up but lighter weight than the boots. They were dark brown, ankle-high shoes to carry me anywhere. They'd last forever and not weigh me down. I set the boots aside and tried on a pair in my size. They fit! These shoes and I belonged together.

A few moments later I headed across the parking lot to my car, the bag of shoes in my hand, a solid reminder of whatever lay ahead. I felt excitement about the future. Not terror, not anxiety, but real enthusiasm, like a well-spring of clear, fresh water bubbling out of the arid desert. Normally, I was filled with apprehension, the dark cloud hanging over me and keeping me from experiencing joy. I swung the shopping bag around recklessly, playfully, like a kid.

I felt my cell phone buzz in my pocket. It was Angela, a friend from work. I clicked talk and said, "Hi, Angela."

"Hey, how are you, Helena? I haven't seen you around for ages. You should stop by the hospital. We miss you tons."

"I know, I should. I've been so busy."

Angela laughed at that, probably figuring it was a joke. After all, how can someone without a job be busy? I had known Angela for years. We'd worked together as travelers at different hospitals, crossing paths now and then. She was outgoing and talkative, one of the few nurses from my previous job who had kept in touch after I left. Because of Angela, I had Amos and Annie.

"Yeah, busy having fun not working! What are you doing now?"

I reached my car, unlocked the trunk and tossed in the shopping bag. "I just left the mall. Bought a pair of shoes."

"See, what did I tell you? Mall-shopping, buying sexy heels for all the partying you're doing now that you don't have to work like the rest of us. Must be nice!"

I slid into the driver's seat, inserting the key into the ignition. "Not exactly party shoes. What are you up to, Angela?"

Funny how Angela, and probably the others back at the hospital, interpreted my current situation: have a bad experience on the floor, quit the job, free to pursue an existence of leisure and frivolity, unburdened by the chains of regular employment. *Ha, if they only knew.*

"Things are slow right now. I'm at work, logged in my details on the computer. I'm taking a break before it gets crazy," Angela said slowly, as if it might make break time last longer.

I tried not to imagine the nurse's station, the halls, the labor and delivery room, the routine of the day. I missed it but not really. When I remembered my last days on the floor, I got shaky, breathless, and my newfound joy began to evaporate.

"Yeah, I should stop by," I said, knowing I wouldn't. It was what one said to show they still cared. My former coworkers had felt like friends before, an era disappearing further into the past each day. It was only six weeks since I'd quit, and it felt like six years.

I wondered why Angela had called. We had no relationship outside of work, never had been to each other's homes. In fact, we lived in opposite ends of the valley. Trying to be friendlier, and feeling a little hungry for news from my old life, I made an effort to extend the conversation. "What's new at work?" I asked.

"Jane was here a second ago. Remember Jane? The traveler with our company? Long brown hair, always wears it in a ponytail?"

"Yes, I know Jane. Why? Did something bad happen?"

"Get this. Her husband's family owns this hotel in Guatemala. He's been down there forever working on fixing it up, trying to get it open. She was showing us the website."

"How cool," I said. "Are they going to move there and run the hotel?" I imagined Jane and her husband leaving the madness of California with its smog and traffic and hordes of people and cars, going to a place of simplicity and beauty. The kind of thing I was thinking of doing, if I could get up the nerve.

"She's going down next month but then she'll be back. She said they need her income to support the renovations. I think they plan on selling once the place is up and running."

"Where is it again?"

"Guatemala. A place called Panajachel, a tourist town on a lake. We saw pictures on the website. It's very picturesque. Mayans and mountainous jungle and volcanoes beside this huge, deep lake."

I pulled a notepad and pen out of my purse. "What's the name of the website again?" Angela repeated it, rattling it off in a Spanish accent. "Okay, I don't know Spanish. Can you say it more slowly, and spell it for me?"

I was poised to write it down when out of the corner of my eye I noticed a green car approaching slowly. "Go ahead, Angela," I said. "Then I should go. I'm sitting in the parking lot at the mall and I don't like how this car is creeping up on me."

Angela did so and told me the meaning of the Spanish words while I wrote it down and spelled it back to her. "Maybe you can go there once it's done," Angela said excitedly. "Fill up your free time. You're so lucky! The things I would do if I didn't have to work."

"It's not all that great actually." I tossed the notebook in my purse. The green car had parked, engine still running, almost like it was waiting for me. "Listen, Angela, there's a car parked behind me and to the side, and I've got a weird feeling about it. I think the driver might be watching me. I wonder if I should wait it out, see if he leaves."

"Where are you again? The mall parking lot?"

"Yes. I was headed to my car when you called."

"Are there many other people around?" she asked.

"Not really. It's barely past noon. What do you think I should do?"

"I'd lock yourself in and wait for the guy to leave. It sounds suspicious to me. I always say to follow your instincts. If your gut tells you to be careful, Helena, you better listen."

"Only that's my big problem, Angela. My instincts *always* tell me to be careful, and it's gotten ridiculous. You have no idea. I can't do this anymore. It has to stop, and it might as well be now. I'm worn-out from resisting life due to my overly sensitive instincts."

"No, really, Helena, you should wait a little. I've been hearing about crooks targeting women alone at malls during the middle of the day. They figure if you're shopping during the day instead of at work you must be rich. That guy could go after you the second you head out, ram your car or something. Are your doors locked?"

"Yes, I'm locked in, and he could just as easily ram me while I'm parked right here. I'm probably overreacting like always. I should go."

"Are you sure? Because I'd be glad to stay on the line with you, to wait and see. That way if anything happens, you can tell me and I'll call the cops for you. What mall are you parked at?"

"Paseo Colorado, in Pasadena. Really, I'm sure it's nothing. It's about time I get past the ludicrous fears. I was even in counseling, and seriously, it's got to stop. It might as well be now."

"If you're sure, but please be careful."

"I will. Thanks for calling, Angela. It was good to talk to you. I'll look up Jane's website. Let her know when you see her next, okay? Say hi to everyone at work for me."

"Of course, will do. We should get together, Helena. Don't be a stranger. Come by and see your old friends slaving away delivering babies."

"I'll do that," I said, thinking I should. Maybe I would. It might be good therapy for me. I figured I'd ask Ruby what she thought about the idea next time I went in, until I remembered I'd ended our sessions. I tried to recapture my earlier feelings, the amazing freedom I'd felt when I first left the shoe store. It was gone, replaced by those persistent silly worries about the green car.

I set down the phone and took another look back at the car. It was most likely an ordinary guy parking his car, waiting for his wife, and I was being extreme as usual. This was the perfect opportunity to ignore my fears and press forward, as I promised myself I would. The way I was when I bought the shoes.

I couldn't sit here indefinitely waiting for the car to leave. This was pointless. He could sit there another hour. I had ended the therapy with Ruby. I'd prove I no longer needed counseling. I would force myself to overcome my fear. It was the only way. Force and pure will power, to ignore the awful feelings always threatening to turn me into a quivering mass of nothingness.

I turned the key in the ignition and started my car, pulling out of the parking space. I maneuvered my way through the parking lot and into the constant stream of traffic that was part of California culture. The green sedan had started up too, but then disappeared. It had been nothing but a random coincidence that a car had parked close to mine in a nearly empty mall parking lot.

My entire life I'd been jumpy about nothing, all in my imagination. Cassie was right. People *could* change, and I was going to prove it.

I felt impatient at every stoplight, each glut of traffic that slowed me down and stopped my progress toward home. I was eager to turn on the computer and find the hotel website. I barely knew Jane, didn't have her phone number or email address; if I needed more information, Angela had everyone's number, was Facebook friends with anyone she'd ever met. I could get to Jane through Angela.

Imagine what a different place this world would be if it were full of people like me—reclusive, keep to themselves people, the kind who break connections with others more than make them. Not that I wanted to be a connector like Angela, but I hoped to at least get the courage to find a new place for myself. Renew my enthusiasm for—what? *Life!* Reclaim my career. Meet someone? Maybe I could actually go on a date without having a panic attack. I didn't want to be alone anymore.

Maybe it would happen in Guatemala! I couldn't help it; already it was becoming The Place. Jane and her husband's hotel. Panajachel, the city by the lake. I didn't suppose most people thought of Central America as the dream destination. Such poverty. And weren't there drug lords? Kidnappings? I'd have to thoroughly drug myself before taking a plane to Guatemala.

This could be the dramatic event to transform my personality, like the woman who had the flu and woke up completely different. That's what it would take. Not motivational sayings or talking it out in endless therapy.

Give it three to six months and I could return a changed woman.

I'd have to research it further before making any major decisions. Harebrained how I was getting excited about somewhere I'd never given a thought to before talking to Angela. I'd get on the Internet and find the website, see photos, look at a map.

I glanced in the rear view mirror and realized the green sedan from the mall seemed to be tailgating me. There was another vehicle, a van, in front of me that kept slowing down. I changed lanes, they did the same. *What the—?*

I was nearly to the onramp for the 210. I'd get away from them once I got on the freeway. Checking the rear view mirror again, I couldn't see the driver. He was in a shadow. I assumed it was the same man I'd seen in the parking lot. It certainly looked like the same car.

I'd heard about this occurring, where the victim is forced into an accident. The car in front stops suddenly, creating a rear-end collision, while another vehicle pulls up and you're robbed. Or sucked into an insurance scam.

I viewed my side mirrors for an opening to get out of this trap. They had me. The green sedan had followed me out of the mall parking lot and this white van had gotten in front, blocking my vision, slowing down. They had me trapped, the van in front and the sedan behind, clearly up to no good. A cat and mouse game.

Never mind. I was not going to be their next victim whatever it was they had planned.

Twelve

I GRABBED MY CELL AND PUNCHED IN 911. AS soon as the operator answered, I gave the coordinates. "I'm being stalked by a white van and a green sedan who have me trapped here on East Orange Grove. I'm still moving, but I think the idea is to provoke a collision."

"Can you see their license plate numbers?"

I read off the plate number of the van. "I can't see the one behind me. Are there any cops nearby? Can you radio for a patrol car to come break this party up? I just need to make it to the next freeway entrance. I should be fine once I'm on the 210."

"I'll do that, ma'am. Hang on."

I could hear the operator calling for the request and felt an immediate rush of relief. A policeman would be here shortly, and these two clowns would disappear. I'd escape to the freeway and be safely home in fifteen minutes. Maybe the cop would follow me to make sure neither of the two stalkers would.

I wondered if a random thief could find a home address from a license plate number, like the police could. Surely not. That would be ridiculous. None of us would be safe in our homes. Anyone could stalk us at the mall, watch us get in our cars, write down the plate number and show up later at our house. Why worry about crime in Guatemala, I thought, there is plenty of it right here.

The 911 operator came back on, interrupting my morbid train of thought. "I've dispatched an officer to your location, ma'am. Keep driving and do not pull over or get out of your vehicle, no matter what happens. Do you understand?"

"Yes, thank you," I replied.

"If they bump you or signal to you in any way, or make any threatening gestures, ignore them. Keep driving. Look straight ahead, don't pull over. You're headed to the 210?"

"Yes, I've still got a couple blocks to reach it."

"Okay, that's good. You should be fine. There's a patrol car in the area who should be there soon. Don't change course or stop the car, understood? If they force a collision before the police get there, stay in your vehicle."

"I understand. Thank you."

"No problem. Do you need to stay on the line? Are you doing okay? I'd prefer you hang up and focus on driving as long as you're feeling okay and staying calm."

"Yes, I'm fine. I'll let you go. Thank you for your help." I clicked off and set down the phone, gripped the steering wheel with both hands and prayed for the police car to show up soon.

"Where is it?" I muttered, checking the rear view and side mirrors obsessively.

Cars passed on the left and right. Occasionally one would slow down as though in curiosity, the driver peering over at me. I kept my vision focused straight ahead, not sure if this were a ploy to get me to pull over or engage and get distracted.

For what I knew, there might be other cars involved, a gang of thieves on wheels who had targeted me for some unknown reason. I was mall shopping at mid-day. A rich husband, a lady of leisure, all the time in the world to shop and spend money. Is that who they thought I was? I didn't drive an expensive car—it was a Toyota Corolla—we all three drove Toyotas. Divorced or not, Simon still could get me great deals through his dealership in Los Angeles.

Still no cop! I debated calling the 911 operator again but then realized the freeway entrance was right ahead. I had the sudden premonition, wondering why it hadn't occurred to me before, of the two vehicles trapping me to keep me from making it. The onramp up ahead was what had kept me from losing it up to now. I visualized it, the one I always took. The oleander bushes on the right side, the slight curve leading to the 210 and freedom.

Panic set in. I had done so well the last twenty minutes. I'd stayed calm, continued at a steady speed toward my destination, called 911. How fortuitous that I'd set my purse close at hand where I could reach for my phone without having to lean for it. What if it had fallen to the floor? Anyway, everything had been fine considering the circumstances.

Until now, when I tried to turn into the left lane to make my turn at the light.

They wouldn't let me. I had no chance.

The light was still green, traffic rushed through. The green sedan behind me zipped to the side to block me from moving to the turn lane. The white van stayed close in front of me. Still no police car anywhere I could see, but then I'd been busy watching the intersection and deciding on my next move.

The driver of the green sedan, a man with indistinguishable features, stayed in position, effectively keeping me from changing lanes. I glanced at his face, wondering why in the world he and his companion in the white van were so intent on me. Why they hadn't given up. It was the nature of thieves, I figured. Not giving up. It was probably the thrill of the chase that kept them at it—the hunters after the hunted.

Jerks! As soon as the police arrived I was sure they'd take off and scatter like cockroaches.

The lane to the right opened suddenly, the light was still green, and I saw my chance. I accelerated, veered right and zoomed through the intersection, heading straight, missing my usual freeway entrance but at least getting past the white van.

With a sense of exhilaration I increased speed, noticing the green sedan had turned and the white van was two cars behind me. No cop in sight. Let one show up now and pull me over for speeding. Ironic if it happened after all my careful driving and waiting for the police to come save me.

I was now well beyond the two vehicles and on my own, still no flashing red lights to the rescue. I was headed to the next onramp six blocks ahead, afraid to slow down, afraid to check my mirrors in case the green sedan would suddenly appear. I dared a glance, seeing neither of the two in sight.

Convinced I'd lost them, I weaved in and out of traffic recklessly. I felt like a crazy video game driver, changing lanes like a maniac, speeding beyond the flow of traffic. I couldn't believe there wasn't a cop flashing his lights behind me to pull me over.

I had to get to that freeway entrance. It was all I cared about. Two more intersections and I'd be there.

Suddenly, there it was—the wonderful green signs pointing to the 210 and away from this nightmare. I wondered about making another appointment with Ruby, in case the fear of the past half hour would prevent me from planning the trip, the one to Guatemala where I'd stay in the beautiful city on the lake. The plan was within reach. My house on the market. The destination in sight. I'd get home, find the website, do the research, make a final decision and solidify my plan.

Barely slowing down as I entered the ramp, I gave one last glance in my rear view mirror. No green sedan, no white van, no cop car. In fact, the traffic had diminished completely, giving me a straight path to the freeway. Freedom! At least I'd been able to give a description to the 911 operator. Maybe the police had gone after the two vehicles and already pulled them over.

As I zoomed onto the 210, still at a speed much higher than normal, I had a microsecond to wonder why the vehicles on the ramp next to me, the off ramp, were heading the same direction I was.

"How odd. Everyone's going the wrong way," I said out loud. And then I was on the freeway at sixty miles an hour, facing traffic head on.

I saw vehicles veering to avoid my car. The last thing I heard were horns, the long endless honking of horns and squealing brakes, before I saw the grille of a truck. There was a sound—earsplitting, deafening, making me want to tear the ears off my head to escape it. I was inside a glass ball dropped from a high building, the clamor of crashing and shattering as the ball hit the concrete.

I saw the bright silver grille, the shiny brilliant red of the truck, something written in white letters, and then the horrible smashing, the crushing of my body inside the glass ball as it dropped, dropped, dropped miles to the ground.

The great explosion, shards of brilliance, light and pain. The glass ball dropped and the darkness came. And the silence.

Thirteen

HELENA RECOGNIZED THE SOUNDS AND smells of a place that felt like coming home, comforting in its familiarity. She struggled to open eyes glued shut, considered turning her head, a wooden block nailed down—solid, dull and immovable. Wiggle her fingers, stretch a leg, curl a toe; the thoughts approached and as suddenly faded away. Her mind and body were disconnected, no messages passing from one to the other.

She was in a bed. In a room. Somewhere special to her, without knowing why or where or what it was. This she realized, in between long periods of nothingness where she found welcome escape. Escape from confusion, from the inability to think or to act. Most important, escape from the unendurable pain.

She shrank away from her body, or perhaps it shrank from her. Mind, spirit—it was like they were separate beings, Mind, Body, Spirit—three in one. The Deity. Only not God. Helena. Herself. Only not Helena either.

Who was Helena?

She kept forgetting, and remembering a different name, right there, on the tip of her tongue, someone else, her but not her. Why did the shuffling, rustling people passing through her wall of pain keep saying "Helena" over and over and over? Helena was this other one, the person she sort of remembered but not really.

If she concentrated, straining not to fall back into the nothingness, she could see the woman Helena. Not tall, not little, just medium. Everything was medium about Helena. Ordinary. Plain. Medium brown hair, not short or long. Medium build, not fat or thin. Face also medium, not smiley or frowny, a plain expression. Normal. Medium. Plain. It was Helena, blending into the environment like a . . . like a . . . lizard . . . small . . . sham . . . sham-y. . . . She didn't know the thing but it was a thing like Helena, blending and retreating, scurrying and hiding.

Afraid. Afraid of everything. That was Helena.

"Helena, Helena, Helena," they kept saying. "Can you hear me? Helena, can you hear me?"

Yes, yes. I can hear you, she wanted to yell at them, to make them go away, to stop calling for Helena. She didn't want to be her. She was not her, this Helena, she would tell them. In her Mind she said it while her Body gobbled the words. Her Body ate them up and didn't share them with the people who kept asking the same questions, repeating themselves like mechanical talking puppets.

"Helena, can you hear me? Blink if you can hear me. I am touching your hand, Helena. Move this finger if you can hear me, Helena."

The Body swallowed her voice before they could hear it. No words, no blinking, no movement of the finger.

She heard a single word.

Mother.

"Mother," she heard. "Oh, my darling mother, please wake up. Wake up, Mommy. I need you." Helena heard choking, sobbing, more words. "Mom, please, can you hear me? If you can hear my voice, can you give me a tiny, little sign, Mom, please? Anything? Are you there, Mommy?"

The horrible, ugly Body swallowed whole what Helena would have said to this girl. The love in her heart for the girl had no utterance. Her love poured into the room, made the darkness go away, and filled the corners of the room with light, wrapping the two of them together in a blanket of light. There were no words. They drifted away before she could catch them, while the girl cried and held on to Helena's hand and touched Helena's hair.

"I'm sorry, Mommy," the girl said, crying tears that dropped on Helena's useless arms like misplaced glistening jewels. "Come back to us, Mom. Grandpa and I are here with you, waiting. Please. Please. I can't bear to see you like this, your body broken and your spirit hiding. Please, if you can somehow let me know you're in there somewhere. I need to know. Can you give us anything, Mom, any kind of sign?"

Helena wept in her own silent, invisible way for this girl who meant more to her than anything. Helena would gather the flowers in the field and bring them to her, for the girl should know about beauty and growth and color. The girl would be pleased, and she would no longer need the grieving, the waiting, expecting, begging Helena for one word, anything, for the bending of a finger, the twitching of a smile.

Instead, Helena would bring her flowers. The little blonde girl would giggle and dance and hold the flowers in her hand, twirling her yellow dress that matched the yellow flowers, the color of sunshine. She'd be happy then and no longer crying or waiting for talk that was impossible, words that disappeared before Helena could think of them. Invisible whispers, were Helena to give them voice, would still be inadequate to express the love she felt for this girl.

When the little girl receded, taking the flowers with her, Helena was relieved to pass into her world of sleep and forgetting. Fading, Helena felt the gentle hands of the man caress her arm, touch her cheek. The man, who was he? She felt devotion pouring from him, always and forever, love beyond what he could say. She understood his heart. He too had no language to say how much he loved Helena, as she had none to express her own profound feelings for the girl.

The man stood by her side, softly crying as he stroked her arm. Helena wished she could open her mouth and comfort him. He meant something to her, this man who whispered roughly at her bedside. She longed to see him, to remember things about him, who he was, what past they had experienced, to view their shared memories.

As Helena traveled onward toward her world of sleep and forgetting, she realized what an immense sadness it would be if she were never to awaken long enough to tell the man and the girl of her love for them.

∞

No longer was there any sense of time or place. When Helena tried to concentrate on where she was or remember what happened to bring her here, it disappeared as though in a dream, and she would return to the strange sleep that went on and on without beginning or end.

She wondered if she were dead, if the strange faint voices she heard, the images of figures moving about, the touch on her skin were the ministering of angels. Surely she had passed on to another sphere of existence. No, she could not be dead. She was in a place of healing, being cared for by . . . by . . . who were they . . . familiar yet strange. She couldn't think of what to call them, and in her quiet, private world she called them Whites.

She would think, I am okay. I am getting better. I'll be leaving this bed soon, go home again, see my daughter. *I have a daughter, her name is . . . her name . . .*

It was enough for Helena to know she had a daughter. The girl was her daughter. The name didn't matter. Patiently Helena would lay there, considering her daughter, knowing there was a name and it would come to her soon, letting the sounds of the Whites soothe her into unconsciousness. Or to sleep. She wasn't sure what it was.

Language escaped her. Instead she saw pictures, sometimes only color, shadows or shapes. Only not actual vision, because her eyes were glued shut. They were images in her mind's eye, perhaps remembered images, or spirits, Helena was not sure. The figures were white, and they seemed to have a white glow about them, and so in her awareness they were Whites.

Helena's thought process was fuzzy and vague: *A White is entering the space. White is moving my arm. The Whites are turning me.* It was like pages of a picture book rapidly turning, not allowing her to read the text or clearly see the drawings.

When the child in a field of yellow flowers came into her consciousness, Helena recognized the girl as blood of her blood, the one close to her heart, the warmest, brightest light approaching her. If only she could remember the girl's name.

For long periods, the light that was like her own heartbeat seemed to disappear, and Helena would almost forget about this Child of Light and Yellow Flowers, her daughter. Until she was there again, and Helena would feel herself warming, opening, remembering bits of something like sharp slivers in her skin, pricking her to pay attention. And for the girl, she would try, who begged her always to try and remember, to wake up, to come back.

Oh, how Helena would try. Before it would close up again, the dream fading, and Helena would go away with a new idea enclosing her as a warm quilt: *You are here. You are alive. You are loved. Hold on.*

Or maybe it wasn't Helena's thought. Maybe it was the child speaking. Or a White. Or maybe it was the man. She believed it was good she was here. She wasn't doing anything, but she didn't mind. It was enough, and it was good. She didn't know if or how anything would change. Or when. It wasn't her job to know. It was up to the Whites, those who were capable and calm and bustling about.

Some were more White than others, and those Helena wanted near her. She felt herself shifting toward them, not so anyone could see, or could tell she was moving. In the same way a plant grows toward the sun was how she did it. She felt herself improved when the brighter Whites were there, murmuring in their soft voices to her, words making no sense yet making her feel better. Helena would remain still and she would wait, as was expected.

Other times Helena wanted to fight, to resist, to climb off the bed and throw things. To scream. She felt if she didn't fight, her body would curl into itself, shrink into nothingness and disappear. Huge and terrible nightmares came to her then, with horrible creatures waiting to devour her and darkness threatening to overtake the room. It would wipe out the Whites, the sweet girl, the gentle man, and Helena would be left alone in the cold and the dark, shivering in horror as awful fiends clawed at her, tearing at her body.

There was something about cars, a red truck—shiny, a pretty bright red—it came straight at Helena like a vicious monster, unstoppable, relentless, evil. Remembering extraordinary pain. Why did the red truck want to hurt her?

There was blackness coming to relieve the torment. She was dying, slipping away, her light fading toward the unthinkable, when she'd lose the chance to tell the girl and the man how much she loved them, had always loved them.

When the agony was most intense, the fear of oblivion ever present, it forced Helena to cry out with her silent, half-eaten words for relief. That's when the other Helena would visit.

Fourteen

T HE FIRST TIME THE OTHER HELENA CAME, SHE looked much like her own self. Medium brown hair to her shoulders, thick and turned under at the ends, slight build, not tall, not short. Medium, like she was, only different.

When the woman told Helena her name—Coriander—the real Helena laughed.

"What kind of name is that? I'm sorry to be rude, but I've never heard of it before. It's a kind of spice. I have a small bottle of it at home in my kitchen. I think I used it once, don't remember for what."

The woman giggled back at her, a sound as lovely as a silver bell ringing in the parlor of an ancient but beautiful home. "It is indeed my name. Coriander. It means 'sweet and savory one,' which I suppose makes sense if you have a bottle in your spice cupboard."

Helena wondered who this person was, why she was here; and of course, why she looked so similar to herself. Helena began to speak again, expecting the words wouldn't come out, but to her surprise she was able to form complete sentences and express herself perfectly naturally.

"Who are you?" Helena asked the woman. "I can talk to you when no matter how hard I try I'm unable to say anything to anyone else. Why do you look so much like me? Or at least how I used to look, before . . . before . . . this . . . thing."

Coriander pulled up a chair and sat down in a graceful manner next to Helena's bed. "How are you feeling, my dear? You do look a bit peaked."

"You look like me but you talk like my great-grandma," Helena replied. "Who are you again?"

"I told you. My name is Coriander."

"It's your name, but who are you really?" Helena wondered if she might be an ancestor from her distant past, visiting from the spirit world to give her a special message.

"I'm someone you know very well. Or should I say, I know *you* very well. I am not a ghost or any such nonsense. Nor am I here to give you a special message."

"Well, you are clearly something very strange because you just read my mind," Helena said.

Coriander laughed in her charming way. "I guess I did. Oops! I do hope it doesn't bother you terribly. I really didn't mean anything by it."

"Are you from the past? You have a rather archaic way of speaking."

Coriander patted Helena's hand. "Now don't worry about any of my history, my dear. I'm not the important one here. You are. You need to rest and get your strength back. There's a long, difficult journey ahead, and battles to fight if you are to recover."

"Will I recover?" Helena suddenly realized how hungry she was for information. Having been given this tidbit, she craved more. Clearly this strange visitor had additional insight.

"Your recovery, or lack of it, is unfortunately out of my hands," the woman said. "I'll do what I can to assist, but I can't foresee the future. It's possible you may not wake up again in this world. I'm not the one to say."

"You're saying I might die?"

"Now, now, did I say that? I'll do anything in my power to give you every chance of recovery, at least to the extent I'm able. I have no control over life or death, you realize. Your body has suffered a terrible trauma, with a great deal of damage."

"I figured as much. This isn't good news. I would've liked something more to cling to."

"You must not give up hope! That's a most dreadful place to be, much worse than where you are now. Don't fret, my dear. I'll sit with you for awhile and we'll chat, and you stop thinking about your dreary notions. Of course, there is hope. There is always hope!"

"I must not give up hope . . ." Helena murmured.

Coriander left the chair and after first smoothing the covers over Helena, she began lightly stroking her hair. "Don't give yourself headaches by trying to think too much," she said.

"If you say so." Helena felt more at ease the longer her visitor was there.

"You have very nice hair," Coriander said. "Thick and brown. Quite lovely."

Helena rolled her eyes at the woman. It felt so fine and natural to roll her eyes, she did it again. "It's exactly like yours, in case you hadn't noticed. We even wear it the same way."

"Oh, dear. It is hard for me to tell, what with the bandages wrapped around your head like an Egyptian mummy. I only noticed the ends here, how it lays against the pillow. How can I possibly see we have the same hair?" Coriander sat back down in a bit of a huff, crossing her arms and one slender leg over the other in a decidedly feminine but annoyed gesture.

For the first time Helena noticed the dress, wondering why she hadn't realized before how familiar it was. Coriander was wearing a summer dress Helena had owned back in college. She had worn it with red sandals, her hair long and loose down her back. The dress had made her feel feminine and pretty. It was white cotton with a long, splayed skirt, no sleeves, tiny red buttons all the way up the front.

Helena couldn't recall when or where she had bought that particular dress, but it had been her favorite. She had often topped it with a light sweater, or a wrap around her shoulders, as Coriander was wearing. Coriander had on an old-fashioned, crocheted white shawl, making the outfit appear more modest and less modern.

Helena wore this dress when she met the boy, and later on one of their dates. They had gone to the sandwich shop near campus, holding hands and laughing at nothing except the sheer joy of being together, the loose, lacy skirt of her dress swirling around her long, tanned legs. Helena had never before felt so confident, pretty or desirable as she had on that long walk to the sandwich shop with her special boy, his brown eyes constantly on her face.

"Where did you get your dress?" Helena asked. She was getting drowsy, unsure if the words came out right. They must have since Coriander answered her.

"From my closet, of course. Do you like it?" Coriander stood, twirling around the hospital room in Helena's dress, in a kind of ballet, singing as she moved, waving her arms in time with the music.

Helena listened to the lyrics of the song, and they faded away as the music and the dance and the dress blended together in a lullaby that soothed her and put her right to sleep, or wherever it was she went—the place of dreaming and remembering and forgetting.

He was watching her with such large brown eyes it was all Helena could do to keep from falling into him like a lovesick schoolgirl. It was a party, a friend's apartment, college, feeling awkward and uncomfortable, such a common thing for Helena. She hadn't wanted to stay any longer, and the tall, slender, handsome boy followed her out. They talked, he walked her home. He asked her out. She turned him down. So much studying. Always studying. No time for dates. No time for anything. Always busy, busy, busy.

As she drifted away, she thought she heard the other Helena singing a silly tune about love and madness, how one leads to the other, round and round, until it brings the world falling upside down.

Fifteen

WHEN HELENA WOKE, CORIANDER WAS gone, and the Whites were talking to each other in their strange language Helena couldn't comprehend. She hoped Coriander's visit had not been another dream. She would be someone to communicate with, to keep her in touch with humanity.

Talking to Coriander, Helena had felt more like herself, more like the old Helena. When she left, Helena once again was a shrinking piece of flesh condemned to her hospital bed.

Before Coriander, her one relief had been disappearing into the world of dreams. The Great Sleep, she called it. There she wandered aimlessly, occasionally seeking a physical release such as needing a bathroom or looking for food. Or she had no body with its physical needs, only a spirit seeking peace, intelligence, companionship, love.

Often it was a dreamless sleep, a soft time of floating away on formless grey clouds, watched over by the Whites who came in and out of her consciousness. During other spells, she would experience realistic scenes as though viewing a film of her life.

Cleaning house, driving her daughter to school, chiding the girl as she slumped at the kitchen table daydreaming instead of finishing her homework. Waiting for her husband to come home. Rushing to work, caring for patients, assisting with the mother's labor and the delivery of a newborn. Shopping at the mall on her days off. This particular dream always had darkness following it. She'd be chased, running for her safety running, screaming, glancing backward, jumping over shrubs, climbing a fence to get away. In the shopping dream, Helena had super powers, yet it also came with desperate panic and the feeling of intense danger.

Once Helena entered a room and saw mounds of food, an enticing variety laid out on long banquet tables: desserts, succulent meats, fresh and colorful fruits and vegetables; beautifully presented, lavish and rich and inviting—a feast for the senses—and she ate and ate without feeling satisfied, never getting full. It amazed her how much she could consume without effect. Eventually she grew tired of it and left the room to wander about elsewhere.

In the Great Sleep, Helena was always alone. It was as though only she inhabited this strange world, a world apparently designed specifically for her. It must not be real, she thought, as she passed through doors into other rooms. Suddenly she'd find herself driving her car along a Southern California freeway, wondering why hers was the lone vehicle on the road. Freeways were always crowded where she lived, before, before . . . this . . .

After Coriander's visit, Helena felt sad and empty, with an increase of both physical and emotional pain. Her suffering grew in intensity until she wondered how she could possibly survive another moment of it. And then she fell into her Great Sleep.

It was different this time. She drifted heavenward like a bird and flew over a land that reminded her of the green, rolling hills of Wisconsin. She saw lakes and forests and picturesque towns. It was as though her childhood was laid out before her. She quickly descended and landed gently upon the grass. She checked her arms and legs to make sure she had not somehow become a bird in this dream, because she had flown so gracefully and easily, like a sharp-eyed eagle surveying the earth below. She was still herself, dressed not in a hospital gown, but in shorts and a tee shirt and tennis shoes. It was a welcome change.

She couldn't wait to go exploring, feeling refreshed by the beautiful blue sky and the far-reaching green landscape. She ran across an emerald field into an astonishing forest, not dark and frightening like a forest might be in a dream. It was musical and golden, with birds singing in the leafy trees, sunlight dappling the path ahead, and the fresh scent of pine all around.

Helena wished she would never leave this beautiful place, until she stopped herself. She could not stay here, no matter how pleasant and peaceful. People she loved waited for her and counted on her return. She did not remember who they were, their names or their faces. A man, a girl. The hope they carried for her was a brightly lit torch.

The light of their hope faded as Helena followed the pathway deeper into the forest, feeling the sweet chill of the air, such a refreshing contrast to the sun beating down on her as she had climbed the sloping meadow to reach the forest. She turned, and saw a door situated between two massive tree trunks, waiting for her to open. Without hesitation she opened it, and saw the doorway led out of the forest and into a town.

Before she could go further, she found herself back in the hospital, her mind slowed down and empty, her senses dull. At least the pain was gone.

Her travels always felt so utterly real Helena wondered if they were actually dreams, or if she was having out-of-body experiences. As she traveled through her strange, sleeping world, her Great Sleep, she often experienced intense feelings of loneliness. She would go from room to room, searching for another inhabitant, wondering why this place had no one in it but her. Whether she traveled far distances in a car, or walked through a neighborhood with many homes, still she saw no one.

When Helena craved companionship the most deeply, crying out for someone, was when she longed for Coriander to visit again. Coriander had been the only one she could actually speak to. The man and the girl and the Whites were in and out; at times she sensed their presence, on other occasions, nothing at all. The inability to communicate with any of them created a huge gulf and increased her sense of aloneness.

Sometimes Coriander did come, sometimes not. There was no telling with her. She came and went as she pleased. Helena had learned she could not summon Coriander or call her, or in any way coerce her to visit. Not even in this did Helena have one bit of control. Not even in this physical manifestation of her own self, which is how Helena chose to interpret the woman. After all, Coriander looked like her, wore a favorite dress with significant meaning to Helena, and seemed to know things about Helena's background she herself had forgotten.

"It wasn't entirely his fault, you know," Coriander said, suddenly appearing in the doorway of Helena's room.

"What are you talking about?" Helena had just awoken from one of her food dreams. If she could have moved her hand, she would have wiped dripping butter away from her mouth, the butter from the morsel of lobster she had savored before waking. She could still smell it, the rich aroma of melted butter and steamed shellfish, like the melting together of land and sea, the swimming creatures and the gentle cattle in the green field created to give her one moment's pleasure as she dipped her forkful of lobster meat in sweet butter.

"Why do you appear dazed?" Coriander asked. "It's not like you haven't seen me before. Do you not welcome my visit today?"

"I barely woke up," Helena explained. "I was dreaming . . . a lovely dream . . . I was eating. . . . At a table with . . . a red cloth, and candles . . . by myself. . . ."

Helena forgot what she had been eating, only that she had enjoyed it a great deal and resented being interrupted in the experience.

"Well, here I am, so wake up." Coriander spoke in a bossy, demanding tone that further irritated Helena.

"When I call for you, when I really need you to visit, you don't show up," Helena retorted. "And when I'm sleeping and having a pleasant dream, you push your way in and force me awake."

"Goodness, make up your mind what you want. I'm not a mind reader. I can't tell if you are calling for me or not, when you are running around in your dream world eating lobster like a fancy Queen of England."

Coriander pulled up the chair as she always did, bringing it close to the bed on whichever side Helena was facing. She lifted the chair like it was nothing more than a vase to move from one table to another, and she would carry it to sit close to whichever side of the bed the Whites had turned Helena toward. Coriander liked to be right near Helena's face and make direct eye contact as they talked.

Helena forgot for a moment how irritated she had been about being jerked back to reality, as she realized how greatly she appreciated this gesture. It made her feel cared for, like she had a true friend—even if her friend was most likely a figment of her imagination. Or perhaps Coriander was an ancient ancestor taking physical form, or ghost form, or something similar to provide companionship to Helena in her worst days. Maybe she was being sent with a message from God. Was she an angel? Is that why she always wore the same white dress, the one from Helena's past?

"You are definitely a mind reader, Coriander, I'd like to remind you," Helena said. "You always seem to know my thoughts, whether I'm asleep or awake. And I know absolutely nothing about you. It's really not fair. Can't you at least tell my why you are here? Is it something I'm supposed to be doing, a message you have for me?"

"You are falling back asleep," Coriander stated, peering straight into Helena's eyes. "Your eyes are droopy. Perhaps I should leave. I don't want to tire you with my chatter."

"I was having a dream, remember? I like going away and dreaming about things."

"You need to stay awake, Helena. I'm here, and you should be, too. Or maybe I should go away permanently and let you sleep without ever having to wake up again."

Helena's eyes flew open. "No! Don't go, please. I'm awake."

Coriander patted Helena's hand in a reassuring manner. "If you say so, my dear. I'll be happy to stay with you, if it's what you want."

Helena nodded. "I do. Stay as long as you want, really. Some days can be so lonely. It's nice to have you to talk to."

Coriander settled in. "Fine then. Now. How have you been?"

Helena sighed. How to answer such a question?

"I've been sleeping a lot lately," she finally said. "But then I would, wouldn't I? Being in this coma and all." It was the first time the word *coma* had come to her. She waited to see if perhaps Coriander would refute the label, give her additional information, maybe how she was not in a coma but simply unconscious for a brief time.

"Not necessarily," Coriander said. "If you are aware of sleeping and having dreams as you mentioned, then you are in a form of consciousness which is most welcome in your situation."

"Really? Then it's not a coma?" Helena asked hopefully. She was still unable to distinguish much of what the Whites were saying. She would catch the occasional phrase when they spoke right next to her in their loud, slow simple sentences:

How are you today, Helena?

Can you blink for me? Move a finger? Smile? Say a word, anything at all?

Try for me, Helena. Let me see your teeth.

These were the usual things she grew used to hearing and could roughly understand, but when they spoke among themselves their words were muted and garbled and indecipherable, whispers in a foreign tongue. Helena had no idea how she was doing or the status of her condition, although she guessed it wasn't good if apparently she had not done so much as blink an eye or lift a finger after repeatedly being asked to do so.

"It's good I am dreaming?" Helena asked, plying for clues. "I was dreaming about food. I assume that means I'm hungry. Although I don't feel hungry. I just see the food and want to eat."

"It means your appetite is active, always a good sign. I'm no doctor. What do I know? I'm guessing, you realize," said Coriander with a shrug and a sideways glance. She pulled the shawl tighter around her shoulders.

Helena guessed Coriander knew more than she let on but no amount of questioning, hinting, cajoling or crying—Helena had once resorted to that—could get Coriander to utter a single thing more than she intended.

"Okay, whatever," Helena said. "I guess I'll resign myself to my . . . my . . . whatever it might be. The people here mutter and murmur so I can't tell what they're saying. You go all close-mouthed on me. Forget it, then. Guess

I'm on a need to know basis. Even though it is me and my future we're talking about."

"Goodness!" Coriander said with a half-smile. "Have you finished your little speech of self-pity? Because if so, I have some news for you."

Helena wanted to say, "If a person in a coma, with only a smirking ghost for company, can't indulge in a little self-pity then who in the world can?" But she held her tongue, not wanting to offend Coriander or scare her off. Coriander could be infuriatingly overly-sensitive at times. Helena desperately wanted to hear this news. Maybe at last Coriander would give her something she could use to assess her situation.

"I'm sorry, Coriander. Go ahead. You said you had news?" This was what Helena actually said, while inside she was crying, *Please please please please, when will I be released from this bondage? When will I see sunlight again? When will I rise from this bed, walk out of the room, see my daughter's face?*

Tears of self-pity and helplessness formed in her eyes. She blinked them away and willed herself to be strong, patient, to listen carefully to Coriander. Perhaps there would be a message at last.

Coriander straightened her skirt and fluffed out her hair. She looked at Helena with bright eyes and barely suppressed excitement. "I won't be visiting you for awhile. I am going on a trip."

"A what? A trip? Like a vacation?" Helena stammered, afraid to say what she was actually thinking. *What about me? What about the trip I had planned? Yes, I remember now. There was a trip to . . . somewhere. Why are you going and I'm not?*

"Yes! Isn't it exciting? I haven't been anywhere for so long, and this opportunity presented itself, and of course, I simply couldn't resist."

Helena stared at Coriander in speechless shock. This was not what she had expected.

"What's wrong, Helena? Aren't you happy for me?" Coriander sat there in wide-eyed innocence, ignoring the Whites bustling around her. Helena could tell they seemed more active than usual, checking her IV, her vitals, lifting her eyelids.

"I swear she blinked," said one of them right next to Helena's ear, enabling her to understand the words clearly.

"Are you sure?" said the one standing next to her, peering into Helena's face, practically tripping over Coriander in the chair. "I didn't see it. Maybe it was just the usual twitch. She seems to be most restless in the afternoons, and I'll notice twitching movements around her eyes and mouth, more so than other times."

Helena focused on making her mouth twitch, but it clearly wasn't anything she could control or force. She wanted desperately to blink as they bustled around her. That would catch their attention. She had no idea how to do it, although she apparently had done it before, from what the Whites suggested.

Coriander appeared irritated by the increased commotion and the close proximity of the people. She let out a huff. "Well! I seem to be in the way. It's time for me to go. When I come back, Helena, you can tell me what has gotten you so upset."

Helena attempted to protest, to plead for Coriander to stay, but her tongue was tied with all the activity, with the Whites discussing whether or not she blinked and how often she had twitched her mouth.

Helena let Coriander disappear as always and let the Whites do their work, while she entered the Great Sleep, the world of dreaming and forgetting. She might always be alone there, but at least she was at peace, unbothered by worry and trouble and fear. It wasn't such a bad place to be.

Sixteen

SOMETIMES IN THE GREAT SLEEP, HELENA would see visions of her past life as though in a fog. Sitting in a classroom, intent on the teacher's instruction. At the dinner table with her parents, the quiet little girl picking at her food.

Running and laughing in the park with her . . . with the boy . . . her . . . She couldn't remember his name or what he had been to her, but she knew they'd been happy.

Sobbing with a broken heart in her lonely bed.

In the Great Sleep she'd be actively moving, her feet on the ground, or in a car driving or sitting at a table eating, doing any number of worldly activities to attract and interest her. And there was another place, a space connected to the Great Sleep. This other area was more restful, with fewer activities to occupy her.

In this world, she drifted and floated in a sort of half-trance state of consciousness. She would pass through like a ghost, seeing nothing, feeling nothing, as though she were there but not really. It was where she wanted to go now, to rest and find escape. Escape from the horrible reality of her existence, where she was unable to communicate with anyone except Coriander, a spirit sent to torment her who was now leaving her alone again.

Why did Coriander have to come in the first place if her intention had been to leave without accomplishing a single thing? Helena couldn't remember any details about the tragedy that had befallen her, and she had hoped Coriander would have filled her in by now. But oh no! Instead, Coriander, selfish Coriander, wearing Helena's dress and copying Helena's ideas, was sashaying off on vacation.

There was some significance about a mall. Helena had nightmares of a huge cluster of stores filled with shadowy figures of ill intent, following her, chasing her; faceless beings trying to hurt her. Helena didn't understand why she had nightmares about shopping, of all things. She thought she had liked shopping, especially trips to the mall when she was a girl and had gone with her mom.

Helena understood her mom was dead, because there was a familiar aching emptiness in her heart when she thought about her. Mom had something bad, an illness, and then she died. Dad grieved for a long time and was alone.

People had been to visit Helena. She knew it in the way you know you ate yesterday although you can't remember when or what. She heard voices, difficult to identify in the foggy haze of her present existence. There was crying, tears shed for her, and Helena felt the power of prayers spoken aloud as someone beloved held her hand. It would be her daughter or her dad, who had come from far away to be with her.

When she thought of these two people, the only family she had left, she longed to see them again, to touch them, talk to them, and tell them about her dreams in the Great Sleep. She could not visualize either of them. They were blurry, like part of the distant world she visited, only they were alive. Like she had been.

The frightening mall of her dreams was so present and fresh, she knew it had to be important. Perhaps she had been attacked there? Or outside? Because she would be running to the parking lot, searching for her car. . . . A man's face, peering at her with hostility, until the face would turn gray and disappear.

Oh, what did it matter how she got here? She was confined to a hospital bed, unable to open her eyes or move or speak, if what she overhead the Whites saying were true. Except Helena could speak to Coriander, and was very glad of it, or she might go mad on top of everything else.

Helena passed through the Great Sleep, happy at last to be free from her cares and worries. Drifting, floating, feeling placid and unafraid. In her old life she had been afraid of a great many things. She could recall some of what had bothered her before, and all that fear seemed silly to her now.

Helena had been afraid of fire, her house burning down around her while she slept, suffocating from lack of oxygen. She'd been obsessive about checking the smoke alarms. It hadn't been a fire that had put her here, she was certain of it. It had something to do with the mall, and a red truck with white lettering. The freeway. An explosion. The truck brilliant red in the California sunshine, crushing her. Why was it coming after her? Why wasn't it stopping? Why was it going the wrong way?

It had to be a car accident based on the images that came and went. She had always been afraid of getting in a wreck, too. Silly Helena, afraid of everything, she said to herself as she passed through the haze of clouds, going nowhere, without sense of time or place, without fear.

She used to be afraid of eating the wrong food, being unhealthy, getting cancer or high cholesterol or heart disease. She took vitamins, ate her vegetables, avoided high fat, high sugar, carbs and processed food. Nurses with their long hours and stressful jobs were prone to poor nutrition and bad skin. She didn't want to fall into that pattern and she had been cautious, being fearful of a misstep.

Nurse. The word came to her in an instant.

It was not White, it was Nurse. And she had been one of them. She wondered if she'd been a whiter White, one who gave solace and peace when near to those who suffered. She hoped so. She hoped she had been a whiter White and not one of the gray ones who pushed around quickly and coarsely, the kind who most irritated Coriander.

When the nurses called her Helena, she sometimes wondered why. It felt strange. Surely Helena wasn't her real name, although she had no idea what else they should be calling her. She couldn't remember her last name. Too much had left her memory. It would be there then it would be gone, like soap bubbles popping in the air, the kind she and her daughter loved to play with outside in the sunshine.

Her memories might come back to stay, perhaps a little bit at a time, as she allowed herself to rest like Coriander was always advising her to do. What other choice did she have but to rest, lying partially curled and stiff, unable to move an eyelash? Surely her body was healing as it lay bent and broken on the bed. She had no way of knowing. She trusted she was getting better, not worse. She could only hope, keeping the tiny flame alive, no matter what.

Often she felt perfectly fine, no pain to speak of. She wished she could share it with those who wept over her, to reassure them. She was doing well, felt no pain, no fear, nor any sorrow really, she wished she could tell them. It was a gift, being freed from all that had bothered her before. She was truly in a state of grace, not part of the everyday strain of daily life, yet not dead either. Not that she was always happy, of course, but she was certainly happier and more at peace than she remembered feeling before, in her old life. It's not like she was in a perfect state. She was not an angel in Heaven floating around on a cloud. Helena knew she was alive, not dead, despite being unable to move or to speak or to communicate in any way with those around her.

Except for Coriander. She could talk freely to Coriander, and as she did, things would occur to Helena. Not suddenly or at once, but little bits of this and that came to her as she visited with Coriander, and Helena knew these were her memories.

All of these thoughts came to her like flower petals dropping around her as she drifted through the endless space. Helena was once more floating through the air without a care in the world, at peace, at least for the moment. Her mind was clear and her body free of pain.

The voices close to her earlier asking their questions, discussing among themselves whether or not she had blinked or shown any sign of awareness, disappeared. Helena didn't know if they were still there or not, and she didn't care. They would do what they would do, come or go, and none of it mattered to Helena who was in another place. A place she supposed she'd return from some day when it was time. She could wait. She felt endless patience at these moments, surprising herself.

When Coriander came again, Helena would pin her down. She'd find out who Coriander was, where she came from, and what counsel she could give Helena, so she could wake up from this coma and live again. As much as Helena found peace in the Great Sleep, it was not where she wanted to stay, forever alone.

Seventeen

WHEN HELENA CAME BACK TO HERSELF, the nurses, which is what she called them now, the word having replaced "Whites" in her consciousness, were no longer attending to her. Not that they dressed in white like the old-fashioned nursing uniforms of the past. They wore their scrubs, familiar to Helena since it was what she had worn herself. But Helena saw them still with the white glow about them as they moved near her.

She was happy the real word had come to her: nurse. She liked saying it in her mind. *Nurse.* Unfortunately, she couldn't count on the word staying. One moment she'd know the meaning of an image appearing in her mind and then it would be gone, leaving an empty space where the word had been, with Helen confused and frustrated by the loss. She was aware of the nurses being nurses, aware too that the girl, whose image was colored in light and love, was her daughter. It bothered her no end how she could not remember her daughter's name.

Coriander appeared suddenly. "At last, peace and quiet! I didn't think those people would ever leave. They can really get in a person's way, how they scurry about like chickens in the barnyard when the farmer's wife tosses the seed out."

"I've been wondering something, Coriander," Helena began without preamble for fear of losing her nerve, "and I hope you'll be open with me. Can you tell me anything? Why this happened to me, how, and what I can do to fix it?"

"I have no idea why you are here. It's a miracle, and one might say you're lucky to be alive, although in your case it would have been luckier to die. Death would have been the easier outcome. Events don't always lead us down the easy pathways, do they?"

"How can you possibly say it would be better if I'd died? That's extremely rude and thoughtless. And mean." Helena felt a bad mood coming on. Sometimes this woman stretched her patience to the limit.

"No, dear, listen. You don't understand. You die, your spirit ascends, your family grieves at the terrible tragedy, and there is closure. Your daughter has a grave to visit, a lovely headstone to place flowers, a tranquil place to come and feel close to you. Where now there is only a living corpse, caught in the betweens and downright confusing to everyone. To you, because of the questions: how long, why, what next, how much longer. To your daughter and your father, for the obvious reasons."

The tears rolled down Helena's cheeks and she wondered briefly if the tears were indeed real, if a nurse could peer at her face and see them. Or were the tears, like everything in her current existence, illusory?

"I still might die. A coma due to brain trauma doesn't generally have a promising outlook." Helena surprised herself with this knowledge she didn't realize she had.

"And especially to your daughter because of her concerns," Coriander went on in her unfeeling way. "She's thinking 'what shall I do about the house, what's next, will my mom get better, is she suffering, can she hear me, is she aware of anything, what is the right decision about her future?'"

Suddenly Helena realized something. Since Coriander seemed to know so much about her, she might know the name of her daughter. "Do you know my daughter's name? I can't remember it, and that really bothers me," Helena asked in a tentative way.

"Well, yes, I do."

"You do? Oh, that's wonderful, Coriander! What is it? What is her name?"

"Sorry, dear, I can't tell you. It's information I'm not at liberty to say."

Helena couldn't believe her ears. "That makes no sense. It's just a name. Why can't you tell it to me?"

Coriander shook her head and tightened her mouth.

There were times—right now, for instance—when Helena wished Coriander would go away and leave her in peace. Coriander was pushing her to the limits today. As though reading her mind, Coriander disappeared in an instant.

Good! Helena thought, then closed her eyes and entered the Great Sleep. She didn't know how long she was there, but it was pleasant and she quite enjoyed it.

She figured she'd be staying out longer, but as soon as she entered the woods, she came to, returning to her hospital room. There was Coriander, sitting in her usual spot, close to Helena, her eyes peering into Helena's.

Helena jumped and let out a squeal. "You startled me!"

"I'm sorry." Coriander laughed as though she were more entertained than sorry. "I like that you said, 'startled' and not 'frightened.' That's an improvement, isn't it?"

"I suppose it is. You know, now that you mention it, I hardly feel fear. I barely remember what it's like."

"Good. Let's keep it that way, shall we?"

"I wasn't sure when I'd see you again." Helena remembered she'd been upset with Coriander about something but could not recall the details.

Coriander waved a dismissive hand. "I can never stay away for long, Helena. You have become dear to me. I value our friendship and enjoy our conversations."

Helena doubted it, since Coriander became easily annoyed and offended by any little thing. But the last thing Helena wanted was to alienate the one person she could have a conversation with.

"I feel the same," Helena said, mentally crossing her fingers. The truth was, Coriander was the kind of friend you love to hate, as annoying as she was charming. Or as her dad used to say, "With a friend like that, who needs enemies?"

Immediately, Helena felt happy she had remembered her dad and how he used to spout off his random sayings. She tried thinking of other things he might have told her, but Coriander was talking, distracting Helena from her memories.

"I am convinced we knew each other in the pre-existence," Coriander said.

Helena was confused. Was the pre-existence another word whose meaning she had forgotten? "The pre-existence?" she said in a puzzled tone.

"Yes. You know, the one we came from before we were born on Earth."

Helena didn't know about any other world, except for her own personal dream worlds, but then she had forgotten so much. "I can't remember it. Sorry."

"Most people can't, no need to apologize. It's too bad though, because it explains a great deal."

"Do you remember it?" Helena asked.

"Bits and pieces, fragments only. When I strive for a fuller picture, sometimes it comes to me."

Helena nodded. "That's how I am with my life prior to . . . to . . . to this . . . whatever it was that put me here." She gave Coriander a direct look. "Do you know what happened?"

"Yes, I know."

"Then why haven't you told me?" Helena blurted. "I can't remember anything, except for images that flash before my eyes then disappear. There's nothing continuous to explain how the pictures relate to each other."

"You never asked me," Coriander said in her matter-of-fact way, pulling the white shawl tighter around her shoulders.

"Are you sure? I thought I had."

"No, my dear, you did not. If you thought you did, well, you can't expect me to read your thoughts," Coriander said gently.

Helena wanted to remind Coriander she had indeed read her thoughts on numerous occasions. Instead she said, "Tell me, please. What happened to me?"

Coriander shrugged. "You know already."

"How can I know? I told you I don't remember!"

"Tell me what images you see."

Helena stopped to think. "It's the red truck going the wrong way. Hitting me. An explosion. Horrible crushing. Noise. Blood. The mall in darkness. People after me. I'm running for my life. A man's face staring at me."

"It appears you have most of it."

"Can't you put it together for me? Explain what happened in a way to make sense?"

"Of course, if it's what you want me to do."

"Yes!" This woman could be infuriatingly stubborn and resistant. It was like Coriander spoke a different language. Realizing her own language skills may not yet be up to par, however, Helena wondered if she had been communicating effectively. Perhaps she used the wrong words, with her sentences disconnected.

"Fine, Helena, there's no need to shout. If you insist, I'll tell you, but don't say I didn't warn you," Coriander said.

"Warn me about what? What is worse than where I am right now, I'd like to know."

"There's no need to get snippy, young lady."

Helena sighed. "Sorry. Please continue."

Coriander smoothed her skirt, spread it neatly around her, and pulled the chair in closer. "Now, Helena, I am going to tell you one thing you need to understand to make sense of the rest."

"I'm listening."

"It works like this. Everything was created spiritually before it was created physically," she said.

"Whatever that means." Helena tried not to sound snippy again. Her head was hurting. "Thinking too much gives me a headache. You'll need to break it down for me, Coriander."

"What it means is in the pre-existence you were created spiritually first before you were born physically on Earth."

There was that word again. "The pre-existence. Right." Helena wondered what this had to do with her accident. "Accident! I have the word, accident, it just came to me! I had an accident. With a red truck."

"That's right. You were hurt very badly. Nearly killed. The air bag saved your life."

"The air bag must have been the crushing sense I had," Helena said. "A feeling like the air being pressed out of me. And the explosion was the crash."

"It was a terrible collision, just awful. Poor, dear Helena. No one could believe you had survived. They finally got to you by the Jaws of Life, to tear apart the mangled metal."

Helena couldn't remember, but she said, "I'm getting the picture. Go on."

"You want to know the truth of what happened. Fine, I'll tell you, but you won't like it." Coriander paused before continuing. "It was first created spiritually."

"Oh, come on now. That's a horrible idea. Who would plan such a disaster to ruin my life? Don't tell me God did, because I won't believe it."

Coriander gazed a long time at Helena before answering in a very soft voice, "No, Helena, it wasn't God. It was you."

"What? Don't be ridiculous. This makes no sense what-soever." She closed her eyes against Coriander's words, wishing she could throw a pillow at the woman, if only her arms could move.

"Let's begin earlier, to help you understand. Think about when you were younger, early on in your marriage per-haps, or when you were a young woman. What did you fear most?" Coriander asked.

"Probably divorce. I didn't want to ever be divorced. My parents were happily married for all those years, and I couldn't imagine anything different for myself. I couldn't comprehend the end of a marriage. What I'd do, how I'd deal with it."

"Yet you are divorced."

"You are saying because I was afraid of getting a divorce, it happened?"

"In a way. Because you imagined it, and not once or twice but over and over in your head. Therefore, you cre-ated it spiritually. Thus it follows the divorce was created physically, in reality. Or what is your reality."

Helena shook her head. "You're saying it is my fault Simon cheated on me? It is my fault he stopped loving me? It is my fault he left me for another woman?"

In an instant, Helena had remembered the brown-eyed boy's name, and worse, she remembered how their sweet romance had ended.

"Absolutely not! I don't buy it for one minute," she said. "I will not take the blame for his infidelity."

"I'm not saying it is your fault, only that you created the scenario through your repeated fearful imaginings. You are certainly not responsible for your husband breaking his marriage vows. I don't mean to say that."

"It sounds like you are saying exactly that."

"I know it is difficult to understand, tied to the physical world as you are, with no concept of the spiritual world existing in the same sphere," Coriander said calmly.

"No, I don't get it. Put it more simply, please," Helena demanded.

"Your husband is accountable for his behavior and will someday be judged accordingly. Then again, you picked him, didn't you? You married him. You chose a willing player for the creation already taking shape in your mind: a cheating spouse, a failed marriage, divorce—what you yourself created spiritually before it took shape physically."

"You are mean," Helena said through clenched teeth. "You are a mean, horrible person, Coriander. I don't know how I ever took you for an angel. You are not a messenger of God, more likely a messenger of the Devil. You are the Devil, that's what you are."

Coriander shook her head, as though in sorrow, which made Helena angrier. "Don't fake how sorry you feel," Helena shouted at her. "Don't pretend to be my friend. Just go and never come back. Go on the stupid vacation you were planning. I'm better off without you!"

Helena's aching head and heart could not process Coriander's ridiculous explanation, nor did she want to. She had analyzed the marriage a thousand different ways for the past two decades, but never in her wildest scenarios had she come up with this scheme.

Crazy Coriander.

Eighteen

HEN HELENA RETURNED FROM THE Great Sleep, where she had been driving alone on an endless freeway, she was surprised to see Coriander sitting next to her bed.

"Didn't I tell you to leave?" It had been an unpleasant dream, the driving and driving and driving across open plains of nothingness without making one bit of progress. Coriander, with her warped view of the Universe, was the last person she wanted to see.

"Yes, you did, but I don't take my orders from you, my dear. Now, are you ready to continue our discussion from before you fell asleep? Are you prepared to hear the truth yet?" Coriander cocked her head, and Helena thought she looked exactly like an arrogant little puffed up bird about to swallow a fat worm.

"Oh, fine! Only never mind my divorce. I don't intend to spend any more of whatever time is left to me thinking about it. What about my accident? You said I created it." *Let's hear the weird ghost woman explain this one.*

"Yes, I know I said that, but one more thing about the divorce, if you will allow me."

Helena closed her eyes and gave a slight nod, her signal for Coriander to go ahead.

She did not hesitate, jumping right in as though she couldn't wait to lay it out at Helena's feet. "You are not to blame for the divorce, Helena, nor did you cause it, but you married the man who did so by betraying his vows. Simon Carr was one who always went after what he wanted until he got it. Remember how he relentlessly pursued you? He was a man who knew what he wanted at any given moment and then went after it. You know that, don't you, my dear?"

"Yes, I do. I'll grant you that. The assertiveness in his personality attracted me. I'm not that way myself, and I tend to admire it in people. My daughter is like her dad. Got it from him, I suppose. Only she's a good and loving person where he was self-centered . . . *is* self-centered." Helena paused, the tears close to the surface, thinking about her daughter. "Half the time I've forgotten I have a daughter. Or had a husband. I can't count on my memories, and I want so much to talk to her, to comfort her, Coriander. It's all I want in the world, really, and I can't even remember her name."

"Of course you do, dear Helena, of course you do. I can't imagine you wanting anything else more than that one thing," Coriander said, with a compassionate tone Helena had not yet heard from her. It encouraged her to go on.

"I try to get out one word, one little flicker of movement when she is here, to give her a sign, any sign at all, to show her I am here. She begs me to, and I want to but I can't, I just can't. Why not, Coriander? What's wrong with me that I can't do this one thing for my daughter?"

"Nothing is wrong with you, my dear. It's the coma, you know. You can't help it. It's not your fault."

"But you said it was, remember? You said we get what we want in life. I want to talk to my daughter. I don't want this coma!"

"Of course. But like most people caught up in their own lives and entrenched in the rules and boundaries of this world, you didn't really understand my meaning."

Helena couldn't stop crying. Through broken sobs she managed to say, "No, no, it doesn't make sense . . . none of it does. . . . Nothing makes sense, I'm so tired of it . . . trying to understand . . . to focus. . . ."

"There, there now, Helena, see if you can calm yourself. I'll give you a bit more information, I promise. You hush now and listen, all right?" Coriander said, still with the unfamiliar compassion that was like balm to Helena's troubled heart.

Helena nodded, managing to quiet herself, stopping the tears and willing herself to listen. Despite her doubts and confusion, Helena did understand one thing. Coriander was strange and quite possibly a figment of her imagination, but without her, Helena would have no one. She would be utterly alone in her miserable coma. To be left alone in this transitional state, neither dead nor alive, would be worse than death itself.

"Now don't get me wrong, Helena, none of what I'm talking about is conscious—neither you nor anyone else in the world are to blame for the actions of other people," Coriander explained. "We are, every one of us, like pieces of a jigsaw puzzle that fit together to form a cohesive picture. Over time the pieces join together with where they fit best."

Coriander's voice soothed Helena's headache, and she was intrigued. She felt her mind opening up. Coriander had a way of explaining things to made her think, Helena realized, now that she had calmed down.

"Tell me more about the pre-existence, about the spiritual worlds you always talk about," Helena said. "I'm sorry I called you the Devil."

"Apology accepted. Are you sure it won't wear you out to have me going on like this? You seem to be tiring quickly."

"I'm fine," Helena murmured. "I'll close my eyes while you talk though, if you don't mind. Don't hold back. This mumbo jumbo of yours is good for my brain waves, I can feel it."

Coriander giggled and pulled her chair closer to Helena. She spread out her skirt and rearranged her shawl, still wearing Helena's favorite white dress of long ago. "If you are sure. Let me know when you want me to stop. I can always come back later, you know, if your brain needs a rest."

"My brain has had way too much resting, I think. You go right ahead, Coriander. I'm listening."

"If you insist," Coriander took a deep breath. "Let's start by saying the source of all light is eternal, permeating from the Universe and filling the Universe with light. A light spectrum with great variety, because light is electromagnetic radiation; and the different types can be twenty to thirty feet tall like radio waves, to gamma rays so small and fast they can penetrate up to seven feet of concrete."

"Okay, I get it. You're saying the Universe is made of light, and light has many differing qualities. I seem to remember learning that in physics."

"The light we see, the visible light, is just a tiny slice from the electromagnetic spectrum. When we talk about God and how He is the source of all light and all truth, then God is also the source of the electromagnetic spectrum, which could actually be larger than what man can detect."

"Yes, I suppose so. Makes sense," Helena said, forcing her eyes to stay open. She imagined the pathways in her brain opening up to welcome this new information. She would force herself to stay awake, to think and to fight this coma with knowledge bestowed on her by Coriander.

"If God is radiating this much light, our physical bodies would be blasted with radiation emanating from His being. Not to mention the spiritual shock of we imperfect flawed beings in the presence of the Perfect One. Neither physically nor spiritually could we stand in His presence. We would have to be changed both physically and spiritually to stand before God, or we would be burned in His presence, as we would if the Earth came too close to the sun."

Helena nodded. "I'm listening."

"Another insight is this. Anywhere our scientists point their instruments of detection toward space, they sense something which can be described as a hum, a quiet hum throughout the Universe. Scientists attribute this microwave radiation left over from the Big Bang, yet it is constant."

"A sign of God?"

"Very likely. It can be the physical manifestation of God's light. But think of this, Helena. Despite His massive governance of the Universe and His presence throughout, He can still speak to the individual and help us under-stand how to fit our own personal jigsaw puzzles together."

Helena felt a stab of longing. She knew this to be true, yet she wanted to feel it personally. She could use God's help in putting together her jigsaw puzzle. "Go on," she said, in a whisper.

"His influence permeates all of space yet can focus on each individual, to help us get through everything here and then return to Him."

"Then why do bad things have to happen?" Helena asked. "Don't say it's our fault like you did before. Because I'm sorry, Coriander, but that didn't make one bit of sense."

"Let me explain it a different way. Bad things happen because the human will is sacred to Him. God will not interfere with our power of choice, although He can bring good out of evil. Your accident was caused by evil as those people went after you, and yet good came out of it."

"Good? You call me being in a coma good?"

"Well, yes, because we were able to meet and become friends," Coriander said demurely. "It may not have hap-pened otherwise. I look forward to my visits with you. I hope they are a help to you."

Helena nodded. "They are, most of the time. If I didn't have you to talk to I'd go mad, I'm sure. You say such strange things. It makes me think, which I know helps to keep my brain active. I've always wondered about God.

I suppose everyone does. I believe in God—I mean, I'm not an atheist or anything, but why does He have to be so distant? Why does life need to be so terribly hard? Doesn't God realize more people would believe in Him if He talked to us, or at least answered our prayers? He is too distant and remote—that's the whole problem with God."

"People are complicated, Helena. You mustn't blame God for our own human weakness."

"Why do people have to be complicated anyway? There's another question I've had, since you bring it up. I've always tried to simplify, thinking it might make things easier. Why is it so difficult to lead an ordinary, uncomplicated life?"

"It's because of quantum mechanics. Our brains use electrical impulses to communicate with the rest of our body. You could look at an electron and measure its speed and position and know where it's going, and know what each person would do, and know the history and future of the world just by knowing about the electrons. But quantum mechanics says no, it is impossible to know the speed and position of the electrons. Simply the act of observing them changes their speed and position because to see them we have to shoot light at them. So by observing these particles you then change what they do."

"I guess it makes sense then, doesn't it, since our brains are made up of electrons," Helena said. "This one thing alone makes us all hopelessly complicated." She could feel her mind expand further with the intelligence Coriander was verbalizing. It was like medicine for her brain.

"Light can be described as a wave, but it can also be described as a photon. A photon is a little light-carrying particle. If you were to set up a device that has two paths light can take, with a mirror that can send light down one path or another, at the intersection the light interferes with itself, like entering a prism. Light enters a prism as white and then comes out in different colors. Instead of sending all the light at once, you send a photon that can't split itself in two. Shoot one photon at a time and you get a dot—one dot after another."

"I get it," Helena said. "This is helping."

"The point of the experiment proves this fact: by observing something you change it. Exactly why people are so complicated. It's impossible to know what people will think or do, because these little electrons are constantly changing. The motions of the particles cannot be predicted, not by others and often not even by ourselves. And thus you see, Helena, why it is impossible to have the simple life you wish for."

"I often don't know why I do what I do. Or why anyone else does what they do. We are complicated and life is complicated and God is beyond our comprehension, and it annoys me when people act like they have all the answers," Helena concluded.

"Is that how I act? Because if so, I apologize. I was simply answering your questions the best I could and trying to get you thinking in the process. Because the mental exercise is good for you, Helena."

"It stimulates my photons? Or is it my electrons?"

"Your electrons. Photons are just light. Thinking is movement of electricity through your brain, and we need to get things moving for you, Helena. We don't want these people here to think there's no activity going on there and pull the plug, as they say, do we?"

In all the conversations Helena and Coriander had had, this was the first time Coriander had mentioned such a possibility. And the first time Helena gave a thought to it herself.

"Really, Coriander? Is this possible? What have you heard about this pulling the plug business?"

"I can't say. What have *you* heard?"

"Nothing. I can't understand them. To me, they're speaking a different language. And they mumble as well."

"There have been tests done. So far you are fine, showing signs of brain activity. We need to make sure it stays that way and gets stronger. It's what we are after."

"Who are *we*? Do you mean you and me, or someone . . . someone else?"

"Never mind. It's a figure of speech."

If only Coriander would give up more information! She'd get so close to saying something meaningful and then back away. "Coriander, do you know how long it's been since the coma? Since the accident?"

Coriander laughed her tinkling bell laugh. "Ah, time. What is time to me? I can't answer that question, and what does it matter? Wondering about such things won't get you better. It will cycle your thoughts around and around in a tiny pointless circle. *When will I get better? How long have I been here? When will I wake up? Am I going to die?* Around and around you'll go with no answers, when meanwhile your body is not getting the signals from your brain it needs."

"Or perhaps my brain isn't sparkling with electronic impulses at the moment," Helena said.

"It's my job to help you there. We have a lot of work to do before I can leave you long enough to go on my vacation."

Funny thing was Helena felt very much alive, similar to how one feels when first waking up. You don't want to get out of bed, don't want to talk or interact immediately with the real world. You prefer to keep inhabiting your fuzzy dream world, half asleep, not ready to jump into the day's activities, thinking a little bit about the dream that might have woken you up. Still you are alive, and a new day beckons.

It was how Helena felt. Despite everything, a new day was beckoning. Things might be unclear and confusing at times, and remembering the details was difficult. But she was alive, she knew it and she felt it. No one was going take her life away from her. She had to get better before they tried.

As Coriander so often reminded her, it didn't matter how long she'd been like this. What mattered was for her brain activity to increase, that somehow the electrical impulses forming her thoughts and directing her body would make their connections. Although she'd try to concentrate on opening her eyes, moving a finger as the nurses would ask her to do, she just couldn't. There was no electricity flowing. The power source failed her. It was like something had been unplugged in her brain and she had no idea how to reconnect it.

Coriander would help her, was already helping her with those long, rambling discussions of whatever seemed to be on her mind at the moment of each visit. Helena wondered if their conversations had a purpose, or if it was dialogue unrelated to anything specific.

You could never be sure about Coriander. Some days she seemed focused and organized and on a mission, with a definite purpose at hand, and other times she rambled on as though meandering along a garden path, simply enjoying whatever delighted her and caught her fancy. Coriander would talk in her lilting tones sprinkled with the bell-like laugh, or sometimes a little huff of annoyance when she was put out by something, such as when there were too many people in the room to suit her.

Helena became as familiar with Coriander's moods and quirks and habits as she'd been with her husband's and daughter's. Surely Coriander had been coming to visit for a long time for Helena to know her so well. Which meant she had been in this coma for a very long time, she assumed.

Was it long enough to make them consider pulling the plug on her?

Nineteen

CORIANDER HAD LEFT, AND HELENA WAN-dered through the familiar path of her Great Sleep feeling lonelier than ever. Empty streets, empty homes. It was such a wilderness. Except for the birds flying above, it was void of life.

Before, she had been content to explore on her own, but after following the same path over and over with the identical scenery, she decided to try a different tactic. She would approach one of the homes and knock or ring the doorbell, to see if anyone was there.

Helena liked how she was dressed today, in her favorite white dress. She was pleased to discover that she instead of Coriander was wearing it, and with no old-fashioned shawl either. Her shoulders were bare, and she felt free and beautiful, such a nice change from how she'd been feeling lately. This would be a good day to take a different approach.

She marched up the sidewalk to a charming, two-story house, one that reminded her of her parents' home, the one she'd grown up in.

Funny how I never thought of doing this before, Helena thought. She imagined it must be Coriander's discourse on the Universe. It must have expanded her brain waves enough to give her thoughts about utilizing more options. And it didn't hurt that she was wearing her special white dress either.

As she approached the front door she felt nervous. It was the old familiar fear of the unknown which had always been with her, with the old Helena. It had been nice experiencing her current world, as limited as it was, without fear. But now, raising her hand to ring the doorbell came the awful, horrible dread pulsing against her ribs like a heart attack, making her feel sick and confused. It had been such a relief to be free of such anxiety in the coma, yet here it was back again, stronger than ever.

What would she say if someone came to the door? How would she explain herself? What if the people inside wanted to hurt her? If they asked a lot of questions, she'd have no idea how to respond. What if she was unable to speak or express herself in any way in the Great Sleep, then what? She hadn't tried to speak, having no opportunity, and didn't know what her capabilities were in this dimension. She might stand there mute and, with someone waiting in expectation, she'd be horribly embarrassed.

It was too much. Helena turned away, feeling nine years old despite her very grown up dress. She felt like she had two cases of Girl Scout cookies she'd committed to sell, unable to bring herself to approach any of the homes in the neighborhood, not even nice Mrs. Parker who surely would have bought a couple boxes. In the end,

Helena gave the all the cookies to her parents. Her mom purchased one case for the freezer, and her dad bought the other one for handing out to his clients.

In a flash, it came back to her: the inexplicable terror of her childhood. Faced with seemingly harmless events, when she felt her throat tighten so no speech could come through, it was all she could do to keep from running away to a safe place. Such as under the covers of her bed, or hiding in her parents' bedroom closet, feeling the familiar comforting touch and odor of their clothing. The Old Spice scent on her dad's side of the closet, the Shalimar and Pond's Face Cream on her mother's side.

The worst part of the panic attacks was the lack of reason for them. "There is absolutely no rhyme or reason for Helena to behave like this," her mother would say.

Her dad would say, "I know, Martha, but to her there must be or she wouldn't do it."

Helena couldn't do it. She ran down the steps, along the sidewalk, hardly daring to look back for fear people were watching her out of the windows. Or worse, if they'd sensed her presence and already opened the door. She couldn't bear to know. The fear swallowed her up and pushed her toward the woods, down the familiar pathway to the meadow, where she would wake up in her nice, familiar, comfortable coma.

The first thing Helena saw when she woke up was Coriander standing rigidly next to her bed, arms crossed, with a scowl on her normally unlined, clear expression.

"Why didn't you do it?" Coriander demanded. "Why, Helena? You were so close. You were almost there, ready to pass to the other side."

"Do what? What are you talking about? I just got back from the Great Sleep, and my brain isn't functioning yet. Don't yell at me."

"I'm not yelling. I am speaking in a commanding and directive tone of voice, and I demand an answer. I want to know why you did what you did."

"Did what?" Helena was utterly confused. First Coriander was mad because she didn't do something and now because she did.

"Run away. You were at the doorstep, ready to knock or whatever it is you modern people do—ring the bell, push the button—you know what I'm talking about. I saw you run away. I want to know why."

"How could you see me? Nobody is there when I sleep."

"That is beside the point. You have no idea of my powers, and if I don't get an answer fast, you may not like what you see."

"Okay, Coriander, please calm down." Helena took a breath to compose herself. She had never before seen this side of Coriander. What was her deal, anyway? Did she want her dead? Was that the other side she referred to?

"No, silly, I do not want you dead. Like I told you before, it's out of my hands whether you live or die. Good gravy." Coriander flopped down in her chair and fanned herself. "Goodness, such exertion. I don't appreciate you getting me worked up like this."

"What other side? I don't get it. I was going to ring the doorbell, see if I could find another inhabitant in my world there, and then I lost my courage."

"Yes. You did. You let fear take over and guide you. That is wrong. Have you ever been guided by faith in your entire life, Helena? Do you have the slightest idea what it's like, to have a life free of fear?"

Helena shook her head, miserably. "Only in my coma. Only when I visit the Great Sleep. It's been wonderful, actually."

Coriander stood again and wagged her finger at Helena. "You know, I've been nice. I've been friendly. I've told you things, tried to help. I don't think any of it has done you one bit of good. Do you want to get better, Helena, or will you choose to stay like this until it's too late?"

"I do want to get better! I was afraid of what might happen if I rang the doorbell. I felt like a scared little kid. Besides, with all your talk of the other side, I am glad I ran away! I'm not ready to die yet."

"I told you, I'm not talking about *that* other side." Coriander shook her head in disgust.

"What then? What other place are you referring to? And why should I want to go there?"

"Listen to me, young lady. It is about time you learn to act in faith, not fear. I can't help you if you aren't willing to help yourself. Must you know the outcome of every single step you take in life before you take it?"

"Sort of. It makes things easier," Helena admitted.

"What a sad, sad way to experience Earth." Coriander sat back down. "Fine. If you can stay awake long enough, I'd like to tell you a story. It may provide assistance in your quest. In the next phase of your journey."

Twenty

I KNEW A MAN ONCE," CORAINDER BEGAN, "LONG ago in a large village on an even larger island in the South Pacific. This man was from a prominent family in the area. He had a rich father, a loving mother who had borne many sons and daughters. Most had married well, some had gone away to get educated then returned to start businesses, build fine homes, contribute to the economy of their island.

"All except for this man, the wayward middle son. He seemed to be without motivation, without focus, except for one thing. He had built himself a humble home near the beach. Each year when the hurricanes came, and his house was destroyed because it was too close to the water, he would rebuild it, always exactly where it was before. Each year the hurricanes would come and tear away pieces of the man's house, and patiently he would go about fixing it again. Always the same as before, never stronger or larger or further away from the danger zone.

"His family wondered why he did this. 'Rebuild closer to our house,' advised his father. 'You will never get anywhere this way. You are right where the hurricanes hit our island. You have to fix up your house over and over again.'

"The man said little. He was used to his parents and his brothers and sisters, as well as his aunts, uncles and cousins—they were all the same. None of them understood or accepted his way of life. He was happy doing his simple work as a carpenter, working for other people when the work was good, and then he got paid. When there was no employment, he caught fish and puttered around his small property along the beach. When the hurricanes arrived one after another, he would no sooner have his house repaired than they would come again.

"This was his life and he was content, until one day he met a beautiful girl. He had passed thirty and figured he would never marry. Until the day he went to a far village to do a job for a man who had hired him. A wealthy man who had heard he was the best carpenter on the island.

"The work had taken many weeks—the man had wanted to expand his home to accommodate his growing family—and when the job was done, this rich man was pleased with the carpenter's work and paid him well, enough to keep him fed for many weeks. The carpenter himself was pleased with the man's oldest daughter, the loveliest girl he had ever set eyes on. She who was so beautiful, the daughter of a wealthy man and twelve years younger than the carpenter, would surely not be interested in him.

"To his great and joyous surprise, she was very interested. At last he had found the girl he loved who loved him back. They planned to marry right after he finished repairing his house from the recent hurricane. The hurricane season had been brief that year and had not done much damage to the little house on the beach.

"He brought his new wife there and they were happy. The man's father was happy as well, because finally it seemed like his son was making something of himself. With a beautiful young wife and a baby on the way, the son stood taller. He took on many new jobs, wanting to provide for his little family as a man should. At last the father began to feel proud of the son he had worried about for so long.

"'He will make us proud in the end, you wait and see,' the father told anyone in the village who would listen to him. There were many who did, for the father was one of the richest, most important men in the village. Many encouraged him to run for governor of the island, sure that he would be elected and bring honor to the village. Whatever this man did brought him greater success and good fortune.

"'Maybe now I will run for governor,' the father told the people of his village. At last his son was becoming a man, and the father was becoming proud to call him his son. He was now doing more than going from job to job, fishing and waiting for hurricane season, only to watch it destroy his house and spend the next year fixing it.

"'Before their baby comes,' the father told his wife, 'I must convince our son to move out of his tumble-down hut on the beach and join the rest of us on the hill. There he and his wife will be safe from the high winds.'

"Except the father couldn't convince his son to make the move.

"'We are happy here,' the young man told his father again and again. 'My wife loves our simple place on the beach as much as I do. We want to raise our child here. Don't worry, we will be fine. I've been here in this spot for ten years, why move now?'

"Three months before hurricane season, their baby boy came into the world, and the couple were still happier than they had been before. The carpenter thought he was the luckiest man alive.

"Only now he began to worry about the approaching storms. What if his little family were in danger? What if harm came to the baby? Or to his beloved wife? He could never forgive himself if such a thing were to happen. Whereas before he used to anticipate the hurricane season and look upon it as the most exciting time of the year, now he dreaded it, thinking of it every moment. He wondered if his father was right, and they should leave this place and move up to the other side of the hill with the rest of the family.

"He and his wife discussed it, and she was agreeable with whatever he wanted. It was one of the reasons he loved her. She was always peaceful and happy and loving, willing to go along with things and not trying to change him or lecture him like everybody else did. When she looked at him, he felt like a hero in her eyes, a man capable of great and noble deeds. He wanted to do right by her, to never disappoint her or their little one, and certainly not to put her in danger. Yet he had been in this house for ten years, always facing the hurricane, and in his own way conquering the elements which came every year to try and destroy his property.

"Should he now leave it, admitting defeat? Walk away? Take his wife and baby to go live in the shadow of his father, like a little boy once again?

"As the season of the hurricane grew near, the man grew quieter, his face as stormy as the winds whipping the tops of the palm trees. He had never before seen such winds this early. He knew it would be a terrible storm, maybe the worst in the history of the island. And the storm in his soul grew larger and louder and fiercer, faced with the decision he did not want to make.

"As the time came closer, the entire village was preparing for what they knew would be the island's worst hurricane. The signs were there in the color of the sea and of the sky, in the erratic behavior of the animals and in the frantic calls of the birds. The man's father called his many children and grandchildren together to stay in the family compound, the largest house in the village, on the other side of the hill where safety lay. One by one his children came and settled in with their families to wait out the coming storm.

"The father and brothers and brothers-in-law visited the man in his house on the beach, begging him to join them, to bring his wife and little baby to safety. 'It will be the most violent hurricane this island has ever seen,' they said to him. 'What are you thinking? You can't stay here like you've always done. You have responsibilities now. You must be a man and take care of your family.'

"'I know this,' the man said, annoyed at them for thinking so little of him. 'What do you think I am?'

"Finally, he chased everyone away in fury, sending his wife and the baby with them. She didn't want to go without him, pleaded with him to come along, but now he was angry and stubborn and could no longer explain his feelings. He had a terrible conflict within him, a turmoil that confused him and which he could not explain, and this is why he sent her away crying, the baby wrapped tightly in her arms. Then he turned back to his house, slamming the door against them all.

"The wind grew louder and the storm was coming. The man's older brother banged on the door, yelling at him. 'Come along now, don't be a fool. Why are you such a stubborn man? You haven't changed at all. You are still a stubborn, rebellious fool of a man who shames his family. Come and join the rest of us right now, this minute, before it is too late. Open the door! What are you thinking?'

"The man opened his door and yelled back, 'Go away! You have said what you came here to say, now go away and leave me in peace. I will do what I will do, and no one will force me to do anything different. You can quit wasting your breath. Go on! The hurricane is coming and I must prepare.'

"The oldest brother left, shaking his head, and hurried off to safety before he got caught in the terrible storm.

"When the man was at last left alone, he came out of his house and viewed the area, to make sure every last one of them had left. He nailed shut the windows, blocked off the front door, all the while knowing it would do no good. This coming hurricane, the strongest one, would completely destroy his house.

"He went through the motions as he had done every year for the past ten years, and then he carried two strong pieces of rope outside. He went to the large date palm tree next to his house. He sat down and straddled the base of the trunk, reached around and tied his ankles together, looping a slip knot around one ankle, pulling the rope toward the other ankle, looping it several times, snugging it tight so his legs were securely fastened to the tree, then knotting the rope.

"With the second piece of rope he made a loop part way down, slipped it around one wrist and reached around the tree, put a couple loops around his other wrist, and then firmly knotted the two ends together. At this point, the man could not get loose even if he wanted to, which was exactly what he had intended. When the hurricane hit, if the storm surge didn't kill him, the debris carried by one hundred mile per hour winds would surely kill him.

"He might outlive it, he might not, but either way he would at least face it on his own terms. Those were his thoughts as he waited, tied securely to the tree next to his house, for the last and greatest hurricane he would face.

"They found him days later when the storm had spent its force on the island. He was still strapped to the date palm tree. The tree was there but the house wasn't. The man's neck had been broken, perhaps by the storm surge, or from being hit with debris, it was impossible to tell. He was bruised and battered, as though he had been in a terrible fight and lost."

Helena had managed to stay awake through Corian-der's long tale. Now, finally at the end of it, she said, "What? That makes no sense to me. Why would he do such a thing when he had everything to live for?"

Coriander smiled with her typical enigmatic expres-sion. "This is what everyone in the village thought as well. He went down in the history of his island as the most foolish of all men. His father was so shamed he never did run for governor."

"What happened to the wife and baby?"

"She of course grieved for a long time, but with wealthy parents and in-laws, neither she nor the child wanted for anything. Eventually she remarried, and last I heard had a houseful of fine, strapping sons, and daughters even more beautiful than she had been."

"Coriander," Helena began, struggling to keep her eyes open. "Did you tell me this story for any particular reason?"

"I'm sure you remember your comment about how complicated people are. And the complexities of life."

Helena struggled to remember anything, but this did sound familiar. "Yes," she murmured, beginning to drift off and hoping Coriander would still be there when she woke up. Helena didn't suppose she would, as she rarely stayed through one of Helena's lengthy periods in the Great Sleep.

"No one knew why the man did what he did. It didn't save his house. It didn't stop the storm. It didn't prevent one bit of the havoc wreaked upon the island."

"Perhaps he was making a statement," Helena said, get-ting an idea or two right as her mind shut down. "Proving a point. He was his own man, not to be ruled by his father or by nature. A last stand. A final sacrifice."

Coriander nodded thoughtfully. "People for miles around heard the story and wondered the same things, speculating as to his motives and intention."

"I can't imagine anyone saw it as any kind of heroic gesture, though." Helena was forcing herself awake.Conversations like this with Coriander were not only interesting but good for her mental processes. Coriander had a way of saying things to make Helena think, despite wanting more than anything to sleep and sleep and sleep.

"No, I don't imagine so," Coriander agreed. "Not heroic at all, really. Although as the years passed, he began to be known as the man who faced the hurricane. That label alone seemed to ennoble him as a legendary figure. His son, who was a mere infant at the time, grew up feeling proud of his father who had faced the hurricane. The son grew up tall and proud, knowing he was borne of such a father."

"So that's good, right?" Helena still wasn't sure about the point of the story. It would be much easier if Coriander would talk straight and explain things rather than doling out these obscure illustrations.

"Yes, it was good, in the end. The boy eventually went to work for his grandfather, taking over the family business and becoming mayor of the village, then governor of the island for many years. He was a most beloved and successful man and would tell people it was due to his father, the man who had faced the hurricane."

"Mmm, interesting . . ." murmured Helena sleepily. "If I could only understand . . ."

"So you see, Helena, how good can spring up anywhere, even when things go wrong and people make terrible mistakes. Life is extremely complex indeed." Coriander stood and patted her hand. "You rest now. I'll be away for a time, to give you a chance to decide what it is you really want."

Helena didn't know when Coriander finally slipped out of the room. She herself was slipping away into the welcome world of dreams and visions, where as she floated by, she saw a large, dark-skinned man strapped to a tree, confronting his demons as his neck snapped, in some misguided attempt to end his life with a noble statement which no one understood.

Twenty-one

*I*T'S TIME I ACCEPT THE TRUTH," HELENA SAID AT Coriander's next visit.

"What truth is that?" Coriander asked, while picking a particle of invisible lint off the sleeve of her dress. Helena's dress again, but not the white one. It was a blue maxi dress she remembered from a few years past. She had bought for a special occasion, the nature of which she could no longer recall.

Coriander always wore Helena's clothing, which made her wonder still if Coriander was a figment of her imagination. Except she seemed real. She kept up her end of the conversation, keeping Helena from sinking into utter despair and loneliness. Real or imaginary, Coriander was now a vital element to Helena's routine.

"The truth of my death," Helena said. "I certainly can't stay like this indefinitely. I'm a nurse, or at least I was in my former life. I know how precious hospital space is. It's only a matter of time before measures are taken."

"What measures are those?" Coriander had a way of asking questions Helena supposed she knew the answers to. Helena went along with it, playing their familiar game.

"You know. Pulling the plug. Cutting off whatever it is keeping me alive."

"They are not keeping you alive, Helena, regardless of what your current traditions or mythology has taught you. You are alive because it's what is meant to be. Besides, if you are appointed unto death, no contraption in your world will stop a scheduled journey to the Other Side. Psh! Machines keeping one alive, what nonsense!"

"It's not nonsense. They take away my food tube, Coriander, I'll starve to death. It's as simple as that. Don't you see how everything pumping into me is to sustain my life? Fluid, nourishment, even a pump to keep air into my lungs and my heart beating. This is costing my insurance company a fortune. They can't be happy, especially with no hope of recovery."

"No hope of recovery? Who says that? What have you heard?" Coriander asked with a suspicious tone.

"I can hear very little of anything. I've told you before. It's so much murmuring and muttering to me, but I realize what must be happening. I did hear my daughter mention a hard decision. I can sense a change in her, in her mood when she's here. I know, that's all, and I should prepare myself."

"Goodness. Such a fatalistic attitude. How can you get better with such words?"

"At the least, they'll move me to a long-term care center. That's the same as being written off in my book. It's a message to the families: Get on with things."

"Is there more?" Coriander said in her scoffing tone.

"Hospitals are a place of transition where work progresses and patients released," Helena continued. "If the work can't be done, if there's a lack of response, they move the terminal patients to a long-term care center. It's procedure. Then the family knows what's what. The loved one has a staff to keep the patient comfortable for as long as necessary."

"It sounds like you have already given up on yourself."

"I'm being realistic. I want to prepare for the worst. It will be better for my daughter. She can go back home without having the constant disappointment of watching and waiting for me to wake up which, let's be honest, may never happen. I can't imagine what this must be doing to my dad."

Helena remembered how her parents used to come visit her in Pasadena and her dad could barely tolerate the traffic, all the people. He used to say living in Southern California was like being trapped in a never-ending, raucous festival. He never understood what attracted so many millions to come and stay.

"It will make things easier for them," Helena said. "If I could talk, I'd tell my daughter to have me moved at once. I don't want to be a burden any longer."

"How long to do you think you've been here, Helena?"

"It feels like months and months, although truthfully I can't say. My sense of time is off. Six months? A year?"

"It's not been a month yet. We're just ending the third week."

Stunned, Helena could hardly believe it. How was this possible? She'd been conservative in her guess of months, instead thinking it felt more like a year. Two years. Although if so, she would surely have been moved to a long-term care center by now.

"Seriously? I've only been here for three *weeks*?"

"Yes, and I thought you should know. I can't have you getting discouraged and giving up on yourself."

"Wow. Thank you, Coriander. I do feel much better knowing it." Three weeks! Why that was nothing! In fact, maybe it wasn't a coma after all, but a long period of unconsciousness while her body worked at healing itself.

"I'm sorry to inform you it is officially a coma, according to their tests for brain and sleep activity," Coriander said, reading her mind yet again. "However, the good news is they are hopeful you'll wake up from it, or at least transition to the next stage."

"Still, it's a huge relief! Oh, Coriander, what would I do without you, my wonderful friend?"

Coriander beamed. "It's nice to be appreciated."

"What should I do? Wait it out? I wish I could force myself awake. I've tried to, you know. To move or blink, focus on someone here, try to wake up."

"Not everything is in our control to fix or change, as you are finding out through your own experience," Coriander said gently. She rose as though to leave and Helena felt sad, not wanting to be left alone.

"I wait it out then?" Helena asked.

"Yes, that's it. Patience. Patience. Don't worry, my dear. Everything will be fine. It always is, in the end."

Helena was not thrilled to hear those words, *the end*. She wasn't convinced everything would be fine either, not by a long shot. What more could she do? She had never felt so powerless. Still, three weeks in the coma! Hardly any time at all.

Twenty-two

ELENA FOUND HERSELF ONCE AGAIN ON the village street. It was empty of any sort of habitation—people, dogs, vehicles—although the homes looked well-kept, the green lawns cut short, the flower beds weeded. Someone had to be keeping up the neighborhood, she thought. Where are they? Curiosity became the driving force behind her second approach to the door.

As she made her way up the front walk, she again felt the horrible fear re-surfacing, feelings she had largely been free of since her coma. She couldn't possibly put herself back there again: to be rid of the bondage and then facing the door, to have it all come back in a rush.

It wasn't worth it. For what? To meet some random imaginary people? There was no guarantee this other place Coriander talked about so enthusiastically would be any better than where she was now. She questioned the wisdom of knocking on the door. According to Coriander, it served as a passage way. It was possible Coriander wanted to trick her into passing through to the Other Side. Death.

Helena couldn't be sure Coriander was trustworthy and had her best interests at heart. She could very well be leading Helena to *that* Other Side, the one she wasn't ready for.

Helena turned back to the street, where she stood and examined the houses lined up along the block. They were similar yet individual, definitely not cookie-cutter suburban homes. Each one had something to distinguish it, such as color, slope of the roofline, type of windows and trim, or landscaping. Maybe it was merely this one particular house that gave her the willies. Perhaps another one would be easier.

She went on, passing three more homes, before deciding to try the fourth one. It was a brick bungalow with rounded windows and ivy growing up the sides, enough to appear charming yet not so much to be spooky.

The door was painted a bright green, with a brass knocker in the center. She looked for a doorbell, uncomfortable hitting the door with the knocker. After all, a knocker was more for decoration than actual use. No door bell. She raised her fist to knock and instead she tensed up, wondering what she'd say. "Hi, do you happen to know why I'm here and what I should do next?"

She'd feel like such an idiot. This wasn't a real world. Who knew what language these inhabitants spoke or what they were like. What if they were hostile? They might capture her and put her in prison for violation of something. She imagined a big bearded magistrate looming over her demanding to see her papers. She had no papers! No driver's license, no passport, nothing but the clothes on her back.

She glanced down to see what she was wearing. It would generally change depending on her mood—sometimes a light, happy spring dress and sandals, sometimes a pair of jeans and bulky pullover. Today she had on black yoga pants and a grey hoodie. Clearly she was dressed for comfort and not for pushing her way into these people's lives.

She headed back toward the woods where she intended to enjoy the cool shade, listen to the bird songs, explore at length through the meadow until she happened to wake up again. She could never control how long she stayed in the Great Sleep, only what she did when there. Right now a little solitude would be welcome. Coriander had been coming at greater and greater frequency, taxing her brain with her stories, her philosophical discourses and her arguments. Helena could use a nice rest, alone in a fresh green meadow.

Finding a large boulder along a bubbling stream, Helena sat down in her sheltering forest glade with a sigh of exhaustion. She was ready to be left alone. Instead, Coriander kept at her and at her. What about the vacation Coriander kept referring to—why didn't she go and leave Helena in peace for a change?

At first, Helena had been jealous when she heard about it, especially when Coriander said she'd be going to Guatemala, which was exactly what Helena had planned for herself before everything bad happened. She was no longer jealous. She wouldn't mind if Coriander left for good, allowing Helena to come and go as she pleased in her Great Sleep. The woods were like a vacation spot, and when she craved sunshine, there was the wide meadow.

Beyond the meadow were the interesting rooms to explore, never with anyone around to bother her. The banquet halls filled with food, the garden areas fragrant with flowers. Oh, so many things to see and do. There was no reason to return to the village with its empty streets and upsetting houses.

She'd stay away from the neighborhood from this point on. It was much too stressful. She'd been through enough with the accident and the coma, not to mention other problems previous to it. None she could recall presently, but she knew they'd been difficult. She deserved a rest, and she would take it. Never mind about Coriander with her warnings and her advice and her philosophies of life. It was her own life she was responsible for, and Helena needed to take care of herself.

Although hoping to relax, Helena instead found herself bothered by thoughts of Coriander, feeling resentment toward her pushiness while pondering the things she had said.

As if in reflection of her own negative mood, the sky turned black and the wind picked up, blowing the tops of the trees around in a furious fashion. Helena stood, troubled and confused. This was a puzzling development! Never before had there been a storm in her Great Sleep. It had always been peaceful, with ideal weather conditions and temperatures in the mid-seventies.

Helena wasn't sure what to do, whether to stay where she was in the forest or retreat to the meadow. Either way was the risk of lightning. In the meadow, she'd be the only upright figure and could easily be struck. In the forest—and who wants to be in the midst of a forest during a thunderstorm when it becomes dark and foreboding—lightning could strike anywhere, even the tree right next to her.

Helena jumped as the thunder rolled, sounding right above her. Lightning followed too closely for her to count the seconds between them. She couldn't stay in the woods another instant. She ran toward the meadow, hoping to soon find herself awake in her bed, like waking up from a nightmare at the most frightening point.

The thunder and lightning was crashing and sparking about her, threatening to bring down the entire forest in fire and brimstone. Helena felt surprised by a few drops of rain on her face, thinking the rainfall wasn't sufficient to penetrate the deep cover of vegetation provided by the tall trees. She ran slowly and clumsily. Unfortunately, her shoes today were flip flops, which didn't function well for running over rocks and brush.

When she finally got to the meadow, she found the rain coming down in torrents, soaking her in seconds. Feeling chilled, she pulled the hood up over her dripping hair and continued slogging over the wet grass in her water-soaked yoga pants. She had not realized before how long the meadow grass was. She had remembered it being short and easy to travel on, but instead it was long and twisty and prickly. In fact, as she struggled through it, the grass seemed to be growing longer still. Soon it was up to her knees and she could barely progress.

"Why aren't I waking up from this hideous nightmare!" she hollered, barely able to hear the sound of her own voice with the noise of the thunder, still rolling furiously onward, as though following her. She looked back and in horror, realized that was exactly what had happened. The sky was blue above the forest, while right above her were the storm clouds in their black turmoil, with lightning hurtling through the clouds and striking the ground around her. She screamed and ran faster, wondering what kind of strange underworld had opened in this once beautiful and peaceful world of escape and solitude.

She stopped her running, unable to break free of the grass wrapping itself around her legs. The running was, in reality, only in her imagination. Her actual movement was a forward and backward rocking, accompanied by increased sobs of frustration. The heaviness of her waterlogged sweat clothes made it difficult to go forward, and the still-growing grass came like ropes entwining around her legs.

She fell, unable to take another step, and then turned on her back, lying in what felt like a green coffin. She felt herself buried in the earth, with water flowing over her, grass strangling her, black clouds lowering down toward her as though some giant hand were bringing a pillow to smash against her face. Now, at last, she would surely die.

This is my punishment for not going up to the house.

"Coriander? Is it you? This is you teaching me a lesson, isn't it? You said I didn't know your power, and you are showing me. I get it!"

Nothing changed. The water flowed, the grass grew over her body, the lightning flashed dangerously close, and the sinister darkness lowered toward Helena until she could hardly breathe.

"Coriander! I'm sorry! I'll go back and knock at the door of whatever house you want. Make it stop. Please! I'm dying here."

Still nothing. *What does she want from me? Whatever it is, I refuse to lay here and suffocate in a grassy grave.* Helena waited for a moment, to see if Coriander would appear with instructions, or maybe she'd end up back in her hospital room, free of the Great Sleep, and life as she knew it would return to normal coma status.

When nothing changed, Helena tried to get up, determined to make her way back to the village and knock on one of the doors. If she wasn't going to magically wake up from this strange Great Sleep nightmare, she'd have to progress forward within it. The village can't be worse than this, she thought.

If I can only break free of the weird Jack in the Beanstalk grass.

The more Helena fought against the grass, the tighter it strangled her. It kept growing and twisting around her body, making it impossible to move. Helena watched the black veil above her seeming to lower its way in her direction. The rain was not letting up, and she felt the water-soaked ground beneath her softening under her weight. She was sinking into it. If she didn't get free she'd be buried alive.

She wondered if this was nature's way of making the coma win. She'd been alive in the hospital, although her diagnosis remained uncertain unless she awoke from the coma. They wouldn't leave her indefinitely hooked up to life-support systems. Eventually, with the passage of time and no hope of regaining consciousness, someone would make the decision to pull the plug. Probably her dad and her daughter together would come to an agreement about what was best for Helena Carr.

The events happening to her might actually be her subconsciously giving into the coma, Helena suddenly realized. While she was experiencing it as a dream, a nightmare really, in reality it could be her body giving in to the natural forces coming to claim her.

Helena stopped fighting and relaxed, thinking *maybe I should give in.* It would spare my dad and my daughter from having to make a horrible decision. I could close my eyes and let the grass cover me as I sink into the soft earth in the meadow, and it will all be over. It's even rather cozy, she thought, like being tucked into bed under a heavy quilt, or sitting in my car with the seat belt on. *I'll never have to be afraid again. My family will not be forced into the unthinkable. I could spare them that at least.*

Rushing into her mind came a deathbed-type vision of her past, seeing how selfish she had been, putting herself above the needs of anyone else, even above the needs of her daughter. Her memory opened to the last phone call she'd had with her, and how at the time Helena knew it was a plea for help, with questions about marriage and about how to communicate with her husband. And she had cut the girl off. Helena felt ashamed.

Same with her dad. The last time she had spoken to him, the pain of his loneliness came in a flash to her as though it was one of those lightning bolts threatening to fry her. How many times had her dad cried out to her in his own way, calling her up at odd times of the day and night, hoping to catch her when she wasn't busy, and Helena had been annoyed at the intrusion, trying to get off the phone quickly to get back to whatever she'd been doing? Things she could no longer remember that had seemed hugely important at the moment.

Helena would let the earth bury her. She no longer deserved to live. The only family she had, the two people who meant more to her than anyone else in the world, and she had no time for them. Selfish, selfish Helena.

She would sink into her grave, and it would be the end of the coma. Three weeks or not, it would be a relief to her loved ones—closure—no longer having to wait and cry over her in the hospital bed, wondering what horrible decision awaited them if she never woke up. This would be one unselfish act Helena could perform for these two who she had turned away from so often.

With sudden clarity, incidents of the recent past were coming back to her in her inevitable journey toward death. Why couldn't she have gone to Wisconsin to be with her dad? Or to be with her mom in those final days? Why could she have not once visited her daughter in Houston? There had been troubles in the marriage, Helena knew—the money issues, the debt, the arguments over who spent how much for what. She could have given guidance and counsel to her daughter and been a comfort to her parents. Instead she had closed herself off to their needs as she buried herself in her own selfish routine.

It was fitting to let herself be buried here in her Great Sleep, in the once lovely meadow that had turned into a graveyard.

If she died, she could see Mom, be with her again, this time for good. The thought brought peace to Helena as she rested in her quiet little grave. She could still hear the thunder and lightning, but it no longer frightened her. The noise seemed far away as the silence was growing within her. She shivered.

Let it roll, she thought.

Mom, are you there? I'm coming, Mom, to wherever you are. I love you.

Twenty-three

*H*ELENA FELT A MOMENT OF PANIC, A FLASH of the familiar terror welling up within her. And then it subsided, replaced by a sense of peaceful joy as she realized it would soon be over. She cuddled herself into her soggy coffin, took one last defiant stare at the dense, lowering fog, and closed her eyes. When the cloud descended down to her face, it would cover her eyes and mouth and nose, and her breath would be snuffed out.

"Good-bye, Coriander," she whispered. "I hardly know what to say. You helped me through a rough spell, despite the scary thunderstorm. Nice touch. Still, without you, I can't imagine what this coma experience would've been like."

"Intense loneliness. Horrible pain. More than the heart can bear," Coriander said.

Helena's eyes flew open, wondering if she'd imagined it. No, there was Coriander, sitting on her familiar hospital chair with its blue upholstery and wooden arms. She was dressed once again in the white dress that had been Helena's, her small pale hands clutching the lacy crocheted shawl. Helena speculated briefly why *she* couldn't be buried in her favorite white dress instead of a pair of yoga pants and a sloppy grey hoodie.

Coriander had her chair pulled right up to the shallow grave where Helena rested. "Hello, dear," she said. "Goodness, this is a fine howdy-do. Look at you, already got yourself buried when you aren't even dead yet." She shook her head and clucked her tongue.

"All right," Helena said, not feeling quite as noble as earlier when she'd imagined herself making the ultimate sacrifice for her family. In fact, she felt rather foolish, with Coriander sitting there the same as always, mocking her. "I didn't have much choice, did I, with everything that's happened, sinking into the earth, literally tied down by this freakish grass. This seemed like the best course of action for everyone concerned."

Coriander tied the ends of the shawl together and folded her slender hands in her lap. Finally, she spoke in such a quiet, gentle voice Helena had to strain to hear the words. "I know something about loneliness, Helena. And fear, too. It's why I was chosen to be your Trusted Guide."

"Trusted Guide?" Another new word.

"Yes. I was there for you many times throughout your life, your Trusted Guide, until I graduated to higher responsibilities. Let me tell you, Helena, it hasn't been easy, watching the things you do."

"Really?" Helena was stunned at the idea of Coriander being with her before the coma. "How? Or are you allowed to tell me?"

"I am. It finally appears you are ready to listen."

Helena did not respond. This was a new side to Coriander, this openness tempered with slight roughness, and she was curious to find out what was next. Coriander was quiet for a long time. Helena waited.

"I was a young girl, approaching marriageable age," Coriander finally said. "I fell in love with a boy from my village. His name was Johnny. He was eighteen, one year older than me. He came from a large family with no wealth. His father was a tailor, his mother a cook for the banker's family. Although my family was not rich, my parents hoped I would marry well. My father was the schoolmaster, and my mother was educated as well. They expected me to do better than Johnny."

The age-old story, Helena thought, twisting a bit to get more comfortable in her grave. Parents desiring more for their children than the children wanted themselves. Helena herself had not been crazy about her daughter's husband. He had seemed full of big ideas with little substance, always jumping from job to job, building up debt, full of unfulfilled promises. *What was his name?* Helen could not remember for the life of her.

"My father refused to let me see him. Johnny and I met in secret. We were in love and no one could keep us apart. We were young, naïve about the ways of the world and what can happen when evil sets out to destroy true love."

"This doesn't sound good, Coriander. I'm almost afraid to ask what happened." Helena held her breath, willing Coriander to continue. At last she'd learn the truth about this strange apparition named Coriander, her Trusted Guide, or whatever she called herself.

"It was a long, long time ago and justice has been served, so never mind about that part of it," Coriander said, her eyes closing for a moment. "There was an older man, a neighbor of ours, whose wife had killed herself some years before. He had taken a shine to me and gave me no peace. Johnny was angry and jealous. I told him not to worry. I could handle myself. This old neighbor had been after me since I was a girl, and I'd always avoided him. As I blossomed into a young woman, he decided I'd be his wife. He approached my father to ask for my hand in marriage.

"My father liked the man, one of those who can smile and shake hands and talk like a gentleman. And he was wealthy. My father said yes, and we were betrothed."

"Oh, Coriander!"

Coriander shrugged. "That's how it was then. Girls had no say in anything, especially in who they would marry. Money and advancing in society was what mattered. Not love. Not free will. My father was only acting according to the rules of our time. He thought he knew what was best for my future."

"What happened?" Helena asked. "Did you marry the neighbor?"

"No, I did not marry him, or anyone. I died young."

"Oh."

"When Johnny found out about the betrothal, he went after the man. I was sitting outside my house on the porch, gazing at the stars and wondering what my future would hold. There was no joy in me. Only sadness. Misery and despair. Fear of this brutal man who had been trying to get his hands on me since I was ten. Yes, Helena, I know something of fear. Fear of real evil, Helena, not the fake kind you have created within yourself to avoid getting close to people. Not strangers either, Helena, but your own flesh and blood."

Helena squirmed. "I know, Coriander, I know! It's why I'm staying here. I won't go back. It's better this way, believe me." She changed the subject. "Did you go to Johnny?"

"No. My father was keeping me inside, for fear I'd run off with him. For weeks I hadn't been allowed to leave the house without accompaniment, usually with my older sister or the housekeeper. The only reason I was alone on the front porch is because it was late at night and the rest of the family had gone to sleep. I'd been in my room, suffering from loneliness and longing for Johnny, wishing I could die right there, and then I slipped out. But I didn't dare go beyond the front step."

"Until?"

"I heard them shouting. I recognized the voices, and I was afraid the man would kill Johnny. I ran to the neighbor's house, where the two of them were fighting in the back garden, rolling around in the dirt like a couple of dogs. I kicked at the man, to stop the fight, and then it happened.

"He had a knife, and he came at me like an animal, hate twisting his face. I couldn't understand. He had been saying he loved me for all these years, since I was little, but what did I know about love or hate? Johnny had truly loved me, and he was hurt. I ignored the man rushing toward me and ran to Johnny. There was a gash on his leg, bleeding badly. I felt a sudden, terrible thrust of pain in my side, twisting, burning, flaring up like a torch of fire. I saw Johnny's face, his eyes wide, and his mouth screaming my name, and then I was gone for a second."

"Gone for a second? What do you mean?"

"I don't remember what happened next. Until I was standing there between the neighbor and Johnny, the three of us staring down at my body crumbled in the dirt, blood soaking my nightdress. Johnny kneeled at my side but there was nothing he could do. The man recovered his knife from my body and held it to Johnny's throat. 'You tell anyone what happened here, and I'll kill you like I did her. Do you understand? It was an accident. She got between us and that's how it was.'

"I was drifting away from the pain and the loneliness and the despair, and was brought quickly to a place of light and love. It was convenient, actually, how I escaped what would have been a life of emptiness and brutality."

"I suppose you're right," Helena said. "I guess I never looked at death like that, but then again I've never talked to someone who died."

"Thus you see, Helena, I understand a little of what these things are. It's been many years, and my heart is healed but I still remember. It's important to remember, in order to help others. To be a solace and a comfort."

Helena barely knew what to say. She would have liked to get up and give Coriander a hug, if only she could move.

Twenty-four

ORIANDER STOOD AND PULLED THE CHAIR aside, peering down at Helena. "You are staring up at death, Helena, and furthermore, you're lying if you say you never saw it as an escape. You think you are doing the brave thing, giving in to the coma, sparing your family hardship, when instead it is one more selfish act in a life filled with selfishness."

"But, but, I thought . . ." Helena started.

"I know what you thought. Remember, I can read your mind. I've always been able to. It's one of the gifts given to Trusted Guides, to enable us to help and assist the afflicted. Helena, there have been moments when it was all I could do to not hit you, or scream at you, to not walk out on you. When I saw your memories, and yes, I could see your hidden memories of your past life. I was present when many of them occurred. When they were closed to you in your coma, I could still see them . . . how you have run away from humanity, ignored those who loved you . . . hidden from opportunities of service . . . I could barely stand it."

"Coriander, stop!" Every word spoken was a whip against Helena, beating her further into the ground. "Haven't I suffered enough? Why are you doing this to me?"

"You are doing it to yourself, Helena. You have always done it to yourself. Driving people away from you . . .

those who would love you, if only you would let them. Building a wall around your heart, saying you are afraid of everything when you are not. You are not!"

Coriander began breaking off grass and tossing it down on top of Helena. "There. You choose to die, go ahead and die. Bury yourself in this place and never return. I lost my chance long ago. I lost my chance at love. I lost my chance at having a husband, a child, a life! My time on Earth was cut short. But look at you! You have had every opportunity and you turn your back on it."

"I'm sorry, Coriander, I'm sorry! I didn't realize . . ."

"Yes, you did! Everyone realizes. The trouble with you, Helena, is you are afraid to take chances. Afraid of risk. Afraid of what you might lose if you jump out of the boat and swim to shore. And you're afraid of what will happen if you stay in the boat."

"No, really, I was working on jumping out of the boat when I had my accident," said Helena. "I remember now! I was heading home to make a big change. Something to do with Guatemala, I think." She paused. "Or am I saying Guatemala because you mentioned going there on vacation? I was going there too, I seem to remember. Something about a hotel in Guatemala, and I thought if I could only make this one last big step, I'd stop being afraid of everything."

And then Helena understood how saying she was afraid of everything was a crutch. Coriander knew it. Helena knew it. She stuttered weakly, adding, "Or whatever it is I'm afraid of . . . I guess. . . ."

"Helena, the first thing you must stop being afraid of is getting close to people. Your Afterlife won't be any better than your Earth life, if you can't learn this simple lesson."

Afterlife? Was she ready for that? "Coriander, why couldn't you have told me any of this before? I've been asking you questions about myself since we first met."

"Goodness, have you not learned anything yet? Simply because someone asks the questions doesn't mean they are prepared for the answers. Remember Ruby?"

"Ruby . . . the therapist . . . You know about Ruby?"

"She tried to help you see the truth and you refused, blinded by your own pride and fine opinion of yourself. Goodness gracious, Helena, the people you could have helped, if only you'd opened up your heart to the possibilities."

"Ruby kept carrying on about my family issues, and I didn't see . . ."

"That's exactly the problem with you, my poor, dear Helena. You don't see. You refuse to see. It's easier that way, isn't it? What about the girl who was bullied and picked on in grade school, the one your mom encouraged you to befriend? You didn't see her either, did you? You are always hiding your eyes from the goodness you could be doing to bless the lives of others."

"The girl who smelled like fish? I was only a kid, trying to get by so I wouldn't be picked on."

"There you go, making your excuses like always. *I didn't know. I was afraid. I was busy.*" Coriander spoke in a mocking tone. "Your mom was busy, too, busy serving others in addition to making things smooth and pleasant for you and your dad. At the end, you were too busy to go out and help her."

This was getting more painful with each word. Helena knew. She knew all of it. "This is like judgment day," she whispered.

"*Your* judgment day," Coriander snapped. "I hope you are paying attention, my friend. Because you are getting a second chance, if you'll only accept it. It's too late for the poor little girl, the one you ignored. I won't tell you what happened to her. Some things it doesn't help to know."

"Oh, Coriander. I'm sorry. I didn't know, I wish . . . You saw that? You know about my childhood and how I ignored the girl who smelled like fish?"

"Yes, I did, and I saw later what happened to that poor friendless girl who was bullied by half the class and ignored by the other half."

"I was no better than the ones who teased and picked on her. I stood silently by when I could have helped."

"Of course you could have. I've been with you for a very long time, Helena, well before you chose to turn your back on that little girl. This was before I got promoted."

"From being a Trusted Guide to something more?"

"The Trusted Guides stay on the Other Side, waiting. They aren't allowed to visit here as I do with you," she ended with a slight toss of her head.

"What are you?" Helena asked, hardly hoping for an answer. She expected any minute to see Coriander stand up, reach into Helena's close quarters to pat her hand as she always did and disappear until next time. "An angel?"

"I am a Friend. A Third-Level Friend, I might add," she stated.

"A . . . a Third-Level Friend?"

"My duties are to comfort and protect. To succor the weak, to lift up the hands that hang down. To minister. To counsel." Coriander counted down the five points on the fingers of one hand as she spoke. "I don't claim to be perfect, not yet anyway, but I think I'm fairly good at what I do." She peered down at Helena and added demurely, "I hope you think so, too. I hope I have been a help to you during your time of need."

"Oh, yes! You have," Helena rushed to say. "If you hadn't been here with me, if I'd been left alone in this condition . . . I can't imagine . . . unable to communicate with or to see those who pass in and out of my room, while aware of them in some strange way. It would've been torture."

"It is why we serve as we do," said Coriander. "There are some things one just cannot bear without assistance, and when there is no assistance to be found within the framework of the experience, it is then we are called upon."

"Who are you, really? Are there others?"

"As many as the sands of the sea, my dear, spread out over the ages of this world and beyond. There are many worlds, many suns, more people in need of help than you could possibly imagine. There's no end of work for us."

Helena's head hurt with the idea of it. "I'm not sure I do see. The way you describe it sounds like you must be angels. Only no angels I've ever imagined. You have no wings."

Coriander smiled and shook her head. "Such a silly idea, that one must have wings to pass from one sphere to another. It is true birds and airplanes have wings or they don't fly. However, they don't go to different worlds. Going from one sphere to another is not flying. It is simply a transition, as one might enter one room from another. You don't need wings to move from room to room, do you?"

"I don't know what I need. I can't even get out of this hole in the ground right now. Wings wouldn't help me," Helena said, trying to move her arms and finding it impossible.

"No, of course they wouldn't. Yet you traveled to this place quite easily, didn't you? Much easier than you can move or speak or see in your physical state, back in the hospital."

"That's true," Helena agreed, thinking of her trips to the Great Sleep she had thought were dreams.

"Those were not dreams," Coriander said, reading her mind. Or had Helena spoken? She wasn't sure. She might have spoken the thought aloud. Then again, if Coriander were an angel without wings who could travel across time and space, being telepathic as well was not much of a stretch.

"People in comas do not dream, not in the normal sense. Although your silly doctors seem to think you are brain-dead. What little they know!"

"How do you know, Coriander? Did you overhear them discussing me?"

"Don't worry about how I know. Surely you don't doubt my abilities? Not after what you've seen and everything I've explained to you."

"Of course not. It's obvious you have special powers or you wouldn't be here talking to me, a coma patient, who apparently is brain dead, who is right now sinking into a grave of her own making." Any hope of recovery was lost to her, Helena realized. Brain dead patients did not wake up from comas.

It wouldn't be long before they stopped the breathing machine, and if Helena were still alive afterward, if somehow her heart and lungs continued on their own, before long they'd pull out the feeding tube and allow her to starve to death. Her family wouldn't want Helena to continue in this advanced vegetative state. That's how it was described—a vegetable. Certainly not human, merely a limp, dying vegetable, like an old carrot tossed away. Not even good enough for the soup.

But she was not dead. Something in Helena was more alive than it had ever been. Her heart? Her soul? The spirit of her personality? She didn't comprehend what it was. She only knew for an absolute fact she was alive and wanted to remain so. She would have to fight, fight for her life, fight for the slimmest chance of recovery. If only she could speak to them! Or make some small gesture to prove there was a vibrant, breathing spirit housed within her withering and broken body.

Helena scrutinized Coriander with pleading eyes. "Coriander, please. Can you help me? If it's true they think I'm brain dead then my future is certain. If there's no hope of recovery, they'll remove the tubes. All of them. The last to go will be the feeding tube. I can't die like that! It would have been better if I had died in the accident, better than a slow death through starvation. Coriander, tell me what to do!"

"I certainly will not tell you what to do. That's not why I'm here, to pave your road with my own decisions. That's your job, Helena, not mine. Have you learned nothing from my visits?"

"How could I? You've avoided my questions. I haven't understood anything."

"I gave you a lot of information today. Too much, I imagine. I always did have a problem keeping my silence. I tend to talk too much, and that's a fact. I need to leave you now and let you absorb things."

"Oh, great," Helena moaned. "Now that information is forthcoming and things are finally starting to add up, sure, Coriander, leave me now. See you in Heaven."

"No need to be dramatic, my dear. Everything which must happen will happen. Patience is a virtue."

"Maybe, but you're not the one lost in a coma, stuck in a hole, facing death by starvation!" Helena cried after Coriander who was slipping away.

"We each have our cross to bear, if you'll forgive the platitudes. Death is simply one more step to take, and it has many doors. Really, more than one could count. Think of how many ways one can die, why you wouldn't be able to do it! It doesn't matter which door opens to get you to the Other Side. You people exaggerate the importance of pointless matters while ignoring what is truly significant. My goodness, Helena, you must stop fretting over every little thing."

Helena wanted to throw something at Coriander's departing back. What an infuriating woman! "Some comfort you are," she called out. "My death is not a little thing! Not to me."

"Good-bye, my dear." Coriander gave Helena a slow wave good-bye. "My sad story had a happy ending. As yours will, one way or the other. I'll be watching."

"*You died!* I don't want to die," Helena said, realizing as she said it exactly how true it was. She would fight. She would do whatever it took to survive.

Right before Coriander disappeared she turned back and said, "Beware of those who profess love when their hearts are closed to it."

Twenty-five

HELENA SQUIRMED WITHIN THE COCOON OF her fresh grave. The rain had stopped. When, she couldn't remember. The vegetation that had grown long and thick in the downpour was still wrapped tightly around her body. Helena wanted out. Staying in this green, growing grave was not an option. For Helena, it no longer mattered whether she lived or died, but for her loved ones to face the decision of stopping the life support—no, she could not do it. To live, to wake up, to return to her hospital bed from certain death in the Great Sleep was the one sure way to prevent it.

If only she could free herself! The more she struggled, the tighter the grassy strands wrapped around her, fighting against her and pulling her down deeper into the soft, giving earth.

She lay still, wondering what to do next. She wasn't sure why Coriander had left as she did. It was apparently no big deal to her that Helena lay dying in the meadow. Coriander must know something Helena did not. Maybe she knew the future. Never mind Coriander, she thought. She left without helping me.

Helena felt the heaviness of the soaked fabric of her yoga pants and the hooded sweatshirt, contemplating what possible reason there was for appearing in the Great Sleep wearing these things. There must have been, or it wouldn't have happened, Helena decided, realizing as she did how Coriander and her spiritual convictions had influenced her. She no longer felt like the spirit world was far away. It was not only close, but it inspired people in countless ways of which they were unaware. She understood this now.

If Helena could figure out why this particular clothing, she'd understand how to escape her predicament. Surely it wasn't to keep her warm in the storm. They had become so wet and clingy, she felt colder with them than without them.

Then it occurred to her. *Without them.*

She pulled her arms close to her and tried bending them inward, freeing them from the loose and heavy sleeves. It was awkward but, after a concentrated struggle, she was able to get first one then the other arm inside the sweatshirt, close against her skin. She was able to move them slightly, up and down, next to her belly. She was glad for the loose sweatshirt, knowing if she'd been wearing something else, like a pair of jeans and a turtleneck, one of the outfits she'd had on during another visit, there'd be no chance of squeezing out of such clothing.

What now? If she could only slide herself downward, and come out the bottom of the shirt . . .

Houdini could have done this, no problem, Helena thought. *I need to concentrate, to focus on small movements. I need to be drawn into myself. No extreme struggling or the strands will tighten against me.*

The yoga pants had a wide waistband which she pushed down with her hands. Down, down, slid the pants, while simultaneously Helena was bending herself up in the middle, as though preparing to do a backbend. The grass was squeezing against her, but her body was within the clothing, and if she could escape the clothing, she could escape the ropes. Or so she hoped.

The exertion and the tension were draining her energy, and the grassy ropes had not loosened their grip on her. How could she have thought sliding out of her clothes was any solution? If she did manage to do so, the ropes were still there on top of the fabric, binding her down. The only way out was to cut through, not slide through.

She remembered the story Coriander had told about the man on the island who had tied himself to a tree and faced the hurricane. What a stupid tale, she thought. Until Helena realized how similar their experiences were, both of them tied down during a storm to face death. Except the man had done it to himself, on purpose, while Helena had simply run into some bad luck, getting caught in the strange, other-worldly storm.

She continued working slowly to slip through her clothing and escape the trap. She was not getting far in the slightest. She felt suffocated by the sweatshirt bearing down on her, reminding her how the massive storm cloud had been pressing downward toward her. There was blue sky above her now, and the water droplets glistening on the grass were like tiny prisms with rainbows inside each one.

A rainbow means hope, she thought, remembering the story of Noah and the flood from her childhood Sunday School classes. *Hope.*

Hundreds of tiny little rainbows were trapped inside the crystal droplets. For a moment she forgot her dilemma and watched the miniature prisms, delighting in such a miracle. She stopped struggling. Resting, she took in her surroundings, absorbing the fresh, natural smell of the earth cleansed after a rainstorm. Helena, practically inside the earth as she was, felt at one with it. Breathing deeply, sucking in the scented air, Helena, in her make-shift coffin, was glad to be alive.

Suddenly she realized why the man had strapped himself to the tree to face the hurricane, his great opponent. It was what Coriander had been trying to teach her—how people cause things to happen by obsessing over them—and not to focus on fear of what might be, but on gratitude for what is. The man did not know this. Instead of appreciating what he had, he could only see what he'd lose if the hurricane won. As a result, he destroyed what mattered most.

Helena had been like the man. She had tied herself down rather than risk loving again. Tied herself down rather than giving of herself to her mother, her father, her daughter. If she pursued it further, she figured there'd be similar parallels in her marriage, but she chose not to go there.

She had been there for her cats and that's about it. *Pathetic.* Abruptly, she remembered she had cats. Gray tiger cats, names . . . she didn't know. Cats . . . what was familiar about that? Cats. And then she knew. Her daughter's name. Cassie. It was Cassie. Cassandra.

At last Helena could see Cassie in her mind's eye, and the sense of her daughter was strong and clear.

The growing baby in her womb was a girl, and she would be lively and funny and strong. When her husband wanted the name Vanessa, Helena had said, "No, she is not a Vanessa."

Simon claimed the privilege of naming his firstborn. "After all, you're the mother and will have such a big part of her life. I'd like to at least choose the name," he had said.

With each name he picked, Helena said no, no, no.

"Alicia?"

"No."

"Jennifer."

"No."

"Tiffany?"

"Absolutely not."

"Candace?"

"Never."

"You come up with something then," he had said.

"We agreed you'd be the one to choose the name. Only it has to fit her."

"How can you know if it fits her? She's not born yet. She's not a person. She'll fit into her name, whatever it is."

"Of course, she's a person! We've seen her in the ultrasound."

"You know what I mean. She's a . . . fetus. She won't be a real person until she's born. She'll grow into whatever name we give her."

"She is a person. I already know her, and none of these names fit our daughter."

He continued until finally hitting upon the right one. Cassandra, Cassie for short. Dreamy yet strong. When Cassandra was born, it was indeed the perfect fit.

Helena longed to see her daughter's face, to reach out and touch her, reassure her that all would be well no matter the outcome. She was trying oh so hard, was she ever trying, to connect somehow with her one and only child. Not even the pure language of the heart, spirit to spirit, was sufficient. Why was it so difficult to express one's true feelings toward those most beloved?

This failure was at the heart of Helena's marriage breakup. She and Simon had not been good communicators, not even at first. Once the physical attraction died away, there wasn't enough left to unite them. The problem was she and Simon spoke out loud too much of what they didn't really mean, the shallow or hurtful accusations that came too easily, and they kept silent on what was more difficult to express—the gentle, caring words that could have bridged the gulf growing between them.

None of it mattered anymore. The marriage was over. What counted now was getting free. Or dying. Waking up in one world or the other, allowing Cassie to have peace either way. As could Helena. The future would be chosen. Settled. She could die or she could live. If she did somehow survive this impromptu burial, trapped in her once lovely meadow, Helena would no longer hide from life. She would speak what was in her heart. She would love. She would hope.

Helena noticed how the water droplets had evaporated in the bright sunlight, and she felt the loss of it. She had been staring at them while pondering these ideas, almost in a kind of trance, and noticing the prisms were now gone woke her up from the dream-like state.

"Now, the yoga pants," she said out loud. "Back at it. See if I can get out of them."

She worked her arms downward yet again, arching her back, trying to push down the pants. It was easier this time. Either the material had loosened or her lengthy pondering had strengthened her reserves. She attempted to push up the sweatshirt. The exertion tired her, and she rested a while longer, feeling encouraged by a renewed hope of success. The grass, in drying out from the rain, seemed to have loosened its hold on her.

Inch by inch, she was able to push the pants down without the grassy chains pressing as tightly against her as before. *Oh, thank you for the sun!* Finally she was able to slide out of the pants, and with a tricky acrobatic contortion, in a long backwards movement, she pulled herself free from the hoodie as well.

Freedom at last!

Helena maneuvered herself between the strands of ropy grass and climbed out of the hole. Standing upright like a newly created being, she knew exactly what she had to do next.

Twenty-six

THE RELUCTANCE TO KNOCK ON THE DOOR, THE turning away from it, had been what got Helena nearly killed in the meadow grave. She would return to the village and remedy her failure. First, she needed her clothes. They lay like a deformed creature, still covered by the grass. She pulled them loose and climbed into the cold, wet uncomfortable yoga pants and hoodie.

"I'm going, Coriander!" Helena shouted. "I know you're out there somewhere and watching me. Hey, thanks for leaving me in the grave, by the way. Rope stretches when dry and apparently grass does as well, so fortunately I was able to get free. No thanks to you."

Helena couldn't understand why she was still in the Great Sleep, never having stayed this long. To stave off loneliness, she continued her one-sided conversation as she made her way through the forest and on to the village.

"Am I dead yet, Coriander? Was this whole experience a transition? I have no clue if I am dead or alive. They say you're supposed to see a light. Since I don't, I'm guessing alive. I'm headed to the village now, Coriander, ready to discover the next step in this bizarre journey. Maybe I'll see the light when the door opens. What do you say?" Silence. No communication from Coriander. She was either not watching or not talking.

Helena approached the house with the green door and the ivy on the brick walls, the second one she'd run away from. It was cute and cozy and charming. Dragging herself up the sidewalk, being weighed down by her soggy clothing, she said, "Coriander, I am going to knock on this door, and guess what? I am not afraid."

She knocked, feeling anticipation instead of fear, wondering what would happen next. Her heart fluttered inside her chest, making her think she surely couldn't be dead or she would not feel so alive. No one answered. She tried again, louder this time, first using her fist then dropping the brass knocker for good measure.

Waiting, wondering if those were footsteps, perhaps only her imagination. She looked around. Not a soul anywhere in the village. There was a robin on the green lawn, pulling out a worm easily from the damp ground.

No, she had not imagined it. Footsteps were coming from inside the house, coming closer. Helena steeled herself, stood firm. She would not run away.

The door opened. Helena gaped, speechless. She could hardly believe what she saw. She opened her mouth to speak. To say hello. To say something. No words came out.

There she stood, looking like Helena always remembered her: the same enthusiastic sparkle in her eyes, the open friendly smile, the quick movements of a woman who loved life and people and was prepared for anything. Surprises were welcome to her. She had always said so.

"Mom!"

Her mom opened her arms and Helena fell into them. She was home. Even the smell was familiar, a combination of the soap and face cream Mom had always used. The clean scent of her mother.

Her mom pulled away and took a long, appraising look at her. "Helena, it is wonderful to see you! How have you been, my darling daughter?"

"Uh, not good, I guess. You know I'm in a coma, I take it? No, on second thought, I must be dead or I wouldn't be here with you. I'm pretty confused at the moment . . . but really glad to see you, Mom!" Helena rushed her words together, wanting to communicate as quickly as possible, in case her mom evaporated. "This makes everything I've been through worthwhile, that's all I know!"

Her mom reached for Helena's hand and led her further into the house. "Let's not stand here in the hallway. Come along, Helena, and have a seat. I like this place, don't you?"

"Is it yours . . . do you . . . uh . . . live here?"

Her mom brought her into a formal living room, reflective of an old-fashioned parlor, with antique style furniture, a large Persian rug covering the wood floors and landscape oil paintings on the walls. A bookcase filled with rows of expensive-looking books took up an entire wall. Everything was spotlessly clean, unimaginably new and fresh, despite appearing like something right out of the 1890s.

"No, it's not mine. I'm just using it for our meeting. We're allowed to utilize places like this now and then, when it is of vital eternal consequence."

"Wow. That sounds very official. You must be someone important, Mom." Helena wanted to examine the features of the interesting house more closely, if she could only stop gazing at her mother's face.

"Helena, one thing I've learned since I've come here is *everyone* is important. The least, most humble person is every bit as important as . . . oh, I don't know . . . the biggest pop star or the President of the United States. Status doesn't matter in this world, not like it does on Earth with the false adulation of wealth and position and power."

"Certainly makes sense," Helena said agreeably, while thinking to herself, *I am talking to my mom! I do not want this to end!*

They sat down together on a flowered settee. Helena sat up straighter, self-conscious as she was about being presented in such a lady-like environment wearing sloppy work-out clothes from the 21st century. Her mom wore an elegant turquoise and white-striped knit dress, modern and expensive-looking, which fit her perfectly and made her look young and beautiful. The dress exactly complemented her dark hair, blue eyes and bold features. She had never worn anything similar when she was alive. Too bad, because it made her look amazing.

"I love your dress, Mom. It's so unlike your typical style, even when you got dressed up."

"I picked it out for this occasion. It's nothing like my old wardrobe, is it? Once we get settled, we're taken to a place where people—experts in design and beauty—fix us up, with the right styles for our hair, with the ideal kinds of clothes to enhance our fresh new spirits, and to make us look and feel fabulous. Who would've thought Heaven would care about something so . . . oh, worldly, right?"

Becoming more relaxed by the moment, Helena let out a laugh of delight. "What a surprise! I'd have never imagined it. I guess we tend to visualize white robes and playing harps and too much leisure time."

"It's nothing like that. For one thing, there's no leisure time. Every single person is busy doing things, regardless of where they are in the journey. For example, getting the new arrivals comfortable and dressed appropriately for their age and style is a job! There are jobs for each individual. It's amazing, Helena, you have no idea."

"You'd like that, Mom. You always loved running around doing things for people." Helena could not stop smiling.

"I do love it, my darling angel. It's what's so brilliantly planned about this place. Everyone stays busy according to preference and personality style. See those books over there?"

"Don't tell me people write books in Heaven?"

"They most certainly do! We read them, too. There are houses along this street where authors and artists work on their creative endeavors, coming to work like someone on Earth would keep office hours."

"Mom, am I dead or what? I'm not sure you'd be allowed to tell me these secrets if I weren't part of things. I don't want to leave you, Mom—this is like a dream come true. I'm okay with being dead, if that's the case."

Helena's mom reached over and embraced her, then stroked her damp hair. "You do look a fright, Helena. I know you've been through a lot. No, you are not dead. You're halfway between. I've been sent to comfort you, just as Coriander was, and to guide you to your next place of assignment."

"You know Coriander?"

"I do now. She's actually one of our great-great aunts, assigned to watch over you from birth. She's quite the character, isn't she? I can't help but love her for the good work she's done with you, especially since the coma. I couldn't bear it if you'd been left alone in your suffering, but then, we are never left alone. We may think we are, but we aren't."

"Coriander said something like that to me as well. She helped me a lot, yes, but it wasn't always easy." Helena wondered how much she should say, not wanting to be a complainer in Heaven, if it's where she was. She went ahead and blurted it out, because after all, this was her mom. "Sometimes she was plain mean, to tell you the truth, Mom. I could never decide if I liked her or not. I think it was more a dependency relationship than a friendship."

"Growth and progress is never easy, Helena. Besides, Coriander died quite young. She was merely a girl, and it's affected her in the Afterlife. Our experiences always do shape us. She's a marvelous person though and always does an excellent job to whomever she's assigned to."

"I did try, Mom," Helena said, not wanting her mom to be disappointed in her. "I was always nice to Coriander, even when she wasn't the most likable person in the world."

"I know, sweetheart, and I'm proud of you for the progress you've made, especially since the accident. The willingness to change, to learn. No more hiding, right, Helena?"

"No, Mom, no more hiding. Only do I have to go back? I'd be perfectly content staying right here with you." Helena finally pulled her eyes away from her mom's face long enough to look around. "What a charming house. It looks like somewhere I'd imagine Coriander coming from."

"It was her childhood home," Helena's mom stated quietly. "She suffered here a great deal, and part of her healing process was to recreate it in its entirety. In spiritual form, of course, since we are in a spirit world."

"Are you saying nothing here is real? Because it feels real," Helena said. She patted her mom's arm. It felt like real flesh and blood, but it couldn't possibly be. Her mom was dead. Helena had seen her in the coffin.

"It feels real because it is. The spirit world is as authentic as our solid, physical world. But, Helena, we do need to get down to business. I don't have long. I wish I did."

"Oh, Mom!" Helena couldn't bear the thought of saying good-bye to her mom. And hearing her say she didn't have long, brought back all kinds of sad memories.

"I wish we could sit like this the whole afternoon and visit. I'd make cookies in the kitchen, and we'd drink hot chocolate. You could certainly use some, as wet and cold as you must be. My darling Helena, I am so relieved you survived it!"

"What was it, Mom? It was such a strange experience. I thought sure it was a dream, a nightmare, and I'd be waking up in the hospital any second, watching Coriander giggling at my predicament."

"It was very real, Helena. Remember the black cloud?"

"How could I forget! I thought sure it would suffocate me, coming right down toward me like that."

"That was death coming to claim you. Since it was premature death, before you were assigned for it, you needed to fight it. Thankfully, you did. It was evil. Someone wanted you dead."

"Wanted me dead? Are you serious? Who in the world would want me dead?" Helena felt faint, and leaned against the parlor settee like a lady of the nineteenth century, fanning herself with her hand. "You know, Mom, if I were given half a chance, I'd definitely change into a dress. I rather like the idea of matching this quaint little room."

Her mom laughed and said, "There isn't time. I'm sorry. Besides, it's not your season. You resisted the evil, you fought back, just as you did when they were after you in Pasadena. I am happy to see you are still very much alive."

She rubbed Helena's back, something that brought back such a flood of warm and pleasant memories. Helena wasn't actually pleased to hear about her present, alive condition. It meant the two of them would soon be parted.

"I'm delighted you are here, Helena, only you'll be returning. You still have work to do."

"Mom, why would anyone want to kill me? I didn't have any enemies."

"Evil rules the Earth, sweetheart. It is everywhere. Don't let the information cloud your vision. When you were young you felt it too intently, and it made you fearful. Afraid of the most common events, the most harmless people. I didn't understand what you were going through, not until much later when I came here and had many lessons. Then I understood."

"You mean my sensitivity made me aware of evil? Wow, Mom. This sure explains a lot, except I'm not sure it's any excuse for how I handled my 'gift,' if you want to call it that."

Her mom put her hands against Helena's cheeks and looked directly into her eyes. "Helena, since I learned this about you, about your gift of extreme sensitivity to the aura of others, I have longed for an opportunity to tell you how sorry I am for having pushed you. I was always urging you into situations you weren't prepared to handle, thinking it would help. I, who should have been your guardian and support, instead caused you pain by trying to make you grow up, as I saw it. I am so very sorry, sweetheart."

"Oh, Mom, you don't need to apologize. You were doing what you thought was best for me."

"You have a good heart, a soft and compassionate heart, Helena. It's made you into a wonderful nurse, and you will return to your job. I know Coriander was pretty hard on you back there, but as your mom I can tell you, the fear that has always been with you was not your fault. It came upon you solely due to your sensitivity to evil. Fortunately, you didn't suffer directly from the wickedness of others, not like some poor souls do—Coriander, for instance. But you felt it, you cringed from people because of it, and it frightened you, not realizing what it was."

Helena began to cry softly. "Mom, it's no excuse though. I should have broken through and been a force for good,

not this person hiding from what she couldn't understand. That's no way to make the world a better place."

"You understand now, Helena, and you will move forward to your destiny. I am very proud of you, my darling
daughter. You have no idea. Never mind about what you
should have done. Every one of us has a list a mile long of
our should've dones. There comes a time when we must
destroy the list, advance and start fresh."

Helena felt panicky. "Start over? After everything I've
been through and learned I've got to start over? Oh, Mom!"

"No, I said start *fresh*. Completely different." She stood
and, taking Helena's hands, gently lifted her daughter up
from the settee. "It's time, my darling angel. We must go."

Twenty-seven

ELENA'S MOM GAVE HER ONE LAST EMBRACE before guiding her through the house, to the back door of the bungalow.

"Go through this door, Helena. I won't be with you as you travel, but don't worry. I'm alive. I'm busy. I'm happy. I'll get to watch over you now and then, when it matters. Please give my love to your dad. Be a comfort to him."

"I will, Mom, I promise! I'll be different. Everything has changed with me."

"Tell your dad I'm well, and contented, but he needs to take care of himself and quit eating that fast food. Get back to cooking real meals in our kitchen, tell him that, and to quit frequenting the bakery. He doesn't need the carbs and fat. He knows how to cook the basics, plus I made sure to leave him a well-stocked pantry. He should eat more fruits and vegetables, because it's not his season yet any more than it's yours, Helena. Time goes quickly here. In fact, it doesn't seem to exist at all, and soon enough we'll be together again."

"Oh, Mom, how can I leave you?"

Her mom had opened the back door and gestured for Helena to go through. Helena wanted to memorize the vision of her beautiful mother standing there in her stunning outfit, smiling at her and nodding and waving her hand in short, quick gestures—the way she always did when she'd wanted her daughter to move along more quickly.

"It's fine, sweetheart," her mom encouraged. "You step into the garden. Isn't it lovely? Coriander created it herself. Gardening can be so healing. It's a very important part of our world. Now, rush along, Helena darling. I love you. Don't worry about a thing. You will remember everything we talked about. If the actual words disappear, the memory will be with you, even within you. I'll watch over you, as I said. We will meet again! Move ahead, Helena. You have a job to do."

Helena turned to see the garden her mother was talking about and as she did, she felt herself passing rapidly through the colorful flower beds, up and up and up, a balloon let free to rise into the atmosphere. She strained to look back at the house, to see her mom one last time, but the place was in a haze behind her.

She had entered another realm.

This realm was different. It felt like exploring another world, perhaps a more advanced one than her Great Sleep. She found herself drifting downward until she was right above a foggy path, passing along the pathway as though pushed from behind by a gust of wind. She could see things—people, buildings, roads going in many directions. Perhaps this was where Coriander had come from.

It was more like the real world than Helena's Great Sleep, yet quite different from reality as she knew it.

In this foggy dimension, Helena could sense what was going on inside the people, almost as though their emotions were tangible entities more obvious and clear to her than were their bodies. It was like taking a person and the sum of who they were, and instead of having a body there was an echo of one, with their emotions and thoughts vibrating around the echo like music.

The way Helena saw and understood these strange people was similar to how one would see and hear music: expressive, infinite combinations of notes combining to create an expression of mood, atmosphere, tone—whether happy or peaceful or sad or furious or searching. Although Helena could see their music, she did not understand it. What made the young man angry or the little girl laugh or that old woman morose? The reason behind each remained a secret known only to them and to whomever they chose to share it with.

Helena got the sense this might be part of the problem for the unhappy souls, with many of them stuck in the middle of their emotions like an insect caught in a web, unable to free themselves of the situation. At least not yet, because it was clear they were trying. There was hope here, a sense of purpose, as the multitudes went from place to place as people do, engaging in the activities of mundane routine: planting a garden, tending to small children, preparing food in a kitchen, working in factories, shopping in stores. Engaging in the aspects of life and work and families.

They appeared to engage in these activities more with their spirits than their bodies. The bodies were of less importance in this world. For instance, if a man wanted to mow the lawn he did it—only Helena wasn't sure if he was actually doing it or thinking about it with such intensity that he seemed to be mowing the lawn, but not really. Maybe it was an actual physical person on Earth mowing the lawn while this man of the spirit realm projected himself into the other mowing individual, until it became real to him and others around him that he was mowing the lawn when he was not.

It was like Coriander. Was she there in Helena's hospital room or did Helena imagine her? Yet Coriander told her things Helena didn't know and couldn't know. Or did she? Coriander was not imagined, as Helena had first thought, because her mother had confirmed it. She was no longer a flesh and blood person, yet she was a person. A ghost? A spirit? Had Coriander simply imagined herself into Helena's hospital room, appearing in clothing from Helena's past?

Coriander was like these people Helena saw as she passed through the fog world—real yet not real. Familiar yet strange. Busy in their own way yet not apparently doing anything. Helena kept watching for Coriander and for her mother, too. She longed to see her mom again, thought of her constantly, expecting any second Mom would round the bend of one of these many intersecting roads and greet her.

"Hello again, my darling angel. I thought I'd pop in and say hi again. Keep up the good work, sweetheart!"

Helena could hear the words in her mind, creating such an ache in her heart she supposed her aura in this world must be one of immense sadness, loneliness and longing for what could no longer be.

Helena was no longer traveling as rapidly. She had descended to a winding walkway where people were headed toward whatever unknown destinations called to them. No one spoke to her, nor she to them. She wasn't sure they could see her. Each one of them seemed very intent on their purposes.

Helena came across a man standing at a crossroads by himself, apparently waiting. It struck her because he was stationery, unlike the others she had noticed in this world.

There was a bench, a green wooden park bench with cast iron arms and feet, and he stood next to it as though at attention. He was an older man, looking close to late seventies, Helena supposed, with soft white hair combed neatly and trimmed close around his ears and at his neck. He had exceedingly blue eyes, alert and intelligent, and a friendly smile that widened as he watched Helena approach. She wondered if he was waiting for her.

She paused momentarily, not wanting to bother him but deciding to give him an opportunity to speak if he was there for her. The man said hello and nodded.

"Hello," Helena replied, taken back that someone in this place had at last spoken to her. She'd been wandering around for how long? She had no idea. She'd gone into the Great Sleep where she was nearly buried alive, then met her mom, and her mom had guided her to this next world. As her mom had said, there was absolutely no sense of time passing. It could have been hours or minutes or days, impossible to judge.

Helena was ready to leave, actually. She longed to be in her hospital bed, safe in her coma, chatting with Coriander. She had a feeling those days were over. She wasn't sure what would happen next on this strange journey, but figured there was no going backwards from this point.

Realizing she was still staring at the man, Helena apologized. "I'm sorry, sir. I didn't mean to stare. I was thinking . . . wondering something. . . ."

He smiled at her kindly. "Quite all right. We do that sort of thing a lot around here. Lose track, I mean." He spoke with a slight accent Helena couldn't place. It was a kind voice, soft with a pleasing timbre that immediately made her feel relaxed and welcomed.

"Were you . . . were you . . . waiting for me?" Helena asked. She'd been able to talk to Coriander easily, but with this man it was a struggle to put her thoughts into words and connect them into a sentence. At least she could speak to him, and he understood her—more than what went on with the nurses.

He peered at her, squinting a little like he'd forgotten his glasses. "It depends. You aren't Katherine, are you?"

"No, I'm Helena. Helena . . . Carr." She was proud of herself for remembering her full name.

"I didn't think you were her. I saw her once briefly. I seem to remember someone shorter than you, stockier. Older, in fact."

Helena was confused. "Is she a friend of yours?"

"I hope she looks upon me as a friend. One never quite knows what to expect in these cases. There may be fear.

Or anger. Often confusion, of course. They might lash out, get violent."

"Who . . . who might . . . do that?"

"Our people. The ones we're assigned to." The man checked his watch. "She should be passing this way any moment now. I suppose I could go to her instead . . . it might be easier. This is only my third time. I'm still a novice at these kinds of things."

The man seemed agitated as he repeatedly checked his watch, peered past Helena, smoothed his white hair across the top, fidgeted from foot to foot.

"Wouldn't you like to sit on the . . . on this bench?" Helena suggested, still stuttering and hesitating as she tried to get the words out. She gestured to the green park bench next to him. "Maybe sit while you wait . . . relax?"

"No, I couldn't possibly. What if I miss her? She might be in a state, anything is possible, and she won't be looking for me. It's my duty to watch for her. If I miss her, well . . . well. That will be too bad. Unthinkable."

"I see," said Helena, trying to be reassuring. He was such a pleasant, amiable gentleman. She wanted to help him out, maybe keep him company until this Katherine woman came by. She could keep him distracted, perhaps calm his distress.

"Maybe I can wait with you . . . help you watch . . . so we don't miss her."

"How very kind of you. I don't want to keep you though. It might delay you in your destination."

Helena almost laughed but didn't, for fear of seeming rude. "I don't really have a destination. Not yet anyway." She spread her arms wide, taking in the expanse of space.

"I am here, not sure why, not sure where. I definitely don't know for how long."

She stepped over to the park bench and sat with a thud. "For some reason," she said, "I got a tremendous craving for barbecued chicken. How strange. I haven't been hungry for I don't know how long, and suddenly I want to bury my face in a plate of hot and spicy wings. With ranch dressing on the side."

The man smiled at her, and Helena was glad to see him cheerful once again. She continued rambling in an effort to distract him. "I was so faint with hunger I had to sit down. I hope you don't mind."

"You go right ahead. I may join you if my assignment . . . no, that's wrong. She's not a job, she's a person. Anyway, if she doesn't come by soon. I no longer feel tired or hungry any more, ever, but I do get bored occasionally. Often quite bored, and also impatient, I'm sorry to admit."

Helena patted the seat next to her. "Help yourself to a seat. We can chat, and I'll try my best not to bore you." She was feeling quite energized, the words flowing better, wanting to keep this conversation going for as long as possible. She hadn't talked to anyone except Coriander in who knew how long. And to her mom, of course, the most wondrous of gifts.

The man sat down with a sigh. "Don't mind if I do, but only if you help me watch for my assignment. My person. An older woman, graying brown hair, a little on the heavy-set side."

"Of course," Helena agreed, wanting very much to see this woman and learn more about who she was and what she was doing there. Maybe she would be like Helena. Not alive, not dead, lost in this strange gray world on the other side of time. Her curiosity was growing right along with her appetite. Did they eat food in this place? Helena could see barbecued chicken—smell it, taste it. She wiped at her mouth.

"Anyway, do you mind me asking: why do you call her 'your person'?" Helena asked.

"I suppose I should call her by name. Katherine. We've not met personally and it feels awkward," he said. Helena waited for more. Suddenly realization dawned in the man's eyes. "I see! You must be new here!"

"I've been around a few times," Helena said, "although, actually a different kind of place. I called it the Great Sleep. There were no people there. It's rather nice to be part of a social order again, even if I don't comprehend any of it. You're the first one to speak to me. Or perhaps to see me, for that matter. I thought I was invisible."

She gave a little laugh of embarrassment, wondering if invisibility were a thing here. She didn't doubt it. She hoped the nice, chatty man would be less evasive than Coriander and possibly shed some light on what was going on in this dimension.

"Not invisible, I'm sure," the man said. "People can see you. Only most of us are distracted. We're either working on a project to help ourselves or to help someone else. Or we are new to everything and utterly confused. Or we've been here too long and want out."

Helena still didn't get it. Although now that he mentioned it, she had noticed how people were either wandering around rather dazed, as she had surely done, or they were rushing to and fro, in groups or one on one, talking intently to one another.

"I myself have been shamefully self-centered in your company, thinking only of my duties." He extended a hand to her. "My name is David. Nice to meet you."

She shook his hand. "Helena. Helena Carr."

"Yes, I remember. You are new here, I believe you mentioned."

"More or less. I come and go . . . places . . . it seems. Truthfully, I understand so very little."

David nodded. "That would be why no one spoke to you before this. You weren't ready."

"Ready for what?"

"To hear them. Or to communicate. In this realm, we know it instinctively and act accordingly. You'll get used to our ways, don't worry."

"I don't want to get used to them," Helena said in a sudden panic. "I really don't belong here. What I want is to get better, return to my own world and be normal again."

"This is normal too, you know," David said in his grandfatherly way. "As normal as anything. It's because you aren't used to it yet."

"I don't want to get used to it. I still have hope of recovery."

"What is it then?"

"A coma. I'm in a coma, in a hospital in Pasadena."

"Pasadena? The States?"

"Uh, yes. Pasadena, California. You mean we aren't even in America here?"

"There's no such thing as time or place where we are, Helena." He patted her knee in a kindly fashion then stood and gazed into the distance. "I believe I see her coming." He resumed his attentive stance, the way he was when Helena had come along. He pointed to his watch and said, "Unless we have specific duties involving meeting those fresh from Earth. Then we get these special watches."

Helena jumped up. "Where are we then, actually?" she demanded, finding her voice getting stronger. "Are we dead? Is this the land of the dead? Because I know I'm not dead. I mean, I almost was, I almost gave in and . . . died, I guess. Coriander talked sense into me, I got free of the strangling grass, then met my mom, and now—"

David made a calm down gesture with both his hands. "There is no such place and no such thing as dead."

"Then what?" she asked eagerly. She sensed her visit with David was short. As soon as the vague-looking woman in the distance got closer, David would run to meet her—Katherine, she supposed—and Helena with her questions would be forgotten. "Because I am not dead, I know that," she insisted.

"How do you know?" he asked with an indulgent smile.

"Because I do. I'm in a coma. Not dead."

"Then why are you here?"

"I'm not sure. That's what I'd like to find out. Sometimes I find myself here, there, other places. Not dreams but somewhat like dreams. Before . . . before my accident, I suffered from such anxiety, I never could have approached you like I did. While now . . . here . . . I feel quite normal. I do like that, I must admit," Helen said.

"Coma patients do not dream. It's one of the signs of coma," David said.

Helena glanced sharply at him. "Hey, wait. You sound like a professional, like you know what you're talking about. Like a . . . like a . . ." Words were disappearing again, and the woman was coming closer. Time was running short.

"Like a doctor, you mean to say? I apologize for finishing your sentence, but you seemed to be struggling for expression." David checked his watch. "I must go. There's my person, I'm sure of it."

He turned again to Helena, who felt panic rising at the thought of losing his company. She knew so little yet had so much she wanted to ask him. The words were fading away faster than she could capture them.

"Yes . . . yes. Then . . . you . . ." she managed to get out.

"Yes, I am a doctor. Or was. I was a surgeon in Capetown, South Africa." He was distracted, and Helena could tell he needed to go to the woman, Katherine.

"A surgeon . . . ?" What kind, she wondered.

"I specialized in traumatic brain injury. I was a neurologist specializing in coma as a result of TBI. How long has it been since your injury? Because the majority of recovery from brain injury occurs within the first six months to a year after a trauma."

"I don't know. I have no idea. What else can you tell me?"

"I'd need to ask questions before I can tell you anything. For example, are you in a vegetative state or persistent vegetative state? Do you know?"

Helena felt like crying. She didn't know a single thing about her condition!

David patted her shoulder. "Please don't cry. Everything will work out, I promise you."

"But you can help me! You are trained for it. Is there anything else you can tell me?"

"In my opinion, it's better for you if you're in PVS, with a short-term coma. You could have locked-in syndrome, where you're aware and awake but cannot move or communicate due to a complete paralysis of the body."

"No, I don't believe it's that. According to what I understand from the nurses, which is very little, I am not awake at all. My eyes are closed. I can't communicate in any way."

"PVS is where the upper portions of the brain are damaged and the lower portions are spared. Locked-in syndrome is caused by damage to specific portions of the lower brain and brain stem, with no damage to the upper brain. Most locked-in syndrome patients can communicate through movements and blinking of their eyes, which are not affected by the paralysis. Some patients may have the ability to move certain facial muscles as well."

"Pretty certain that's not me. I apparently can't move anything."

"Sounds like you're either in a vegetative state or have advanced to PVS—persistent vegetative state."

"Is that good?"

"It depends. PVS with a short-term coma gives you best chance of full recovery, as long as you get proper rehabilitative care. Most patients with locked- in syndrome do not regain motor control. One more question, before

I go." The woman was approaching quickly. Helena could make out the features of her face. She was probably in her mid-sixties, had a big smile on her face, and was rushing forward toward David. Funny, Helen thought, since according to David they had never met.

"Okay, what? This is extremely helpful, I can't thank you enough," Helena said. "What else did you want to ask? Quick, here she comes."

"Are you an educated person? Any college?" David asked, glancing at Katherine.

"Yes, I graduated with a bachelor's in nursing."

"Good, that will help. Those with higher education are more likely to attain disability-free status after a TBI than the less-educated. Those with greater cognitive reserve tend to be more resilient, with greater ability to function in the face of damage."

"This is good information. Thank you, Doctor . . . Doctor . . . David." Helena wanted to shake his hand, give him a hug or something. She felt so happy and close to this elderly man who had helped her, a complete stranger, out of his past experience and knowledge of her situation. She held back, however, not sure what the protocol was for physical contact with spirits.

David smiled warmly at her, as though understanding and acknowledging her gratitude. "I do wish we had more time to talk, Helena. I must go. Perhaps we will meet again. Remember, make sure you get proper physical and cognitive rehab when you wake up. I can't emphasize it enough. It will be key to your recovery."

He was gone, walking briskly down the path with Katherine trotting along next to him, leaving Helena to look after them with empty longing, wondering how she would ever find him again in this vast place. There were so many more questions.

The next thing, she was back in her hospital bed, trying to understand the muttering of these infernal nurses. *Why for God's sake didn't they speak up so a person could hear them?*

Twenty-eight

HELENA DECIDED TO PAY MORE ATTENTION to the cycles and symptoms of her coma, in order to know where she was, according to David's analysis. Apparently her choices were completely brain dead, vegetative state, progressive vegetative state, or locked-in. During her conscious and mentally active phases, she kept reviewing the different names in her mind, so she could remember. Her plan was to analyze and determine where she might be in the process, then return to the Fog and find David to discuss it with him further.

Unfortunately, there were long periods when she was not in a mentally active phase. She worried about David's information disappearing into the endless void of her mind during those phases.

Without the cooperation of her body, Helena could not feel emotions in a normal way. With her brain on partial shutdown, her emotional life had changed, leaving her unable to quantify or analyze the changes. Odd things would happen. She might feel frustration at not being able to clearly hear the people standing near her, and then the frustration would give away to numbness, as though it went away on its own without her paying attention.

She felt almost an animal instinct taking over her human side, the side that made decisions, effected change, took control. Without any options or abilities to control a situation, Helena would go numb, like a rabbit or deer suddenly aware of danger.

She waited. Waited for something to change. Waited to revisit the strange realm where she had met the white-haired man, David. Doctor David. She had to go there again, find him and get additional information about her condition. She must pay close attention to her symptoms in order to relay it to him and see if he could diagnose her.

She waited for Coriander to return. Helena had no idea how long it was between visits, or how long she had been in the Great Sleep and then in the Fog. It might have been a very long time since she last saw Coriander, or mere minutes. Helena couldn't tell.

And so she expected someone to come, something to happen. Not in a restless, impatient state, but more like a peaceful mellow anticipation of things to come.

Questions would occur to Helena, things she wanted to remember to ask when she saw Coriander again, or when she might find herself strolling along the path in the place of fog and spirit people. She wondered if her brain function had permanently changed, wondered why she could remember certain things from her past so vividly and others not at all.

She remembered how she used to experience mild fear and anxiety nearly every waking moment of her previous life. Although she had no idea if she would become whole again or how long they'd let her stay on life support before giving up on recovery, she felt no fear about the outcome—only determination to hang on to life as she knew it with every tool in her very limited arsenal. Coriander was a tool, and now David, if only she could find him again. They would both be useful to help her out, otherwise why had they entered her life?

Helena realized how unusual it was how everything she valued had been taken from her, yet she felt no despair. She was still relatively content, an astounding thing to her. She was the same person as before the accident, but not really. She was not afraid when she used to always be afraid.

Where is God in all of this? Helena wondered. Is Coriander a messenger from God? An angel? If so, why isn't she more helpful? What is her purpose in coming to visit? If it's to answer questions she's not been doing a very good job of it, thought Helena. There were so many questions.

Are my expectations too high? Should I not expect answers? Or improvement? Is it enough that I am here, alive, a semi-conscious being, getting medical attention, getting visits from Coriander? Is it wrong of me to want more, to expect more? What am I supposed to be doing? Is it enough to simply be? That I exist, even in an altered state? Am I wrong to want more?

Helena wondered what the point was, and why her life was spared. In her visits to the other dimensions, she would have liked to have seen God, to ask Him about her situation. She wondered if she had displeased Him and was being punished. She had no idea what she could have done better, beyond pushing past the fear and reaching out to people instead of avoiding them. When she was in the Fog, she had reached out to David, making an effort to soothe his nervousness as he waited for Katherine. Helena felt this was a positive step. She would do more of it as she got the opportunity.

She reflected on how by knocking on the door, she had received the unbelievable privilege of speaking to her mother. Also, by speaking to David and thinking more about him than herself, she had drawn him into conversation and therefore learned significant information about her coma and what she should watch for.

For not being a very religious person, one who rarely stepped inside a church or gave much thought to God, Helena now found herself surprised to realize she desperately wanted to please God . . . or at the very least, to not be a disappointment to Him. She supposed it was due to the nearness of death with its mysteries.

She understood her willingness to overcome her personal anxieties and be less self-centered was pleasing to God. It was an important step in her healing. In helping others, people bring blessings upon themselves.

Helena had never thought much about life after death before her coma. Now there was no doubt in her mind people passed on to another sphere of existence, close to this one where they continued on whatever path they were directed to go. She had seen it distinctly in the Fog. Similar to this world, the people there had a destination they set out for with varying degrees of success.

Helena's destination was to get better. To regain health and consciousness and continue on where she'd left off. She couldn't remember what she'd been doing at the time of her accident that had been so important. She could not recall the details of the event. Only that she'd been going extremely fast on a road she thought would lead her to an important destination. When the red truck hit her and changed everything.

"Isn't it funny how life does that?" asked Coriander, suddenly at Helena's bedside, leaning forward in the chair.

"Oh, hello!" Helena said in surprise, sure Coriander hadn't been there a second ago. "Where did you come from?" A rhetorical question, really, not expecting Coriander to reply as succinctly as she did.

"Guatemala."

"What did you say?" Helena asked.

"I said, 'Guatemala.' That's where I came from. Did you miss me?"

"Yes, I did actually. I don't have a very clear sense of time, you know, but it did seem like you've been gone awhile. I was beginning to wonder . . ."

"If you'd see me again?" Coriander asked cheerily.

"Yes," said Helena. "After what happened in the Great Sleep. I transitioned to another place, another realm. My mother and I had a really nice conversation, in your home apparently, and she told me I should go to this different world."

"A foggy, misty place?"

"That's exactly it. With people who didn't seem aware of me. Finally, a man spoke to me."

"And?" Coriander prompted.

"It was nice. Enlightening," Helena said. "He noticed me, the first time anyone had, and he initiated conversation. He was nervous about meeting this woman, and I tried to help him take his mind off things by chatting with him."

"About what? Did he tell you anything? About himself perhaps, or what he was up to?"

Helena had never known Coriander to ask so many questions. Usually it was she who took the inquisitive role in their relationship.

"He said he was waiting for someone. The woman approached us later, although I never found out exactly who she was. Her name was Katherine and apparently she was dead. This David told me he was a neurologist from South Africa and could help me understand my coma, until the lady was coming closer and he had to go. He got very distracted once he saw her."

"It sounds like he was a First-Level Friend. Was he standing at a crossroads next to a bench?"

"Yes!" exclaimed Helena. "I was walking along the path, when he appeared there like he was waiting for a bus."

Coriander nodded. "A First-Level Friend. Not there for you though obviously. Plus, you have *me*." She smoothed her skirt, seeming pleased with herself.

"What is a First-Level Friend?"

Coriander waved her hand dismissively. "Nothing to do with you yet. That's something for you later. Much later, let's hope."

"What do you mean?"

"It's someone assigned to assist the newly dead to their destination, to help them navigate their way across the deep abyss. To tell you the truth, I was a bit worried when you mentioned him," she huffed. "Because it's my job to keep you here. I don't like to think someone is pushing his way into my affairs and trying to change my job description. I have no use for bullies like that."

"He was as nice as could be. I can see why he was a . . . a . . . friend. He seemed trustworthy and genuinely concerned about his duties to help this Katherine woman." Helena paused a moment in reflection. "You're saying she had just died?"

Coriander nodded. "Clearly the case. And this man, David, was assigned to meet her and accompany her to the Light."

"How interesting," Helena murmured, glad at last to be getting some clarity on the various worlds she'd been inhabiting lately.

Coriander slipped away suddenly, and Helena could sense someone else entering the room. Of course her eyes would not open, although she was working very hard at it and thought she could actually sense movement beneath her eyelids. Then the moment of awareness was gone, right when she heard the words: "Mother, it's me."

Helena wanted more than anything to wake up, to open her eyes and see her daughter, to give her some small sign she was there. Alive. Not brain dead. Not ready to be let go. A sound, a movement, the flicker of an eye— anything to show she was here in this uncooperative shell of a body. With every force of will available to her, Helena tried to concentrate, to focus on a word, one word: Cassie. Cassie. The word formed in her brain but would go no further. Or perhaps it was in her soul, the place of feelings without expression, where the name took root. And it stayed there.

The effort caused Helena to feel like she was expanding, and then shrinking in upon herself, tighter, tighter, like a coiled spring. As she moved back within herself, she was disappearing from the room where her daughter sat next to the bed as Coriander had moments before. Cassie held her hand and cried softly while stroking her hair.

As Helena disappeared into darkness, she heard the scattered words, *". . . difficult decisions to make, Mom . . . I don't know what to do. Keith keeps saying things . . . I'm not sure . . . I don't want to lose you. It may be too late. I don't know . . ."*

Twenty-nine

HELENA PUSHED THROUGH THE FOG, THE road barely visible ahead of her. Before she had stayed on whatever path she found herself until she was suddenly transported back to her broken physical body. This time she had other plans. She had to find David, the neurologist from South Africa, the First-Level Friend. She needed to know what to do next, how she could relay the message to Cassie that she was alive and would surely wake up from the coma. Helena could not possibly be moving toward death when she felt so energized. She would recover, she was sure of it. She had to let Cassie know. Before it was too late.

Perhaps this David person could tell her how to make herself open her eyes, speak, move a finger—anything!

Coriander had been absolutely useless, barely answering Helena's questions, always lecturing her about getting upset. Of course, Helena did appreciate the company, and she understood Coriander wasn't as sympathetic to Helena's situation as she could have been, considering her own sad history. She wished someone more helpful had been assigned to her case. Someone more suitable who could empathize and understand her, like David.

Helena was tired of going around in circles, getting nowhere. Visits from Coriander, traveling to the strange spirit worlds, and back again with Coriander. No progress, nothing. The same eternal round going nowhere and getting Helena no closer to waking up, as though time didn't exist. Helena was running out of time. She had no more use for the pointless round of visits.

Helena was determined to get well. She needed another chance, *a fresh start*, her mom had called it. Helena would redeem herself, prove she would embrace life rather than avoid it. To do good. But first she had to wake up from this coma.

Helena picked up her pace, her eyes flicking to one person after another she passed along the way. No one she recognized. She felt desperate. How would she find one lone man out of these hordes of people? They were everywhere, she suddenly realized. The visit before she had focused on the road ahead, caught up in her own movement, amazed at being in a different realm, one populated by others, so unlike her Great Sleep.

As she scanned the faces to find David, she saw how many inhabitants there were, and how fascinating to see the diversity of people and the variety of expressions they wore. All ages, races, cultures, although no small children. Helena wondered if perhaps the little children went somewhere else. She hoped so. She didn't want to think of toddlers wandering alone and lost in this strange world of fog. How sad that would be. As Helena looked, she realized those who were alone were few and they, instead of seeming lost and neglected, moved quickly as though to an appointment, with expressions of purpose and confidence.

The people who seemed most confused were accompanied by another, who Helena assumed was their appointed First-Level Friend. She wondered why she hadn't been assigned a First-Level Friend, until she realized the obvious. She was not dead. She was Coriander's assignment while still among the living. Coriander, who was meant to be her comfort, her friend, her own Trusted Guide.

Helena had to find out what was going on with her life, such as it was, and where she was headed. She couldn't stay in the hospital, in a coma. Soon enough, they'd transfer her to a care center for the permanently damaged. She couldn't bear the thought of being left alone to wither and die, and she didn't want her daughter forced to arrange her life around visits to the mother who was there but not there. It was unthinkable. The only viable options left to her were to either wake up or die.

Wake up or die, what a dilemma. Did she have a choice in the matter after all?

Helena joined the throng moving along the road. To the side were groups clustered together, chattering and rejoicing before getting back on their journey to somewhere. She saw a few walking alone as she did, but most were accompanied by a companion or friend, leading the assigned charges along, like her doctor who had waited for the woman.

Where are these people going, anyway? Helena wondered. Was this Heaven? It sure didn't fit her preconceived notions of what Heaven would be. There were no harp-playing angels floating by on clouds. No clouds at all, except for this foggy mist around one's feet, making it difficult to see much beyond the path directly ahead. Helena couldn't see very far in the distance. It was veiled from sight by the thick white mist. She saw people headed into it, and this frightened her a bit. Where were they headed? What made them follow this trail into nothingness?

As Helena wandered further, she felt her senses awakening. Smells and sights and memories came to her as though from a world far away, like remembering life experienced on a distant planet.

She would definitely have to put herself out there to get answers. She had gotten the same message from her mother, from Coriander sort of, and from her experience with David. Among all these people, and peering into the thick white mist where so many were headed, she didn't feel up to it. How could she possibly approach a complete stranger and say, "Hi! I am Helena Carr and I'm in a coma. Do you know a neurologist named David?"

She felt a sudden urge to forget the whole idea and go back; to stay curled up, protected and secure in her hospital bed, safe in the coma that had removed her fears. She was much too anxious about approaching anyone. What would she say? How would she express to them what she needed? Everyone seemed engaged, preoccupied with their own journeys. Helena couldn't interrupt this important work. What if she happened to intrude on a newly dead person who was vulnerable and confused?

"Hi! It's me, Helena Carr. I need something. Pay attention to me!"

Impossible. She could not, would not do it. It would be less an act of bravery than one of self-centeredness. It would be unseemly to allow herself to carry out a selfish act in this world where selfishness did not exist.

Helena had no place here. Her plan wasn't going to work. She'd never find David, and he was the only one who could possibly help her. Helena paused, wishing she could think herself back to the hospital where she felt comfortable and safe.

Without David's help, waking up from the coma was an unlikely outcome. This meant death, and Helena was fine with death if it was meant to be the next step in her journey. At least it would be closure for Cassie, and for her dad. She had not died in the grave because, as her mom had said, it was not the right time. Now it must be. She would be reunited with her mom sooner rather than later, a pleasant scenario that brought a smile to Helena's face.

As Helena was turning back, she saw an older woman approaching. *Seeing* Helena. Helena looked around, not sure if the woman was coming toward her or someone else. No, it was unmistakable. She was walking directly toward Helena.

"Hello," the woman said. "You are Helena, aren't you?"

"Uh, yes, I am," Helena said, not sure if her voice would work. It did! The words came out clear and distinct. Since the woman had talked to her first, Helena decided to take the opportunity. "I hope you don't mind me asking," she blurted, "but do you know a man named David from around here? He's a neurosurgeon. From South Africa."

"No, not David, Helena. Daniel. My grandson. You recently spoke to my grandson." The woman had a Southern accent, reminding Helena of someone she had met recently. If only she could remember who or when.

"His name is Daniel. Danny Boy, I always called him."

"Daniel?" It came back to Helena gradually, the young man at the barbecue. He had the same kind of accent as this woman. Helena remembered him speaking fondly about his grandmother. "Yes, I think I remember Daniel. He was a very nice boy."

Daniel's grandmother beamed, her round face pretty with a sweet smile and thoughtful brown eyes. "That's him, sugar. My Danny is such a nice boy. I can't tell you how I miss that boy."

"I am so sorry," Helena responded instinctively, before the irony hit her. Daniel's grandmother was dead and Helena was consoling her.

"He's been struggling with a personal issue. I'd like you to take a message to him, if you would kindly."

"I don't know if I can," Helena said. "I'm in this kind of halfway zone between you people, and I'm not sure where I'll end up."

Daniel's grandmother patted Helena's arm. "Now, don't you worry about a thing, sugar. I got special permission to come find you, and I'm pretty sure it wouldn't have happened without a reason. Nothing here happens without a reason, or in your world either. It's one of those old sayings people like to say without thinking, and once you're passed over you come to know how true it is. No indeed, nothing happens without a reason. You can take my word for it."

"I think I believe you," Helena said, wondering what in the world was going on here. As she stood there in the road with people graciously moving around the two of them, Helena kept eyeing each one, finding it increasingly difficult to concentrate on the woman's voice. She might see David! She desperately needed to find him. This might be her only chance.

"You don't need to worry about where you're going," the woman was saying. "I wouldn't have gotten permission for nothing. It's been eating away at me for some time, this problem of my Danny's, and finally I was given the go-ahead to do something about it."

"Which is?" Helena asked, still wondering what she had to do about it. "I don't mean to be blunt, but the fact is I could disappear at any moment, back into my coma. If that happens, I'm pretty sure I won't be able to find you again next time. I'm having a hard enough time finding the man I met before. Do you know a doctor named David?"

"Honey, you need to calm down. We don't go running around here like chickens with their heads cut off. Save that for Earth. Things are different in this place. I told you, it's not David. It's Daniel. And this is very important, if you don't mind."

Helena nodded, saying, "Sorry, sorry," while looking

around at the others passing her and ignoring the woman who was some relation to Daniel from the barbecue.

"I'll get right to the point," the woman said. "I came especially to find you and tell you."

"Tell me what?" Helena asked. Before the woman could respond, Helena saw him. The white hair, the friendly smile, leading along a young man who seemed rather confused and bewildered. The young man kept wandering off and David would put a hand on his back and guide him back in the right direction.

"It's him! It's Doctor David. I must go to him," Helena said, pleading with the woman and her yet unspoken message. "Please, I've got to run before I lose him in the mist. It's important. Life or death."

The woman stood there in silence, a vision of sadness, as she gazed at Helena. Finally she said, "But you are the one, the only one. I got special permission for it. I've been praying, watching, waiting for a person, an opportunity to help my Danny. Finally, my prayers have been answered. And it's you. You're the one who can help me and Danny."

Helena felt bad for her. She was the one? How could that be? She didn't even know this woman, but she nodded. "Well, if it's not too long." Clearly the message was extremely important to Daniel's grandmother. She couldn't hurry up the dear Southern woman without appearing rude, but she kept one eye on David. "Go on, whenever you're ready," she said.

"I have a message for Danny. Now, here it is. You listen up, and you listen good, sugar, because it's important you get it right."

Her Doctor David was disappearing as the woman began. Helena was losing her chance! She watched as the doctor and his young charge entered the deep fog, on their way to wherever. To the light, she supposed. She should run ahead after them.

Doing so would mean ignoring this poor woman and leaving her disappointed, unable to deliver the message she seemed to think only Helena could hear. Helena was in turmoil. Without the doctor's advice on waking up, or at least how she could somehow make herself blink or move or raise an eyebrow—giving Cassie a sign she might *eventually* wake up—Helena was doomed. They would take her off life support. She would die in her coma.

She was losing her only chance, watching it disappear into the mist.

She still might catch the doctor, but she could not leave. Not with the little grandmother with her love and concern for Daniel enveloping the two of them like a blanket of light and warmth. Helena turned her attention back to the woman.

"I'm sorry. I got distracted by someone I saw, who I used to know. Never mind. He's gone. I am listening," she said, "and I'll remember."

The moment she said the words, Helena knew it was true. She would remember, and she would carry the message to Daniel. This idea gave her hope beyond anything she'd felt previously, even more than her plan to talk to the doctor. She would wake up! Helena hardly dared express the idea, the hope of healing, while in her heart she knew it would come to pass.

The woman patted her arm. "Yes, we often see familiar faces. Meeting old friends is the greatest joy. Don't worry, sugar, you'll run across him soon enough."

"I'm sure I will. It's okay. I'm ready to listen. What is the message again?"

"Thank you, dear. Now here it is. I want my Danny Boy to not be afraid of honesty. He must be honest and truthful in all things. He must move forward with those decisions which are clear to him. Do you have it so far?"

"Yes, I do," Helena said, concentrating to not forget a single word of it.

"I want him to know the pain and trials and heartache he has faced for so long are for this life only. After he has lived as well and as honestly and as generously as he possibly can, when it's time to move on, his burdens will be lifted and he will receive his reward. He must not hate himself or others. He must return hatred with compassion, fear with faith, meanness with generosity and be kind to all he meets, and joy will be his. He must not falter but do his best and continue forward in love and trust."

"What beautiful words," Helena murmured. "I'm not sure I can remember them, or express it as well as you did." She looked around for a piece of paper and a pen, seeing nothing but the mist upon the road where she and Daniel's grandmother stood to one side as people continued on past them. "I should write it down," Helena said.

"You will remember. Don't you worry about a thing, sugar. I'll be helping from my end. A message written on the heart is always more powerful than one written on paper."

"Of course," Helena said, feeling silly. This was not the kind of world where people had to write things down to remember them.

"Now please tell him every word of it, won't you? It will mean everything to me, and to my grandson. You *will* remember this message, and you'll know you promised to pass it on to Danny. Well, Helena. Do you promise?"

Helena paused. She had been ready to mindlessly blurt out the "I promise" at first on her lips. Until she considered that promises made here were probably different than those made at home. She wondered how much was at stake if she somehow broke her promise.

Daniel's grandmother waited patiently, watching Helena like she knew everything going through her mind. It reminded Helena of how Coriander had watched her and read her thoughts. Were they all mind readers in this dimension, or just super sensitive?

"I appreciate how you are thinking it over carefully, Helena. That's good. Because if you promise something in one sphere of existence meant for completion for another, you had darn well better keep it," Daniel's grandmother said. "You understand what I'm saying, sugar?"

"I didn't before, but I think I'm getting the picture. I had no idea promises carried over from one existence to another."

"You bet your biddy, they do. Why, I've met people who promised something in the pre-existence and never kept it. They spent their entire Earth life in frustration and depression despite every blessing poured down upon them, and despite many opportunities where they could have fulfilled their commitment. Why did these people finish up what should have been a good life feeling so bad? It was because of the unsettled feeling of something missing. Sugar, that something was their unkept promise."

There was that word again. *The pre-existence.* "How is this possible, when we can't remember from one sphere to the next? It hardly seems fair."

"You follow the twinges of conscience that are your guide. We can't expect to know the end from the beginning before taking action. That would be arrogance," Daniel's grandmother said.

"So it's the conscience who is the Trusted Guide?"

"I'm sure you've heard the old expression, 'let your conscience be your guide.' Them old expressions exist for a reason, you know. Mainly 'cause they're true, sugar."

She pronounced it "sugah." Helena smiled. Of course she would deliver the message, if only she got the chance.

"If you are sure I will wake up and return to life. And also, that I'll remember—those are the two main concerns on my end," Helena said. "Will you be there somewhere to guide me?"

"You can count on it. We are never left alone, never left without guidance, no matter where we are in the Universe. There is always a guide. Always," Daniel's grandmother said emphatically.

Coriander was Helena's guide. Helena could remember her saying: "Ignoring one's guide will lead to great unhappiness. Why must mortals make it so difficult?"

Finally, Helena spoke the words Daniel's grandmother was waiting to hear. "I agree to this promise. Yes, I will give Daniel the message."

The grandmother bowed her head and murmured, "Thank you."

"Will he listen?" Helena asked.

"He will listen with his ears. I hope he listens with his heart. That part is out of my hands and entirely up to him."

Helena watched as the grandmother faded away, back to where she'd been before finding Helena on this path.

Thirty

ONCE HELENA MADE THE COVENANT WITH Daniel's grandmother, she returned from the Fog and no matter how much she tried, she could not go back. She often thought of David, how important it was to find him. And there was always the hope she might see her mom again. Helena would try drifting away, but it never worked like it had before. Instead, she seemed to be spending more time in the present world than the foggy one. As for the Great Sleep, it was a thing of the past. Helena never was able to go back there either.

Coriander was pleased.

"I'm thrilled to see your progress, dear Helena. I may not go on vacation after all," Coriander said, appearing suddenly as she so often did.

Another vacation? One second Coriander was gone, the next she was sitting in the chair pulled up next to Helena's bed.

"What progress?" Helena asked, longing for a hint of what might be going on with her. "Am I close to waking up?"

"The nurses are excited is all I can say," Coriander said with a wink. "What's more, I've been given another assignment. It's time to say good-bye, Helena."

Suddenly Helena realized how large a part Coriander had played in her recovery. She lifted up her arms, her spiritual arms, and said, "Coriander, come and give me a hug. I will never forget you, or what you've done for me. The philosophical rants, the strange stories, the coming and going, the chastisement, even wearing my favorite dresses. I know what you were after, and I thank you. Everything you did was to test me, to bring about my healing, wasn't it?"

"You are welcome, Helena," Coriander leaned in for an embrace. "I did my best to challenge your brain waves right along with your spirit. You did well, my dear friend. I've been with you for a lifetime, and I've seen more growth and change these past weeks than in all your forty-some years. I couldn't be more proud of you and what you've accomplished."

Coriander was fading away as she spoke. Helena could hardly bear to see her go. "I couldn't have done any of it without you, Coriander. Good-bye, my friend. Please tell me we'll meet again soon."

"I'll be there, off and on, as I've always been. You won't see me, however, until the end. Until we meet again, my dear." And Coriander slipped away, first moving the chair to its original place, as she always did.

Thirty-one

HE DAY I WOKE UP, MY DAUGHTER WAS THERE. I opened my eyes and tried to focus on her face. Everything was a blur with a strange dark aura, as though I had left a brightly lit room and entered one with the lights dimmed. At first I thought I was back in the Fog. But no, this was decidedly different. The air wasn't so much foggy as . . . dirty. And familiar. A hospital room.

Cassie, who had been sitting in the corner chair writing something in a notebook, looked up and screamed. "*Mom!* You're awake!" She rushed into the hall, hollering for the nurses as though I might drift off again if someone didn't come immediately and witness the awakening.

That day was the beginning, and each day after I made further progress. Mentally, things came back quickly. It took a bit longer for my speech to catch up to my thoughts, but I kept working on it. Soon I could express words and phrases with little hesitation. Eventually, conversation followed.

I was moved to a physical rehabilitation center to get my limbs and muscles back in motion. Cassie visited daily. I took this for granted until one day I remembered Cassie lived in Texas with a job and husband. Keith.

"Honey, I need to ask you something," I began. My speech was still slow and awkward, but with practice it was getting better. Sometimes I felt tired of the effort and didn't talk much, and I'd fall behind in my progress. Cassie would prod and engage me, never allowing me to be silent for long.

"Sure, Mom. What is it?" Cassie set down her book and looked at me expectantly.

"You are with me day in and day out. What about your job?"

"I quit my job, Mom."

"What? Then what are you doing?"

"I'm here in Pasadena with you. Helping you get better is my job right now."

"But you . . . you live in Houston . . . Texas."

"Not anymore. I left there and moved into your house."

I remembered the realtor and how she'd put a for sale sign in the front yard. "Is it for sale?"

"No, I took it off the market. You're going to need a familiar place to return to when you're ready to go home."

"That's a good idea. You did the right thing. I'm glad you're at the house."

"Thanks, Mom. Me too. It seemed like this was where I was needed most."

"What about Keith? Where is he?"

Cassie closed her book and set it in her bag next to the chair. She didn't say anything for a minute or so. I watched how her face turned hard and sad all at once.

"Mom, I have to tell you something."

"Sure, honey, go ahead." Something about Keith, I knew. Something bad. I shifted in my bed.

"Keith came with me at first. We were in the hospital with you a lot, do you remember?"

"No, I really don't. It was like I was in another world."

"Yeah, he was there, acting all like the devoted son-in-law. Until you weren't waking up and the doctors talked to me about our options."

"Options?"

"Yes, you know. How long should we continue the tube feeding and the artificial means of keeping you alive. I hated those conversations. I wanted to scream at them whenever they'd bring it up. I knew you would come back, as much as I knew anything. I could tell you were there, inside somewhere, only needing to heal a little more until you were well enough to wake up."

"Resting in the Great Sleep. Moving through the Fog."

"They'd say, 'If that's what the family wants. We'll give it a little more time,' and that sort of thing. Then Keith started in on me. He was pressuring me to give up on you, to take away the feeding tube. 'Let you go peacefully,' is how he put it. 'For your own good. It's what your mom would want.' How would *he* know what you'd want?"

"I almost died once. It was like someone was trying to suffocate me. I was trapped in the grass, the cloud dropping down to my face."

"There was no way I'd have allowed them to remove the feeding tube and have you starve to death, Mom. No way. The idea was appalling to me. It still is, to think about people doing such a thing to their loved ones. It makes me sick. And here was Keith saying it's what we should do. That it would be 'the greater good, an act of compassion.' Grandpa was with me, totally against it."

"Dad?" I remembered seeing him after I woke up. Seeing my daughter and my dad together.

"Grandpa said absolutely not. We weren't giving up on you. He and Keith got in a fight over it."

I had never seen my dad angry. "A fight? What kind of fight?"

"Not hitting each other or anything. A lot of shouting. Keith started it by swearing at Grandpa when Grandpa sided with me. Grandpa let him have it. He told Keith to stay out of it, it was none of his business, and as far as he concerned, Keith wanted you dead because he was after your money. He called Keith nothing better than a murderer."

A laugh burst out at the sight of my laid-back dad yelling at Keith and accusing him of murder. Laughing felt good, like it was something fresh and new and healing. I tried it again.

"Yeah, it really wasn't funny at the time, Mom. I was afraid Keith was going to hit Grandpa, until someone came into the room and Keith backed down. We were in one of the hospital waiting rooms. Grandpa went back home shortly after their shout-out, he was so upset. This whole experience was extremely hard on him, and that particular incident was the worst. Before he left, Grandpa made me promise I would not listen to Keith, that I'd stay strong and believe in you coming back to us. He promised to return when you woke up."

"I remember seeing him in the hospital, I think. Before I was moved here. And now?"

"He went back home soon after. I encouraged him to, Mom. I was afraid for his health and mental state, with everything coming so soon after Grandma died and all. Grandpa needed to get back to his own home and routine."

"I'll go see him when I'm better. I'll get on a plane and go out there for a good long visit. There's something, something I have to tell him. Something important, I can't remember it, but it's there. I'll know later, when it's time. Only now that it's over, with all the tension of the situation, you should go back home too, don't you think?"

"I don't know, Mom. This experience changed my relationship with Keith in such a profound way. He actually seemed to want you to go away. I don't know if I can be with him again. It was like he cared more about your money than about you. He showed his true colors, and it wasn't pretty. There was a violence in him that shocked me. Scared me a little, too."

"Cassie, I love having you here, but . . . well, I don't want you to end your marriage over me."

"It's not like that. It's not you, it's him. I need to be away from him, to think things over. And I want to help you anyway, so this works out perfectly. Keith is in Houston, I am here. We aren't together at the moment, and I'm not sure we will be again. We'll see if anything changes later with Keith and me, but for now, I'm fine." Cassie paused then added, "I mean, if it's okay with you. I can help you at home, get settled again, whatever you need. As long as I'm not in your way or anything."

"Oh, Cassie, no. Never. I know I've been a distracted mother at times, and not always there for you like I should have been. It's going to be different from now on."

Cassie raised her eyebrows, and I hurried to say, "Don't worry, I won't get in your business and treat you like a child. Nothing like that. My heart has changed, is the thing. It's like I was closed off for so long, afraid of getting hurt or damaged, I don't know. Afraid of something bad happening. And now my heart center has opened, expanded, and the fear is gone."

"Mom, don't worry, you were fine. You were busy with your life, and I was busy with mine. I always knew you loved me. There was no question of it. I could count on you if I really needed you. Don't be too hard on yourself."

"No, it's not that. It's just, well, hard to explain. The words don't come easily."

"You never were much of a talker, Mom. That was Dad's department. I think I know what you're trying to say, in a way, and I want to say this: You have been a wonderful mom. An example to me my entire life of a caring, giving person."

I tried to speak but the words had disappeared.

"You gave me space to make my own decisions. That is love, too, Mom, even more than those mothers who can't let go. I have friends with moms like that. It cripples them both, mother and daughter, and what's worse, it ruins any close relationship they might have with the woman who *could* be their best friend in the world."

"Thank you, Cassie. It means a lot to hear you say it. As for me, I'm free, Cassie . . . free from the binding fear I've suffered from my entire life, for as long as I can remember. And I am free to love."

Epilogue

MY HOME HAD NEVER LOOKED THIS beautiful. Or this messy. The kitchen was spread with cooking preparations, chaos expressing life and creativity and sharing and openness. People were starting to arrive. Cassie let them in as I put the finishing touches on our feast.

It felt good to be cooking. To load the dishwasher. To put a basket of salsa ingredients in the sunshine and see the light reflect the colors of the red tomatoes, the deep green shine of the jalapenos, the curving white bulb of garlic next to the yellow skin of onion. It was completely, utterly wonderful. Unbelievably fresh and alive and brilliant. I had never felt happier or more at peace.

I pulled out a massive pan of lasagna from my oven. The smell of cheese and oregano and tomato sauce filled my senses. The heat from the oven warmed my face. It was late August and I had not yet turned on the air-conditioning. I wanted to feel heat, feel sunshine, feel everything that had almost been lost to me. I would bring the outside into my home, not shut it off with closed windows and cooled air. Dust, dirt, weather, smells, heat, people: I wanted to see it and feel it and be part of it.

Trudy and Tom rushed in and both wrapped me in hugs. "Welcome home, neighbor!" Tom said in his loud voice. "It's great to have you back!"

Trudy wiped away tears, at a loss of words. She kept shaking her head, and holding me, and then looking at my face, and holding me again. Finally she said, "You are cooking! What is this? Why aren't you resting? Cassie said you wouldn't let me bring a thing over."

"Trudy, I am resting by cooking. I'm messing up my kitchen like never before. I don't know when I've had such a thorough rest."

"You look amazing, Helena. I've never seen you like this before. You're ten years younger if a day. I can hardly believe it. What a miracle!" Trudy started bustling about in the kitchen, finding things to do. Tom was calling for my kitties, hiding under their loveseat in the family room. He pulled Amos out first and sat down to pet him.

I was proud of Amos, cuddling up on Tom's lap. My kitties weren't accustomed to people in the house, and Amos was stepping out of his reserve, just a little. Annie was fond of Cassie. She would always let Cassie hold and pet her.

The doorbell rang several times in a row, and I heard a familiar voice in the hallway. Soon Ruby entered, her arms outstretched and a big smile on her face. "Girl, look at you! In the kitchen, of all places. It's amazing to see you, Helena. Here you are, recovered and better than ever. You look brand new!"

I had not seen Ruby since my last session, before the accident. "Thanks for coming, Ruby. I'd hoped you could, but I know Saturday afternoons can be tricky for busy people."

"I wouldn't have missed this party for the world, Helena. If you hadn't called to invite me, we'd have had words for sure." Ruby did what Trudy had done—pulled back to examine my face, hugged me, then away again to look at me. "My golly, this transformation is hard to believe. You are a different woman. Open and joyful. You literally shine, glowing from within. I wouldn't believe it if I didn't see for myself. What happened to you in that coma of yours?"

Others had asked me the same question. I never knew what to say, how to explain the change. I couldn't talk about a lot of it or I'd sound crazy. Visits from Coriander, meeting David, the First-Level Friend. Talking with my mother who's been dead for months, and who looked better than I'd ever seen her. Coriander's stories about 'people she knew' and the function of light in the Universe. Trusted Guides. The pre-existence. It was inside of me, and it had changed me, yet I didn't know how to explain any of this to people without going on and on and saying more than anyone was ready to hear.

Finally I had settled on a simple explanation: "I guess facing death made me realize how much I have to live for. And to appreciate each moment." It was clichéd and generic but people got it. It was simple and straightforward and in terms the living could understand.

"It sure does appear like this accident of yours did more for you than I ever could have, that's for dang sure. You are a changed person, Helena. Can I ask the obvious question?"

I smiled at Ruby, knowing what she meant. "Yes, you can, and the answer is, I've got a contract that starts in three weeks. I can't wait to get back!"

"No anxiety or fear about it? No panic attacks?"

"I have never felt less anxiety about anything in my life. In fact, when I try to remember how I used to feel before the coma, I can barely comprehend it. It's like something far away in my past, a fuzzy memory of something that might have happened once but no longer matters."

Everyone was listening with eagerness. It was like I had information which, simply by hearing it, freed them up as well. As though I was giving them a message of hope and light. I remembered the two messages I had promised to share when I returned. One to my dad and the other to Daniel. I'd fly out to deliver Dad's message. He deserved to have me come to him.

As though following my thoughts, the doorbell rang and Trudy said, "I'll bet that's Danny. He's bringing his dad. You said he'd be welcome, didn't you, Helena?"

"Of course! When I called Daniel, he said his dad was visiting from West Virginia, and I insisted he bring him over."

When Cassie went to get the door, Trudy whispered to me, "Danny and Charlie, they've got some real issues to work out, you know. It's been very difficult for both of them. I hope this doesn't turn into an awkward situation."

"I'm sure it will be fine. Also, Trudy, I'd like to have a moment alone with Danny at some point. Could you make sure his dad is occupied so he and I can visit privately?"

"Of course, I'll do it. Give me a signal of some kind when you're ready." She looked around as though assessing the situation. Tom and Ruby had migrated to the shaded patio and appeared to be deep in conversation. They each had a cat in their arms. I was so proud of Amos and Annie, coming out of their shells like this.

"I know!" Trudy exclaimed. "Hand me an apron and tell me to help out in the kitchen. I'll ask Charlie to assist. We'll wash dishes or something."

We had no sooner finalized our plan than Cassie entered with Danny and his dad in tow. Trudy rushed to hug them both. Charlie was her brother-in-law, having been married to her sister Bernie, who had died some fifteen years ago of breast cancer.

"I think this is everyone, right, Mom?" Cassie asked.

"I invited my friend Angela from work, but don't bother watching for her," I said. "She's late for everything. We'll hear the doorbell when she arrives. She told me she'd drop by later for sure and to not wait the meal."

"Okay, let's start then. I'm starved. It's nearly two," Cassie said, nodding in a meaningful way toward the kitchen clock.

"Sure thing. The table is set up outdoors and the food is ready. Come help me carry everything out." I had really gone crazy in the kitchen. Besides lasagna and a huge tossed salad, I'd made salsa and guacamole for tortilla chips, garlic bread, cut up fresh vegetables and dip. There was mint lemonade or water with lime to drink. For dessert, lemon bars.

My guests exclaimed over the food as Cassie, Trudy and I brought it out to the table. "I know it's ridiculous, all this on a hot August day. I was in the mood to cook, so here it is," I explained, feeling somewhat ridiculous at the sight of everything.

Charlie, Danny's father, looked around happily at the feast. He was quite handsome, tall and slender, probably in his late fifties, with slightly graying, dark brown hair. When we'd met briefly in the house, I'd noticed he had the same slow drawl as his son, spoken with a slightly deeper voice.

"Well, now, Helena, no one should have to apologize for creating something as beautiful as this meal you are so kindly sharing with friends," Charlie stated. "Although we just met, I'd like to call you a friend, if I may. Ya'll are a true artist. I for one cannot wait to dig into this lasagna."

It put me immediately at ease, no longer feeling ridiculous for having cooked a large meal and offering it to friends.

The others here-here'd him, thanked me just as profusely for my efforts, and especially for inviting them to help celebrate my miraculous journey back from unconsciousness. And then we dug into the lasagna.

After dinner, Trudy kept to her vow and steered Charlie, as well as the others, to the kitchen for clean-up duty. As she shooed them inside, their arms full of dishes and things to clear the table, I heard Trudy explaining, "Helena and my nephew share a special bond, you know. They met over at our house and had quite a conversation. Let's give them a minute to catch up."

Danny and I pulled our chairs to a corner of the patio, away from the shade where I'd set up the table. I craved sunlight. Knowing others didn't share my current obsession, especially on a hot day in the high 80s, I offered to move back if he'd be more comfortable.

I barely knew where to begin.

"Not at all," Daniel said, pulling out a pair of sunglasses from his shirt pocket. "I'm prepared for sunshine. Looking cool in the heat." He put on his sunglasses with a flourish. "I can quite understand your desire for the sunshine, after what you've been through. I can only imagine. I'd like to hear all about your experience someday. I know this sounds strange, but I've always wondered what it would be like to be in a coma."

I laughed. "I found being in the coma more interesting than coming out of it. It's funny, because I learned more and felt more in my coma, in that almost death-like state of unconsciousness, than I ever had when fully alive."

Daniel gave me the look I'd come to see quite often on people. The expression of eagerness, hopefulness, like there truly was life after death and I was there to prove it. When I didn't say anything more, he finally broke the silence. "I know you saw things. I can see it in your eyes. You have more understanding than the rest of us."

Again, words failed me. I truly wanted to tell what had happened with the coma at some point in the future, when my language skills had improved and I could do it justice. People seemed hungry for information, eager to hear what I had experienced and learned. I was committed to this responsibility, as soon as I was able. Besides going back to nursing, I had this other work. I would find a way to share my story with others.

Daniel watched me, waited, then spoke aloud my own thought. "You will find a way. It will come, Helena. You have a gift. I am honored to know you. I look forward to seeing what you do with yourself now. Everything is different. Everything is changed for you."

"Yes, it is, and I plan on talking more about it. Because people want to know. Their eyes are begging me for information, and believe me, I know what that feels like."

"Can I just say I am feeling a little bit jealous of you at this moment?" Danny said. The sun had gone behind a cloud and he removed his sunglasses, gazing intently at me with his sky-blue eyes. "You have been given something special, Helena, and you will never again be the same person you were before. It's what every one of us wants, isn't it? To have a miraculous event that changes us and suddenly creates our best self."

"Danny, there's a reason I wanted to talk privately with you." I glanced around. Everyone was still inside. Trudy, like always, had come through for me. "I don't know if what I'm about to say will be one of those things that permanently changes you, as you mention, but it's something I have promised to share with you."

He sat up intently. "Go ahead."

"I hope you don't think I'm crazy, Danny. When I was in my coma, I visited these other places, other realms."

"Like Heaven?"

"I don't know. Heaven is a big place. I used to visualize it like this small area, you know, white and clean and spare with nothing really going on, and that's just not accurate. Heaven is huge. And busy. Think of a bustling city or community that goes on and on, people learning and communicating and working, each with a purpose, and that's way more like Heaven than the white rooms of our imagination. Sounds and scents and activities, similar to Earth only with much greater purpose and clarity."

"You went there? To Heaven?"

"I have no idea if I did or not. I don't know what those places were called I visited. I had my own names for them. Part of it must have been Heaven, because I got to talk with my mom who had passed away." I paused then fearlessly blurted it out, "And I spoke to your grandmother, Daniel."

He gasped, opened his eyes wide, staring at me. Still as a statue, he was focusing to not miss a single word of what I'd say next.

"She sought me out. She told me I would recover and there was a message I was to give you, from her."

"Oh, my, this is like everyone's secret wish and what makes them go to séances. What was her message to me? Go on, I'm listening!" He leaned forward in his chair.

"Okay, here it is." I took a deep breath. "She said she wants you to know the pain and trials and heartache you have faced for so long are for this life only. After you have lived as well and as honestly and as generously as you possibly can, Danny, when it's time to move on, your burdens will be lifted and you will receive your reward. You must not hate yourself or others. You must return hatred with compassion, fear with faith, meanness with generosity and be kind to those you meet, and joy will be yours. Danny, you must not falter but do your best and continue forward with love and trust."

Daniel was gazing at me with a big smile at first, eager to hear the message, but when I finished, he bowed his head, just as his grandmother had done. I waited for him to speak. I did not want to interfere with her message by intruding with words of my own.

Finally, he raised his head, tears brightening his eyes. "Thank you, Helena. I don't know what else to say. It's like you saw right into my heart. And you know what? As you were speaking, your voice sounded like my grandmother's. I half expected to hear you call me 'sugah.'"

I grinned. "Yes, she called me that numerous times. It was quite charming."

"Oh, dear, I should have written this down! I don't want to forget it." Daniel rummaged around in his pockets, and pulled out a smart phone. He stared at it dumbly. "You know, this piece of electronic crap seems so out of place right now with our talk of Heaven and angels and messages from beyond and my grandmother." He put it back in his pants pocket. "I don't need to write it down. The words are engraved on my heart. I will never forget them. Thank you, Helena."

"You're welcome, Danny. I hope it helps with whatever struggles you are facing."

"It does. More than you could ever know." He shifted his eyes toward the house, where loud, companionable voices were wafting out from the open patio door. "It has to do with my dad, and something I've got to tell him . . . about myself . . . and, well . . . my problems. It's my cross to bear. I can't change it, I've tried. God knows I tried, but . . . I just can't. I don't know how to fix this, and I can't keep fighting it. The fact is, I've accepted it, and well . . . I've got to tell my dad."

"And you are afraid to tell him."

"Yes. I'm afraid he will stop loving me. We've always been close, especially since Mom died, and I can't bear for him to hate me. Only he might, when he knows this thing about me."

The words came to me then, as though his grandmother was whispering them right in my ear. "Danny, you must live honestly, remember. And not falter but do your very best, always, and continue forward."

He nodded and sat up straight. "Yes, I know. Thank you. I will remember. I'll talk to Dad tonight. He goes back to West Virginia next Saturday. I can't put it off any longer. Tonight will not be too soon." Danny looked past me to the kitchen window. "He's enjoying himself, I can tell. This has been good. We're both relaxed after being here. Being around you is the best medicine, Helena, do you realize that? I'll talk to him tonight."

"Good. I'm glad I could help. Let me know, okay?"

"Yes, we will definitely keep in touch." He smiled at me then, a bit mischievously. "And I think Dad would like to see you again. He's dated here and there, nothing very serious. I know he's lonely. He's awful picky when it comes to women. Mom was just too perfect, I guess. You're the only one I've met who can match her—her inner strength, her compassion, her tranquility. I think Dad sees it, too."

I blushed and looked away. "Oh, I don't know."

"Sorry if I embarrassed you, Helena. I feel like I can tell you anything. And oversharing has always been one of my weaknesses. Let's go inside and join the party."

Before Danny and Charlie left later that day, Charlie turned to me and in his casual, gentlemanly way asked, "Can I call you, Helena? I'd like to see you again once or twice before I go back to West Virginia."

I smiled up at him and without a moment's hesitation replied, "Yes, of course, Charlie. I'd like that."

Acknowledgements

WHEN I AM WORKING ON A NOVEL, PRACTIcally anything and everything that occurs to me during the process may end up in the pages. Telephone conversations that intrude while I'm trying to get my pages in for the day. Long road trips when I say, "Someone tell me something interesting to put in my book." Visits with friends, when dialogue stays in my mind to write down later.

Therefore, I'd like to acknowledge and thank the following people whose intriguing remarks and/or conversations ended up in *Afraid of Everything*: Rob Hall, Travis Gowen, Liesel DeVaul, Allie Maldonado, Bruce Gowen. Thanks, guys!

Thank you to Vrai at WiDo Publishing for your close, careful edit of the final draft. Thank you as well to my family members who read and gave valuable feedback during the editing process.

As always, I thank the readers of my work who leave positive reviews and encouraging comments and emails, inspiring me to keep going in the ups and downs, the hard work, long hours and occasional disappointments that come with being a writer of books. I write for you.

About the Author

*B*ORN AND RAISED IN CENTRAL ILLINOIS, Karen Jones Gowen attended Northern Illinois University in DeKalb and the University of Illinois in Champaign-Urbana. She transferred to Brigham Young University, where she met her husband Bruce, and there graduated with a degree in English and American Literature.

Karen and Bruce have lived in Utah, Illinois, California, and Washington. They currently reside in Panajachel, Guatemala. They are the parents of ten children. Not surprisingly, family relationships are a recurring theme in Karen's writing. Her author website and blog is at http://karen jonesgowen.com.